KRISTY A
DISASTER

"Hey," said Bart, "I've got an idea. Just to show you that I think your team is as good as mine, even if the kids are younger, how about a game? Bart's Bashers challenge Kristy's Krushers."

A game? A real game? Against Bart's team? I didn't know if the Krushers were ready for something like that, but I wasn't about to say no. I couldn't let Bart think I was afraid of his team. Besides, if we arranged a game, I'd be sure to see him again—soon.

"Fine," I replied. "How about two weeks from Saturday? Is it enough time for the Bashers to get ready?"

"Of course! But what about the Krushers?"

"Oh they'll be ready."

When Kristy sees how much her little brothers and sister want to play softball, she starts a team of her own. Now Kristy's Krushers have been challenged by Bart's Bashers. Not only are they a better team, but Kristy has a Gigantic Crush on their coach!

Also in the Babysitters Club series:

Look out for:

KRISTY AND THE WALKING DISASTER

Ann M. Martin

Hippo Books
Scholastic Children's Books
London

Scholastic Children's Books,
Scholastic Publications Ltd,
7-9 Pratt Street, London NW1 0AE, UK

Scholastic Inc.,
730 Broadway, New York, NY 10003, USA

Scholastic Canada Ltd,
123 Newkirk Road, Richmond Hill,
Ontario, Canada L4C 3G5

Ashton Scholastic Pty Ltd,
P O Box 579, Gosford, New South Wales,
Australia

Ashton Scholastic Ltd,
Private Bag 1, Penrose, Auckland,
New Zealand

First published by Scholastic Inc., USA, 1989
First published in the UK by Scholastic Publications Ltd, 1991

ISBN 0 590 76548 5

Printed by Cox & Wyman, Reading, Berks.
Typeset in Plantin by AKM Associates (UK) Ltd, Southall, London

10 9 8 7 6 5 4 3

*This book is for
the members of
the Lunch Club*

1st CHAPTER

"We're here! We're here!"

The front door to my house burst open and in barged Karen and Andrew. Karen and Andrew are my stepsister and stepbrother. Karen is six and Andrew is four, and Karen was the one doing the yelling. Andrew is quite quiet and shy. In fact, he's very quiet and shy. He's the opposite of Karen. It's hard to believe they're brother and sister.

"Hi, you guys!" I called. I was on the upstairs landing, looking down. I ran to greet them. "I'm so glad you're here early. I'm glad your mum had to go out."

"Me too!" exclaimed Karen. She slung her rucksack on the floor.

Andrew put his down more gently. "Me too," he whispered.

I hugged Andrew and Karen, and then Karen ran off to check on things—her

1

room, Shannon (our puppy), and Boo-Boo (our cat).

Andrew glanced at me and said, "Maybe David Michael wants to play catch." He looked terribly hopeful.

"He might," I said. "He's out in the back garden. Why don't you go and see."

Are you confused yet? I'll stop here so I can introduce myself and explain who all these people are. My name is Kristy Thomas. I'm thirteen and in the eighth grade. One of the most important things to know about me is that I am the chairman, founder, and creator of a business called the Babysitters Club.

David Michael is my brother. He's seven. I have two other brothers. They're in high school. Sam is fifteen and Charlie is seventeen. Until recently my three brothers and I lived with our mother in a small house on the other side of town, here in Stoneybrook, Connecticut. (Our parents are divorced.) Then my mum met a guy called Watson Brewer, a divorced millionaire. Practically before we knew it, she had married him and he had moved us into his house—which is a mansion.

Karen and Andrew are Watson's children. They live with us every other weekend and for two weeks during the summer. The rest of the time they live with their mother and stepfather.

To be honest, I didn't like Watson much

at first. Oh, all right. I hated him. I didn't want anything to do with him, even though he likes baseball as much as I do. I even refused to meet his kids. You know what brought us together? The Babysitters Club. Once, in an emergency, I got a job sitting for Karen and Andrew. By the time the job was over, I thought they were the greatest kids in the world. Now I am so, so glad they're my stepbrother and sister.

It was a Friday afternoon, almost five o'clock. Mum and Watson were both at work. Sam was around somewhere. He was probably doing his homework. He likes to get it out of the way on Fridays so he can watch TV for the rest of the weekend. Charlie was out, but I was waiting for him to come home. Three times a week he drives me to and from meetings of the Babysitters Club, which are held from five-thirty until six o'clock in my old neighbourhood on the other side of Stoneybrook.

I decided I had better go and check on the little kids. I never know *what* Karen might be up to. She's not naughty, but she's fearless and has a vivid imagination. (Watson calls it "fertile," I suppose he means that any idea could grow there.)

Trying to keep track of all the people (not to mention animals) in my house is not easy, especially when Karen and Andrew are staying. Can you believe that my mum has been talking about wanting *another* kid? I

3

can't. I love children, but there's plenty of confusion at our house as it is. Besides, my mother is at least thirty-seven.

I found Karen, Andrew, and David Michael in the back garden. They were trying to play three-man softball.

"This is so stupid!" David Michael was saying. (He was only saying that because he had just missed the ball.)

"David Michael," I said, "watch the *ball* when it's being pitched. Don't look at your *bat*. I know you want to connect the two of them, but believe me, you won't hit the ball if you don't look at it."

Karen pitched the ball again and David Michael watched it like a hawk. He swung. *Crack*! The ball sailed across the garden.

"All right! Home run!" I yelled.

I just love sports.

"Boy, thanks, Kristy!" exclaimed my brother. "That was a good tip. . . . I really wish I could play softball or baseball in a real team, with a coach and everything."

"Me too," said Karen and Andrew.

"Hey, Kristy!" someone yelled.

"Coming!" I shouted back. It was Charlie. He was home and ready to drive me to my club meeting.

"I've got to go, you guys. Behave yourselves, okay? Sam's home and Mum and Watson will be here soon. We'll talk about softball later."

I ran to our front drive and jumped into the car, next to Charlie.

"Ready to go visit your little friends?" he teased me.

I scowled. They are not *little* friends, and Charlie knows it. They are Claudia Kishi, Mary Anne Spier, Dawn Schafer, Mallory Pike, and Jessi Ramsey, and they are all different and special. And none of them is little. Claudia, Mary Anne, and Dawn are thirteen, like me. Jessi and Mal are eleven and in the sixth grade.

I used to live next door to Mary Anne (she's my best friend) and across the street from Claudia. We thirteen-year-olds are eighth-graders in Stoneybrook Middle School. (Most of the kids in my new neighbourhood go to private schools, but Mum let my brothers and me stay in our normal state schools.)

Mary Anne Spier is the most sensitive person I know. Sometimes she's too sensitive. She'll cry over the slightest thing. And she's shy and quiet, like Andrew. But once she's your friend, you've got a friend for life. She is very loyal. Maybe that's part of the reason Mary Anne was the first one of us to have a steady boyfriend. His name is Logan Bruno. Mary Anne lives with her dad and her kitten, Tigger. Her mum died a long time ago, so long ago that Mary Anne doesn't even remember her.

Even though I have a big mouth and I'm

5

far from shy, Mary Anne and I are alike in some ways. For one thing, we look alike. We both have brown eyes and brown hair and are short. I'm the shortest kid in our grade, believe it or not, but Mary Anne has grown slightly. For another thing, we don't care much about clothes. Truthfully, I don't care a *thing* about clothes. My friends tease me because I always wear jeans, a sweater, and trainers. (Well, not in the summer, of course.) And Mary Anne used to have to wear babyish stuff that her father chose for her, but now he's not so strict and lets Mary Anne choose her own clothes, so she is more interested in what she wears.

Boy, are Mary Anne and I different from Claudia Kishi! Claud is super-sophisticated —and looks really great. She's Japanese-American and gorgeous, with long, long silky, jet-black hair; dark, almond-shaped eyes; and a complexion that I'd die for. She's funny and talented—you should see her artwork—and she practically has boys drooling over her, but she doesn't have a steady boyfriend like Mary Anne does. One thing about Claudia that's a problem is that she's a terrible pupil. To make this worse, her older sister Janine is a genius. Janine is in high school, but she already takes college courses.

Claudia and Janine live with their parents and their grandmother Mimi. Claudia's special likes are: junk food, mysteries (especially Nancy Drew mysteries), and, of course, her art. Her artistic flair runs over into her clothes. You should see how she dresses—wild! Baggy jeans, skintight trousers, miniskirts, odd layers of things, bright colours, and weird jewellery. Also, she wears her hair differently every day, and she does things like paint her toenails with sparkles. Once, she went to school with glitter in her hair.

Dawn Schafer, who is Mary Anne's other best friend, is originally from California. She and her mum and younger brother Jeff moved here when we club members were halfway through seventh grade. They moved because her parents got divorced, and Mrs Schafer had grown up here in Stoneybrook. A sad thing is that Jeff was so unhappy that not long ago he moved back to California to live with his father. Now Dawn's family is divided in half—and separated by a continent. In a way, this is like my own family, since my dad took off for California years ago and I never see him, but I feel luckier than Dawn. I have a new family now.

Dawn is really great, even though sometimes I'm a little jealous of her since she's so close to Mary Anne. But Dawn is independent. She "does her own thing" and couldn't care less what anyone else thinks. She's super-organized, a health-food nut, and has her own style of dress. I think of it as "California casual". Also, Dawn has the

7

palest blue eyes and the longest, blondest hair I've ever seen.

Now—about our two younger members, Mallory Pike and Jessi Ramsey. They joined the club some time ago after one of our original members, Stacey McGill, had to move away. (I'll tell you more about Stacey later, I promise.) Mal joined first. She's the oldest of the eight Pike kids. Our club sits for the Pikes a lot. Mallory had always been a big help to us sitters, so now that she's eleven, she's allowed to sit in the afternoons and on weekends. She's great with kids! She's patient and practical. She thinks her parents treat her like a baby, though. She desperately wants contacts instead of glasses, but she's getting braces instead. She wishes her hair were straighter. She wishes a lot of things. Mal loves reading, writing (poetry and stories), drawing, and horses.

Jessi (Jessica) Ramsey is Mal's friend. Her family moved to Stoneybrook pretty recently, and both Jessi and Mal were in the market for a best friend. When they found each other—*POW!* They have so much in common. They have the same interests (Jessi is also a talented ballet dancer), they both think their parents treat them like babies, and they both come from really great families, although Jessi's is much smaller than Mal's. Apart from Jessi and her parents, there are just her eight-year-old sister Becca (short for Rebecca) and her

8

baby brother Squirt, whose real name is John Philip Ramsey, Jr. Here's the one big difference between Mal and Jessi. Mal is white and Jessi is black. That hasn't mattered to either of them, but being black in Stoneybrook can be difficult. Let's just say that some people here didn't exactly make the Ramseys feel welcome at first, but things are improving. Jessi is adjusting—and she's a great addition to our club!

So. These complicated people are the "little friends" Charlie mentioned. The more I thought about them, the more I looked forward to seeing them. I always look forward to club meetings.

When Charlie pulled into Claudia Kishi's driveway (our meetings are always held in Claud's room) I leaped out of the car. I couldn't wait to get things started.

"'Bye, Charlie!" I called to him. "Thanks! See you in half an hour!"

"'Bye, kiddo. Have fun!"

Have fun? No problem! We always do.

2nd CHAPTER

"Claud? Is that you?" I asked.

Claudia's grandmother Mimi had let me in and told me to go up to Claudia's room. So I had—and now all I could see was a pair of legs sticking out from behind an armchair.

"Yeah, it's me," said a muffled voice.

"What are you doing?" I asked

"Looking for my packet of Quavers. I know they're around here somewhere . . . but I don't think they're under this chair. Look what I did find, though."

Claudia's legs disappeared. A hand clutched the back of the chair. Then she stood up. She was holding a paintbrush. "I've been looking for this. I wonder how it got under the chair. But where are the Quavers?"

I giggled. Claud is just like a squirrel. She hides food—then forgets where she hid it.

"I'll look under your bed for you," I volunteered.

I flopped onto my stomach, scrunched underneath the bed, and poked around in the art supplies Claudia keeps there. "Jackpot!" I exclaimed. "Here are the Quavers *and* a whole packet of Kit-Kats."

"Oh, goody!" said Claud. Even though our meetings are held just before dinner, Claudia always provides us with snacks, since we're starving by five-thirty. Well, she provides most of us with snacks. Dawn won't touch much of Claud's junk food.

"Hi, you guys!" Mary Anne came in just as I was crawling out from under the bed. "I brought Tigger over. I hope you don't mind. He needed a change of scenery." Mary Anne put her grey kitten on the floor. Tigger immediately found a piece of ribbon and began hitting it.

Dawn and Mal turned up next, and Jessi appeared last. She usually does. She's very busy in the afternoons, between ballet classes and a steady sitting job.

My friends were all crawling around on the floor playing with Tigger, so I called the meeting to order.

"Any club business?" I said loudly.

At the sound of my voice, everyone scrambled to their usual places—Claudia, Mary Anne, and Dawn on Claudia's bed, and Mal and Jessi on the floor. I always sit in Claud's director's chair. And I wear a visor.

I am the chairman and I must look as though I mean business.

"The treasury is getting low," spoke up Dawn, our treasurer. "But when I collect subs next week, I think we'll be okay."

Maybe I had better stop for a moment and tell you how our club runs.

As I've said, I'm the club chairman. This is because the idea for the club was mine. I got it at the beginning of seventh grade when my mum and my brothers and I were still living next door to Mary Anne. Mum was just getting to know Watson then. Anyway, one evening, Mum realized she needed a sitter for David Michael. Sam and Charlie and I were all going to be busy. So Mum had to find someone else. I watched her make call after call. And as I was watching, it occurred to me that Mum could save herself a lot of time if she could phone one number and reach several sitters at once.

That was it! A brillant idea! I already did some babysitting in my neighbourhood. So did Mary Anne and Claudia. We decided to start a babysitting club. We also decided we should have a fourth member. That was when Claudia introduced us to Stacey McGill, a new friend of hers who had moved to Stoneybrook from New York City. Stacey had lots of experience and was a terrific sitter, too. We asked her to join us, we began advertising, and just like that we had a babysitting business.

12

We decided that if we were going to be serious about our business, then we had better run it professionally. First, we agreed to hold regular club meetings three times a week. We told our clients they could reach us at Claudia's number on Mondays, Wednesdays, and Fridays from five-thirty until six. (Claudia has her own phone and personal, private phone number.) One of us was certain to be free to take any job that came in.

Then we voted ourselves officers of the club.

I was made the chairman . . . for obvious reasons.

Claud was made the vice-chairman, since we would always be meeting in her room and using her phone. Also, people would probably be calling the club number even when we weren't meeting, and Claudia would have to deal with that extra work.

Mary Anne, who's the neatest and most organized of the four original club members, was named secretary. Boy, does she have a lot of work to do. It's her job to arrange sitting appointments, to keep all our schedules straight (such as when Claudia goes to art lessons or when Jessi has ballet classes), and to keep the club record book up to date. The record book is crucial (that's a really good word, meaning "very, very important") to the running of the club. In it, Mary Anne keeps track of all our clients and their addresses and phone numbers. And on the appointment calendar pages she schedules our sitting jobs. (The treasurer also uses the record book, but I'll get to that in a minute.) Mary Anne is a wonder. I don't think she's slipped up yet. None of us has ever been booked for two jobs at the same time or anything like that.

Last but not least, we made Stacey McGill our treasurer. It was her job to keep track of how much money each of us earns (just for our own information), to mark it down in the record book, and to collect subs for our treasury. What do we use our treasury money for? Two main things. 1. Entertainment, such as pizza parties. 2. Funds for supplying our Kid-Kits.

The Kid-Kits were my idea. I thought that a good way to entertain the kids we sit for would be with a box of fun. So we each decorated a cardboard box and filled it with our old games, books, and toys. Then we bought some things like colouring books, activity books, and crayons. We take the Kid-Kits on our sitting jobs so the kids can play with them and not be bored. We use the treasury money to replace things that get used up.

How did Dawn, Jessi, and Mal join the club? Well, Dawn joined not long after she moved here from California. She and Mary Anne had become friends quickly, our business was growing, and we needed extra help. So Dawn became our alternate officer. That meant that she could take over the duties of any other member if someone had to miss a meeting. That didn't last long, though. Unfortunately, Stacey had to move back to New York City. (This was *especially* unfortunate since she and Claudia had become best friends, and now they really miss each other.)

Anyway, after Stacey left, two things happened. Dawn became our new treasurer —and we realized we needed lots more help. Our club was doing lots of business. (Don't get me wrong. I'm not complaining. But we did have a problem.) We'd already signed up two associate members, kids who don't come to meetings, but who are good sitters we can call on in a pinch. They are Shannon Kilbourne, who lives across the street from me in my new neighbourhood— and Logan Bruno, Mary Anne's boyfriend! But they weren't enough. We needed a regular member to replace Stacey. My friends and I thought and thought. We liked Mallory Pike, whom we already knew is good with kids, even if she is younger than the rest of us, but the problem was that her parents don't allow her to sit at night, except at her own house. Finally, we took on Mal *and* her friend Jessi. We thought that if they could take over a lot of our afternoon jobs, the rest of us could handle the night-time stuff. So far, it's working

15

just fine. Jessi and Mal are our junior officers.

There's one other thing I had better tell you about—our club notebook. The notebook is different from the record book. It's a sort of journal. We're all responsible for writing up every single job we go on. Then, once a week, we're supposed to read about the jobs in the notebook. It's really helpful. We can find out if the kids we sit for are having problems the rest of us should know about, or how one of us sitters handled a sticky situation, and other important things, like if any kid has food allergies or special fears. The notebook was my idea and I know it was a good one. I also know that most of the other club members think writing in it is a big bore. Well, too bad. Writing in the book is one of our few club rules.

"Okay," I said, from the director's chair, "the treasury is in good shape. Anything else?"

"Aw, look at Tigger!" Dawn said suddenly. Tigger was sitting in one of Claudia's shoes, which was pretty cute—but I was trying to conduct a meeting.

"Anything besides Tigger?" I said sternly.

Five heads snapped to attention. And just then the phone rang. I was nearest to it, so I answered it. "Hello, Babysitters Club . . . Hi, Mrs Rodowsky." (I heard Dawn groan, and I waved my hand at her to make her be quiet.) "Tuesday?" I repeated. "Okay,

I'll get back to you . . . Yes . . . Okay, good-bye."

I hung up. Mary Anne had opened the record book to the appointment pages. "This coming Tuesday?" she asked.

I nodded.

"Let's see. You're free, Kristy, and so are you, Dawn."

"You can have the job, Kristy," said Dawn quickly.

I grinned wickedly. "Is Jackie too much for you?" I asked.

"Nooo. Not exactly. You know I like him. His brothers, too. It's just . . . . Well, you never know what's going to happen at the Rodowskys'."

That's true. And it's all because of Jackie, the middle of the three Rodowsky boys. Shea is nine, Archie is four, and Jackie is seven—and a walking disaster. He's just totally accident-prone. And he doesn't have little accidents like skinned knees. No, he's more apt to lock himself in the bathroom and then get his hand caught down the plughole. I could understand why Dawn preferred not to sit for him.

"Book me in for Tuesday," I told Mary Anne. Then I rang Mrs Rodowsky back to tell her that I would be sitting.

I had just put the phone down when the phone rang again. Then four more times. For quite a while, all we could do was arrange jobs, although Claudia did manage to pass around the Quavers and Kit-Kats.

The meeting was almost over when Mary Anne suddenly said in a sort of strangled voice, "Uh, where's Tigger, you guys?"

We searched Claud's room from top to bottom. We found a bag of peanuts, a box of Maltesers, some Mars Bars, and a packet of Wine Gums—but no Tigger.

Mary Anne was just beginning to get tearful when we heard someone say, "Perhaps you are looking for this."

Standing in Claud's doorway was her sister Janine, cradling Tigger. "I found him sitting on my computer," she said. She was trying to look cross, but you could tell she wanted to smile.

Mary Anne greeted Tigger as if he'd been missing for a year or so, and then the meeting ended.

Jackie Rodowsky, I thought as Charlie drove me home. Would my afternoon with the walking disaster be fun . . . or well, a disaster?

3rd CHAPTER

"Hit it! . . . Hit it! . . . No, *hit*—Oh, never mind," said Max Delaney crossly.

"Don't yell at me!" retorted his sister.

"Anyway, *you* never hit the ball," Karen accused Max.

Max stuck his tongue out at Karen, and Karen stuck hers out at Max.

It was Saturday, the day after our club meeting, and it was a gorgeous afternoon. I was babysitting for Karen, Andrew, and David Michael. We were in the back garden and a group of kids had come over to play softball . . . or to try to play softball. Amanda and Max Delaney were there (Amanda is eight and Max is six), and Linny and Hannie Papadakis had come over, too. Linny is David Michael's friend, and Hannie is one of Karen's best friends. The girls are in the same class at school.

The kids had a pretty pathetic game going.

Most of them were old enough to be in Little League or to play T-ball, but I could see why they hadn't bothered to join a team. They all worked and worked and worked —and nothing happened. I'd never seen so many kids play so hard with so few results.

Hannie really couldn't hit. She never connected with the ball. Max dropped or missed every ball he tried to catch. David Michael was simply hopeless. He tripped over his feet, the bat, even the ball, and no matter how he concentrated, he somehow never did anything right, except pitch. Karen wasn't a bad hitter. And Andrew might have been a good catcher if he weren't so little, but he's only four, so balls went sailing over him right and left, even when he stretched for them. Amanda and Linnie were no better than the others.

"You guys," I said to the kids, "come over here for a sec, and let me help you get organized. I'll give you some tips, too, okay?" (I happen to like sports a lot.)

Karen, Andrew and David Michael, Hannie, Linny, Max, and Amanda dropped their gloves, bats, and the ball. They gathered around me.

"First of all," I said, "Hannie, it helps to watch the *ball* when you're trying to hit it. Don't look away from it, even to look at your bat."

"Yeah," said David Michael knowingly,

as if I hadn't just told him the same thing the day before.

"And Max, the trick for holding onto the ball after you catch it is to close your glove around it right away. Otherwise, the ball will fall out. And keep your eye on the ball when you're trying to catch it, just like when you're trying to hit it. Don't look at your glove or the batter. Got it?"

The kids nodded.

Then Andrew said, "What about me? I could catch those balls if I were taller."

"I know you could," I replied. "So let's work on your hitting and pitching instead. The only way to make you taller is to give you stilts. Or else hold up this game for a year or two while you grow."

Andrew giggled.

I divided the kids into teams—the four younger kids *versus* the three older ones. "Now!" I cried. "Let's play soft ball!"

David Michael pitched to Hannie. Hannie swung her bat. She missed the ball by about two feet. Three times. He pitched to Karen. Karen hit the ball. *Smack*! It sailed right to Amanda, who appeared to be looking at the ball—until just before it reached her glove. Then she glanced at her glove to see how things were going. The ball flew over her head.

Everyone groaned. Even Karen, who was running bases.

I gathered the kids around me again.

"We're going to stop the game," I announced, "and have a softball clinic instead."

"Clinic?" repeated Amanda nervously. "You mean, like a hospital?"

"No. No, I mean when I work with each of you on your weak points—the stuff you need help with. I'll be your coach and trainer."

The kids looked excited. And David Michael said, "If I were in Little League, there'd be a coach to help me all the time."

"You should join," I told him. "The rest of you should, too. Or play T-ball."

"I can't," said Andrew. "I'm not old enough."

"I can't either," said Karen and Hannie.

"Why not?" I asked. "Girls can play."

"Yeah," said Karen, "but no one would want me."

"Or me," said Hannie.

"Or me," said Linny, David Michael, and Max.

"I don't want to join," announced Amanda. "I don't like playing soft ball *that* much."

"Well, the rest of us do," said Hannie, who does not get along with Amanda and probably never will.

"We want to be in a team," added David Michael. "We just don't want to embarrass ourselves."

"No Little League?" I asked, knowing what the answer would be.

22

"Nope," he replied, and the other kids agreed with him.

Then Amanda spoke up. "Hey, Kristy, do you know Bart Taylor? He coaches his own team right here in the neighbourhood. A whole group of kids belong. His team is called Bart's Bashers."

"Maybe we could join!" exclaimed David Michael.

"I could talk to Bart," I said slowly. "Where does he live, Amanda? And who is he, anyway?"

"He's a kid who goes to Stoneybrook Day School. I think he's in eighth grade, just like you, Kristy." Amanda told me where he lives, which isn't too far from my house.

Well, I thought, I could go and talk to him. I wouldn't like it—but I would do it. Why wouldn't I like it? A lot of reasons. For one thing, you can never tell about eighth-grade boys. Half of them are normal, the other half are wallies. And in this neighbourhood, about half of both groups are also snobs. I worked out my odds. I had a twenty-five percent chance of getting a plain wally, a twenty-five percent chance of getting a snobby wally, a twenty-five percent chance of getting a plain snob, and a twenty-five percent chance of getting a normal, nice guy.

The odds were not great, but I would risk them.

If only my brothers and I went to private

school like the rest of the kids in this neighbourhood, then the kids wouldn't have to lord their snobbishness over us. On the other hand, we might be wallies ourselves then, and besides, I wouldn't be in the same school as Claudia, Mary Anne, Dawn, Jessi, and Mal.

Mum and Watson came home at three-thirty that afternoon. At four o'clock, I put Shannon on her lead and walked her over to Bart's house.

A very, very, very cute guy was in the Taylors' yard, raking up dead grass and twigs and things. It couldn't be Bart. Most people around here have gardeners to take care of their lawns.

The boy saw me slow down and look curiously at him.

"Can I help you?" he called.

"I'm, um, I'm looking for Bart Taylor," I replied.

"Well, you've found him." Bart grinned.

I grinned back. So far, so good. Maybe Bart was from that normal non-wallyish twenty-five percent.

Bart dropped his rake and crossed the yard to the pavement. "That's a great-looking dog," he said, as Shannon put her front paws on his knees and wagged her tail joyfully.

"She's a Bernese mountain dog," I told Bart. "Oh, my name's Kristy Thomas. I came . . . I came to ask you something."

Why did I feel so nervous? I've talked to boys before. I've been to dances with boys. I've been to parties with boys. But none of them had looked at me the way Bart was looking at me just then—as if standing on the pavement was a glamorous movie star instead of plain old me, Kristy Thomas. And, to be honest, none of them had been quite as cute as Bart. They didn't have his crooked smile or his deep, deep brown eyes, or his even, straight, perfect nose, or his hair that looked as if it might have been styled at one of those hair places for guys—or not. I think it's a good sign if you can't tell.

"Yes?" said Bart, and I realized I'd just been staring at him.

"Oh. Oh," I stammered. "Um, what I wanted to ask you is, well, I heard about your softball team, and I wondered whether you need any more players."

Bart laughed. "You're a little old," he replied.

"Oh, it's not me!" I cried. "It's my younger brother, and my little stepbrother and stepsister, and, let's see, one, two, three other kids. My stepbrother, Andrew, is only four," I rushed on. "I feel I have to tell you that. And none of them is very good. Well, Karen's not a bad hitter, but David Michael's useless, and Linny's—"

"Whoa!" exclaimed Bart. "Hold it. You're talking about six kids? I could take on one more, *maybe* two, but not six. I've already got more kids than I need."

Bart and I talked a little while longer. I decided two things. Since Bart couldn't handle any more kids, I would start my own team. I would take on any kid who really wanted to play in a team, no matter how young or hopeless or uncoordinated he or she was. I would phone the other girls in the club and tell them to keep their ears open for kids who'd want to join. Maybe Jamie Newton, or some of the Pikes or Barretts would be interested. I could talk to Watson about the team. Watson loves baseball. In all honesty, he's not the most athletic person I can think of, but he's a huge baseball fan, and he's good at organizing and running things—even better than I am, and I don't mind admitting it. If I wanted to start a softball team, Watson was the person to go to.

The other thing I decided was that I had a Gigantic Crush on Bart Taylor.

4th CHAPTER

Monday

This afternoon I baby-sat for Myriah and Gabbie Perkins. What can I say? We always have a good time together. If Kristy had to move away, and a new family had to move into her House, I'm glad my dad and I got the Perkinses as our new neighbours.

Anyway, I suppose I'm off the subject. Our afternoon went well of course. And I got some kids for Kristy's ball team, but you already know that, Kristy, since I called you as soon as I finished sitting. What happened was that when Mrs. Perkins left, Jamie Newton and Nina Marshall turned up to play with Gabbie and Myriah.

*Things got sort of out of hand, so
I suggested playing catch in
the backgarden...*

Rowf! Rowf! Rowf!
   "Hey, is that you, Mary Anne?"
   "Toshe me up, Mary Anne Spier!"
   The door to the Perkinses' house hadn't
even opened and already there was happy
noise and commotion as the girls and
Chewy clamoured for Mary Anne. The
Perkins girls are Myriah, who's five-and-a-
half, Gabbie, who' two-and-a-half, and
Laura, the new baby. Chewy (short for
Chewbacca) is the Perkinses' big, friendly
black Labrador, a great dog, even if he is
sort of, well, high-spirited.
   Myriah was the one calling, "Is that
you?" She knows she's supposed to find out
who's at the door before she opens it, even if
her mother or father is home. Gabbie was
the one calling, "Toshe me up." That's her
way of saying, "Pick me up and give me a
hug, please." No one knows where that
phrase came from. She just invented it. And
she almost always calls people (except her
sisters and parents) by their full names.
   "Yes, it's me! It's Mary Anne!" Mary
Anne replied.
   The door was flung open. There were
Chewy, Myriah, and Gabbie in an excited

28

group on the other side of the screen door. Mary Anne let herself in, and Myriah threw her arms around Mary Anne's legs in a happy hug. She and Mary Anne have been special friends ever since Mary Anne showed her how they could look out of their bedroom windows and see each other, just like she and I used to do. (Myriah's room is my old room.)

Even with Chewy barking and leaping around, and Myriah gripping her legs, Mary Anne leaned over to toshe Gabbie up.

"Look, Mary Anne Spier," said Gabbie, holding out her finger. On the finger was a plaster with pictures of Baby Kermit printed all over it. "I have a cut," she informed her sitter.

"A cut!" exclaimed Mary Anne. "Oh, no. How did that happen?"

"I was playing, and by accident, my finger went *WHAM* on the other side of the TV. I was running, and it just went *WHAM*!"

"It's only a little cut," added Myriah, looking up at Mary Anne and Gabbie.

"No, it's a big one."

"No, little. How could—"

"Girls!" called Mrs Perkins. "Let me talk to Mary Anne for a moment."

Mrs Perkins came down the stairs with Laura bundled up in a baby blanket. We sitters would love to take care of Laura sometimes, but she's just too little. Mrs

Perkins usually takes her wherever she goes. I suppose one baby is a lot easier than one baby *and* two kids.

Mrs Perkins made sure that Mary Anne knew where the emergency numbers were, where she was going, and when she'd be back. Then she left. She hadn't been gone long when the doorbell rang.

"I'll get it," said Mary Anne. "You guys hold Chewy."

Chewy just loves to charge up to visitors. All he wants to do is greet them, but sometimes people don't know that. The sight of a huge dog running straight at you can be scary, especially if you're only four or five years old and not much taller than Chewy.

Mary Anne opened the door. There were Jamie Newton and Nina Marshall. They're both kids in the neighbourhood and they're both four years old. Jamie was no surprise, but Nina was. Our club sits for Jamie all the time, and for Nina and her little sister Eleanor sometimes, too, but while Nina hardly ever goes to the Perkinses', Jamie often does.

Mary Anne was glad to see both of them, though.

"Hi, you guys!" she said. "Did you come over to play?"

"Yup," said Jamie and Nina at the same time.

Mary Anne had just let them in and closed the front door when she heard a *rowf*!

30

Chewy had struggled out of Myriah and Gabbie's grasp. He made a skidding dash through the hallway. Mary Anne caught him and led him out into the fenced-in back garden. Chewy is a handful—a happy handful with a doggie grin.

When Mary Anne went back in the house, she found things a little out of hand. Nina was running after Myriah with a giant foam-rubber banana. "Zonk! Zonk! Zonk!" she kept crying as she hit Myriah over the head with it.

Gabbie had found a plastic jug from her tea set. She had filled it with water and was carrying it through the house, crying, "Drinks for sale! Drinks for sale! Who wants to buy special water?"

"I do!" Jamie replied. "How much does it cost?"

"Four hundred dollars."

"Okay." Jamie reached into his pocket. He pretended to give Gabbie some money.

"Thank you," she said. Then she handed Jamie the water and he drank it straight from the jug.

"Mmm, yummy. May I have—"

"Zonk! Zonk!" cried Nina. She and Myriah were tearing towards Gabbie and Jamie and the jug. Every time Nina zonked Myriah, Myriah replied, "Boi-oi-oi-oing!"

"You guys!" Mary Anne said desperately. "Look out!"

Too late.

Myriah and Nina crashed into Jamie and Gabbie. Water splashed everywhere.

"I think," said Mary Anne, "that it's time to play outside. May I have the jug and the banana please? And would the four of you clean up the water before you put your jackets on?"

Mary Anne had never seen so many paper towels used to clean up such a small puddle, but at least the mess got mopped up. Then she took the kids into the Perkinses' back garden.

"How about playing catch?" she suggested, remembering my phone call about starting a softball team.

"With Chewy around?" replied Myriah. "We'd better put him inside."

"Oh, poor Chewy," said Mary Anne. "He'll miss out on the fun. Let's leave him outside for a little while."

"Okay-ay," said Myriah in a singsong voice that clearly meant she thought Mary Anne's idea was not a very wise one.

The kids found two bats—a plastic bat and a normal one; three balls—a plastic ball, a softball, and a tennis ball; and a couple of gloves.

"I'll be the pitcher," Myriah announced. "Nina, you be in the outfield. Gabbie and Jamie, you're the batters. You're on the other team."

Mary Anne was impressed. Myriah seemed to know a lot about playing softball.

32

"Okay, here comes the ball!" Myriah announced to Jamie, who was ready with the bat.

Jamie took one look at the softball flying towards him, dropped the bat, put his hands over his head, and ducked.

Guess who caught the ball? Chewy. Everyone ran after him. Chewy had the time of his life. He loves games. But when the kids couldn't catch him, they gave up. Besides, it was Gabbie's turn to bat, and since she's so little, Mary Anne told Myriah she'd have to pitch the plastic ball. Then she gave Chewy a bone to keep him busy while the kids played.

Myriah tossed the plastic ball.

Whack! Gabbie hit it. She looked extremely pleased with herself. But she just stood by home plate, holding the bat. "Now, what do I do?" she asked.

"Run, you dope!" exclaimed Nina.

"Nina, no name-calling," Mary Anne admonished her.

The kids barely heard Mary Anne. Myriah went after the ball, caught it, ran to home plate, where Gabbie was still standing, and hit her sister. "You're out!" she cried.

Mary Anne told me later that the game went on in pretty much the same way the game at my house had gone. Jamie ducked all balls, whether he was supposed to be hitting them or catching them. Gabbie wasn't too bad at hitting and catching—but she didn't understand much concerning the game of softball. (What can you expect from a two-and-a-half-year-old?) Nina, like Hannie Papadakis, tried hard, but wasn't particularly coordinated. Then there was Myriah. She was actually a pretty good player.

"Why don't you try for Little League?" Mary Anne wanted to know.

"Can't. I'm old enough for T-ball, but not Little League."

"Would you like to play in a real team?" Mary Anne asked.

"You bet!" replied Myriah, and Mary Anne was surprised when the rest of the kids said, "Yes!" as well.

"Really?" she asked. "You too, Gabbers?"

Gabbie nodded solemnly.

"Well," said Mary Anne, and she told them about my softball team.

The kids were enthusiastic, especially Myriah. They spent the rest of the afternoon hitting balls (or ducking them)—and then rescuing them from the jaws of Chewbacca, who had long ago given up on the bone.

5th CHAPTER

I always step onto the Rodowskys' front porch with a feeling of trepidation. (I like the word *trepidation*. It means alarm or dread, but somehow it seems less awful than those words.) The reason for the trepidation is, well, you know—Jackie, our very own walking disaster. Things happen to him. Sometimes things just happen because he's *around*. Imagine Paddington Bear. Imagine the little girl Eloise from the book called *Eloise*. Then put all that energy and mischief inside a character as nice as Charlie Bucket from *Charlie and the Chocolate Factory*. That's Jackie Rodowsky.

Because Jackie is basically a nice kid, I like to sit for him. But because I never know what's going to happen, I feel that trepidation. I feel it the whole time I'm at the Rodowskys'. It comes over me as soon as I reach their house, and it leaves the

35

moment my sitting job is over.

I rang the Rodowskys' bell.

Mrs Rodowsky answered the door, gave me the usual instructions, and began to put her coat on.

"Where are the boys?" I asked.

Mrs Rodowsky smiled. "They're in the games room," she said, lowering her voice. "Peek down there."

I peeked. The room looked ready for a party. Streamers crisscrossed the ceiling, and bunches of balloons hung here and there. The boys were busy blowing up more balloons and opening packets of paper plates and cups and party poppers.

"Aww," I said smiling. "Whose birthday is it?"

"Bo's." Mrs Rodowsky looked at me meaningfully.

"Bo's? . . . Oh, the dog's!" I giggled.

"He's two today, and the boys decided they wanted to give him a party. They've even wrapped up presents for him, and on my way home this afternoon, I'm supposed to pick up a birthday cake—a *small* one— with Bo's name on it. Can you believe it?"

"I think it's great!" I said. "We never did anything like that for our collie Louie, even though we loved him a lot. But maybe when our new puppy turns one, we'll have a party for her. We'll even invite Bo, since he'll know how to behave at a dog party."

Mrs Rodowsky laughed. "Well, I had

better get going. Let the boys do whatever they want for the party—within reason. Then take them outside for a while."

"Okay," I said. I walked Mrs Rodowsky down the stairs to the games room.

"'Bye, boys!" she called as she left through the back door.

They barely heard her.

"So, you guys," I said, "what did you get Bo for his birthday?"

All three boys looked at me in surprise.

"Where'd you come from?" asked Shea, the nine-year-old.

"I've been here for about five minutes," I told him. "Your mum just left. I know all about Bo's party. You look like you're doing a great job."

"There's not much left to do," said Shea.

"Nope," agreed Jackie, who's seven. "Just make the lemonade and find the birthday candles. And finish setting the table." Jackie glanced at a folding table that had been covered with a paper cloth. It looked like a table for a kid's birthday party.

"I'll find the candles!" volunteered Archie, the four-year-old.

"I'll finish the table," said Shea.

"Then I suppose I'd better make the lemonade," Jackie said, and added, "I'm making pink lemonade. It's more special."

"I'll help you!" I said quickly.

"*No* I can do it myself. I'm not a baby."

"Okay, okay. Sorry."

This is what I mean by trepidation. I didn't want to hurt Jackie's feelings, but I knew (well, I was pretty sure) that letting Jackie make lemonade would lead to a disaster.

I let him do it anyway.

"It's just a mixture," he said. "All you do is add water."

That didn't sound too dangerous. The one thing I insisted on, though, was a plastic jug. Letting him fill up something glass was plain foolish.

"Kristy? Can you help me look for the candles?" Archie said then. "Shea told me they're in a box in the cellar, and, um, I don't want to go down there by myself."

"Of course," I replied. I held out my hand. "Come on, Red."

"Red!" exclaimed Archie. "That's not my name."

"Red is a nickname for anyone with red hair," I told him, "like you guys have." The Rodowsky boys all have flaming red hair and plenty of freckles.

Archie and I left Jackie in the kitchen with the lemonade mixture and Shea in the games room, setting the table. Hand in hand, we descended into the cellar. I had to admit, the Rodowsky's cellar *was* a little spooky.

We had just found the candles when, from above, we heard a *thunk* and a *whoosh*. Then we heard Jackie say, "Uh-oh."

Archie and I didn't waste a second. We ran up the stairs to the games room and then to the kitchen. Shea was already there. He and Jackie were staring at a large pink puddle on the floor, and pink drips down the sides of the cupboards, the dishwasher, and the table and chairs. Jackie was blushing as red as his hair.

"It was an accident," he told me.

With Jackie, it's always an accident. And once he gets started, it's hard for him to stop. Have you ever heard the saying that "bad things happen in threes"? Well, with Jackie, they happen more like in fifteens.

"Come on, let's clear up," I said. I'd meant just Jackie and me to clear up, but Shea and Archie pitched in, too. They're used to helping their brother out.

When the kitchen was clean and non-sticky again, and another jug of lemonade had been made (we made it in the sink and *I* carried the jug to the refrigerator), I said, "Is everything ready for Bo's party now?"

"Yes," answered the boys.

"Good. Then we're going outside." I was not about to wait around for another disaster, and disasters were less apt to happen outside.

"What are we going to do?" asked Archie, as he and his brothers were putting on their jackets.

"*I* need to practise for Little League," said Shea importantly.

Of course, my ears pricked up at that. "Little League?" I repeated. "Jackie, are you in Little League, too?"

"Naw," said Jackie, staring at his feet.

Shea snorted rudely, but I ignored his behaviour. "Go and get your baseball equipment," I told him.

A few moments later, the Rodowsky boys were swinging bats, and tossing balls in the air. I was standing on a flat rock which Shea assured me was the pitcher's mound. "Okay, batter up!" I called.

"Me first! Me first!" cried Jackie. He leaped next to an old magazine (home plate).

I pitched the ball. It was a good pitch—I mean, an easy one. If I'd been pitching in a real game, it would have been like saying to the other team, "Okay, just go ahead and score yourself a run." But Jackie missed the ball. Not by much, though.

Archie missed my next easy pitch, too, but then he's only four, and also left-handed, which makes things a little more difficult.

Shea, on the other hand, slammed the ball so hard, and it travelled so far, that even Bo couldn't find it.

"Home run! Home run!" shouted Shea. He jumped gleefully up and down on the magazine.

"Kristy, Kristy, can I pitch now?" asked Jackie. "I want to try pitching."

"Good luck," Shea muttered sarcastically, but I was the only one who heard him.

Jackie took his place on the rock. He wound up his arm like professional ball players do. He threw straight to Shea—and somehow, *some*how, the ball hit the house next door. *Boing, boing, boing, slurp.* It bounced down the roof and landed in a rain-filled gutter.

"Jackie!" exclaimed Shea.

"Oh, brother," I said. "Now we're going to have to go over there and tell your neighbours there's a softball in their gutter."

"Don't worry about it," said Shea. "Four others are there, too. Our dad's going over on Saturday to get them out. He can just get this one while he's at it."

"Do you have another ball?" I asked.

"We'll use a tennis ball," said Jackie, heading for the garage. "I'll get it. I want to try batting again. I *know* I can hit the ball."

Jackie was a disaster on the softball field, just like he was anywhere else, but he was determined to play. And he did hit the ball from time to time. He reminded me of David Michael. I really admired him.

While Jackie was getting the tennis ball, we heard a huge crash in the garage. Since I was tired of disasters, all I said was, "Whatever it is, pick it up, Jackie!"

"Okay!" he shouted back.

Jackie returned with the tennis ball.

"Anything broken in there?" I asked.

"Nope."

A miracle.

Jackie handed the ball to Shea, who pitched it to him.

"Keep your eye on the ball!" I called.

Whack! Jackie slammed the ball. "I hit it!" he yelled, and made a dash for first base.

Shea caught it as it flew through the air, but Jackie kept running. He ran all the way around the yard to home plate, where he was met by Shea. Shea held the tennis ball in Jackie's face. "I caught it," he informed him. "You're out. Jackie, you will never be in Little League." He didn't have to add, "Because no one would want you," but that's what he meant, and we all knew it.

"Yes, I will," replied Jackie stubbornly. "I *will* be in Little League. I'll practise and practise. I'll get as good as you. I'll get *better* than you. I'll be the best player in the universe." Jackie punctuated his speech by tripping over his shoelace.

Sheesh. He's even worse than David Michael, I thought. But I was pretty sure I had a new member for my softball team. A few minutes later, I was positive. I noticed that the worse Jackie played, the harder he tried. He wouldn't give up. Maybe he just needed some confidence and coaching. Watson had said those things were very important. (Watson, by the way, had been extremely flattered when I'd gone to him about organizing a team. He had also been extremely helpful and extremely nice.)

I told Jackie about my softball team. Jackie's face lit up like candles on a birthday cake. I really wished Watson could have seen that smile.

That night I got some interesting phone calls. The first was from Jessi Ramsey. "Guess what," she said. "Matt Braddock wants to be in your team."

"Great!" I exclaimed. Matt's a terrific kid and a terrific ball player—but he was born deaf. He can't hear or speak. You have to communicate with him using sign language. Luckily, a lot of the kids in Stoneybrook learned some sign language after they met Matt, so this isn't much of a problem.

Then Mallory rang. "I talked to my brothers and sisters. Nicky, Claire, and Margo want to be in your team," she said. "I tried to talk Vanessa into it, but she's not interested. And the triplets are in Little League."

Next to phone was Dawn, saying that two of the three Barrett kids she often sits for were interested, as well as three friends of theirs (whom I didn't know).

The last call was from Claudia. "I haven't found a single kid for your team," she wailed.

"Don't worry about it," I told her. "I've got twenty already."

"Wow!"

"Yeah."

It was time for a planning session with Watson.

6th
CHAPTER

Boy. I had no idea what I was getting myself into when I decided to coach a softball team, even after I had talked to Watson. It seemed like such a nice thing to do—organize a team for kids who were too embarrassed or too young to be in Little League or to play T-ball. Well, it *was* a nice thing. I knew that. And Watson knew that, which was why he was so encouraging. But it was also . . . . Well, you'll see what happened.

Anyway, as soon as I found out that twenty kids wanted to be in my team, I got to work. First, I made a few lists. The Babysitters Club is always doing this, and it's very helpful. One list, the most important, was of the names and ages of kids in the team, and their special problems. It looked like this:

Gabbie Perkins - 2½ - doesn't understand game yet
Jamie Newton - 4 - afraid of the ball
Nina Marshall - 4 - probably just needs work
Andrew Brewer - 4 - just needs work
Suzi Barrett - 4 - ?
Myriah Perkins - 5 - ? (probably just needs work)
Claire Pike - 5 - ?
Patsy Kuhn - 5 - (haven't even met her)
Laurel Kuhn - 6 - (haven't even met her)
Karen Brewer - 6 - just needs work
Max Delaney - 6 - just needs work
Buddy Barrett - 7 - ?
David Michael Thomas - 7 - absolutely hopeless
Hannie Papadakis - 7 - poor hitter
Matt Braddock - 7 - excellent player; uses sign language
Jackie Rodowsky - 7 - a walking disaster
Margo Pike - 7 - ?
Nicky Pike - 8 - ?
Jacob Kuhn - 8 - (haven't even met him)
Linny Papadakis - 8 - just needs work

I looked at my list. I did a little maths.
The average age of my team was 5.8 years—
just under six. These were *young* kids. Of
course, if they were older, they'd have
joined Little League. Well, some of them
would have.

Then I made a list of questions to answer:

46

Would anyone help me?
What would be the purpose of my team?
Does Bart Taylor think I'm cute?

A zillion phone calls later, Watson and I had found answers to all but the last question. Thanks to Watson, we got permission to meet at the playground of Stoneybrook Elementary School. This was convenient since a lot of the kids lived nearby. We would meet on Tuesdays after school, and on Saturday afternoons.

Some of the club members volunteered to help me. Some of them also sounded pretty uncertain. For instance, Jessi said, "I'm a dancer, not an athlete. I barely know the difference between a football and a baseball." And Claudia said straight away, "I hate sports . . . but I'll help you." Mary Anne and Dawn were more helpful, and said, "We don't know much about sports, but we love the idea of your team. Just tell us how to help." Mallory was a great help: "I've lived with Little League for two seasons now. I know all there is to know about kids and ball games. I'll do anything— except watch Claire have a tantrum."

Tantrum? Uh-oh.

The purpose of the team? Watson and I talked about that for a long time, and

Watson did not say a single stupid thing. We agreed that the purpose of the team was the reason I'd started it—to coach kids who wanted to improve their playing skills, but more importantly, just to have fun. I thought I could put the twenty kids on two sides each time we met, and we could have a game—after coaching. Coaching first, I decided, then a game. Maybe just a seven-innings game, or an even shorter one. Coaching (and I promised myself I would *never* lose my temper with any kid, no matter what) followed by a game should be a lot of fun.

Does Bart think I'm cute? Well, how would I know? Maybe the better question was, *Had* Bart thought I *was* cute? I hadn't seen him since I'd walked Shannon over to his house. And I'd probably never see him again, considering we went to different schools and had different friends. I tried to put Bart and my Gigantic Crush out of my mind.

That was not too difficult. On Saturday afternoon, we held our first team meeting. Every single kid turned up! So did Dawn and Mallory.

"Where'd you get all that equipment?" Dawn asked me in awe, as she looked at the things surrounding me—four bats, five gloves, a catcher's mask, a softball, and a plastic ball (for Gabbie).

48

"Oh, it's all ours. With six kids in your family," (I count Andrew and Karen as part of my family, of course), "two of whom are guys in high school, you'd be surprised at what accumulates. Some of it's mine. The only thing we're low on is balls. All Sam and Charlie have are hardballs, and I couldn't find any tennis balls."

The twenty kids gathered around me eagerly. We were standing at the edge of the playground. I saw that a few parents had come along, and I began to feel nervous. I felt like a teacher on her first day at school when some parents have stuck around to see how good she is. One of the mothers was Mrs Braddock, and I knew she was just there to translate everything I said into sign language for Matt, but still. . . .

The kids were looking at me expectantly. I edged away from the playground and said, "Let's sit down. I want to talk to you for a few minutes."

The kids plopped down in the grass. Dawn and Mallory sat on either side of me. The parents hovered in the background (except for Mrs Braddock).

"First," I said, "I just want to introduce myself to the three kids I don't know, the Barretts' friends." It was easy to spot them in the crowd. They were the only faces I didn't recognize.

I pointed to the oldest-looking one. "You

must be Buddy's friend," I said. "I'm Kristy Thomas."

The boy nodded. "I'm Jacob Kuhn, but call me Jake. I'm eight," he added.

The other Kuhns turned out to be Laurel, who was six and so shy that Jake had to say her name and age for her, and Patsy, who was five, Suzi Barrett's friend.

"Well," I said, "I want you guys to know that we're here to play softball, but mostly we're here to have fun. I'm going to coach you and teach you skills during the first part of each afternoon, and then we'll divide into two teams and play a game. If you think you're not a good player, don't worry about it. There's no pressure here. This is *just fun*. Got it?"

I saw a few eyes light up, Jackie's among them.

David Michael raised his hand, just as if he were in school. "I'm hopeless," he said.

"I don't care," I replied. "Everybody here is good at some things and not so good at others."

Jamie Newton raised his hand. "I'm afraid of the ball," he admitted.

"I can never hit it," Claire Pike announced.

"Then those are the things we'll work on," I said, smiling. "Now. How many of you are friends with Matt Braddock?"

A few hands went up, including the Barretts' and the Pikes'.

50

"Matt is deaf," I explained to the others. "He can't hear and he doesn't talk. But I'll tell you something. He is one super ball player." (Matt beamed when his mother signed that to him.)

My stepsister Karen raised her hand. "We can talk to him, though," she informed everyone. "We can talk to him in his secret sign language, just like his mother is doing now."

"That's right," I agreed. "I'll show you the signs you need to know to play softball with Matt."

"I already know them!" said Nicky Pike proudly.

"Me too," said Buddy Barrett.

"Great. Now today, instead of having a practice first, I think we should just hold a game. I haven't seen many of you play, and—"

"Wait!" cried Jackie. "Don't we need a team name? If we're going to be a softball team, we need a name like the Mets or the Dodgers or the Red Sox."

"Yeah!" cried all the kids.

Suddenly they were shouting out dozens of suggestions—the Stoneybrookers, the Tigers, the Big Leaguers. But when Jackie yelled out, "How about Kristy's Crushers?" everyone agreed.

"And we could spell 'Crushers' with a 'K'," added Margo Pike. "You know, to go with Kristy. Kristy's Krushers."

"No!" cried Karen. "That's wrong. That's not how you spell 'crushers.' You spell 'crushers' with a 'C'!" (Karen takes her spelling very seriously.)

But she was voted down. Every other kid liked "Kristy's Krushers-with-a-'K'".

"And we should have team uniforms," added Jake Kuhn. "The kids in Little League do."

I hadn't thought about that. It seemed expensive. "Where will we get uniforms?" I wondered aloud. Even Watson hadn't thought of that.

"How about team T-shirts?" suggested Mallory, coming to my rescue. "If each of you could get a plain white T-shirt, you could iron on 'Kristy's Krushers'. You know, with those letters you get at Woolworth's."

This seemed to appease the kids, even though we all knew that T-shirts were not as good as real uniforms.

"Well," I said, "let's get a game going here. Everyone stand in a line."

It took a few moments, but the kids organized themselves into a long, straggly line.

"Now pair off," I instructed them. "One, two, one, two. . . ."

I gathered the Ones and the Twos. "These are your teams," I said. "We'll toss a coin to see which team will bat first. Then I'll assign positions to the rest of you."

The game began. Linny Papadakis was the pitcher.

He pitched to Claire, who missed the ball by a mile.

He pitched to Jamie Newton, who, at the last moment, dropped the bat, covered his head, and ducked.

I winced, then hoped that none of the kids had seen me.

Over in right field, I caught sight of Laurel Kuhn making a daisy chain. "Hey, Laurel!" I yelled. "Watch the game, okay?"

Laurel nodded, but over in left field, Hannie Papadakis was looking for four-leaf clovers.

"Hannie! Heads up!"

"Left field is boring!" she replied.

Linny pitched the plastic ball to Gabbie Perkins, who made the first hit of the game. She even ran for first base, but halfway there she got a fit of giggles, which slowed her down. The first basewoman caught the ball before Gabbie reached her.

Jackie went to bat next. He made the next hit of the game—right into the woods behind the school.

"Foul ball!" I cried.

Eight children went looking for the softball. They couldn't find it, and no one wanted to play with the plastic ball.

"Game over," I announced.

"Thanks to Jackie," someone muttered.

But all I said was, "You guys were great!

"Keep up the good work. I'll see you on Tuesday."

" 'Bye, Coach!" called Linny Papadakis.

Coach? . . . Coach! I liked the sound of that.

I couldn't wait to tell Watson about our first practice. No one had cried or got hurt. The kids had been excited. They'd had fun. They'd come up with a team name. As far as I could tell, the practice had been a success.

7th
CHAPTER

Monday

Mallory! What a game!

I'll say, Claud. Kristy's Krushers are terrific. We hardly had to babysit today.

Nope. We were fans instead.

Except for that one tantrum.

Well, those are bound to happen every now and then. I warned Kristy about them. Claire may be silly, but she's also got a temper. Especially when she's doing something, you know...

Competitive?

Well, competitive. And only when it has to do with baseball....

Sometimes I think the Pikes are the best thing that ever happened to Matt Braddock and his nine-year-old sister Haley. When they moved to the Pikes' neighbourhood, Haley thought it would be the end of the world. She thought that because Matt's deaf, kids would think he was weird—and if they thought he was weird, they would think *she* was weird, and that neither one would ever make new friends.

Luckily Haley was wrong, thanks to Jessi and Mallory. Jessi started bringing the Braddock kids over to Mallory's house, and Mallory and Jessi told the Pike kids that Matt knew a *secret language*. What a mystery! They all wanted to learn it, too. Now they can talk to Matt pretty well. If there's trouble, Haley helps out, since she can sign almost as well as she can speak. Also, Haley has got to be friends with Vanessa, and Matt is friends with the Pike boys.

Anyway, on the day that Claud and Mallory were sitting for the seven other Pike kids, Jessi brought Matt and Haley over as usual. Claud and Mal were in the back garden with the Pike kids. It was a sunny day, and everyone felt like being outdoors. Margo was skipping on the patio, Vanessa was teaching Claire to play jacks, the triplets were trying to do acrobatics in the grass, and Nicky was examining a scab on his elbow.

"That drives me crazy," said Mal, watching the triplets. "They're going to break their backs or something. I just know it."

"Oh, they are not," said Claud. "How many times have you tried things like that?"

"Just once," replied Mal, "and I sprained my wrist."

"Oh."

Claudia was saved by a shout of, "Hi!"

Vanessa had spotted Jessi, Haley, and Matt. She left the jacks game and ran to them, waving to Matt. Waving is the sign for "Hi!" (Easy, huh?) Matt waved back, then joined the triplets. The triplets stopped fooling around (to Mallory's relief).

"Do you want to play a game of softball?" they asked Matt with their hands.

Matt nodded vigorously.

"Can we play, too?" asked Claire. "Nicky and Margo and me? We're in a softball team now, you know. We're Kristy's Krushers, just like Matt."

Mallory could tell that her brothers wanted to laugh—obviously, they didn't think much of the Krushers—but they didn't want to hurt Matt's feelings.

"Hey!" Adam cried suddenly. "How about Little Leaguers *versus* the Krushers? That would be an, um, interesting game."

"Oh, but it wouldn't be fair," spoke up Nicky. "There are only three of you guys . . . and four of us Krushers."

"Believe me, that'll be very fair," said Jordan snidely.

By that time, Matt was looking angry, as he often does when he's left out of a conversation. (It must be awfully frustrating.) Haley rushed over and signed to him. When Matt understood what was being planned, his face lit up. He signed furiously to his sister.

Haley burst out laughing. "Matt says the Krushers can beat the pants off you Little Leaguers!"

"Oh, yeah?" said Adam, leaning toward Matt menacingly.

No one needed to translate that, and Matt's response was to draw his finger across his throat, clearly meaning, "You *die*!" But he was smiling and so was Adam.

"Are we on?" said Byron.

Claire, Margo, Nicky, and Matt were facing the triplets. Their answer? *Yes*! And Claire added, "And we'll beat you, all right!"

"Oh, sure," said Jordan. "You know what Claire's batting average is? *Zero*. She has *never* hit a ball."

"But I've caught a lot of them," she pointed out.

Adam and Byron headed into the Pikes' garage and returned with some gloves, bats, and softballs.

"Because we're so nice," said Byron, "we'll let you Krushers bat first." And he signed to Matt, "Your team first."

Matt nodded, looking as if he thought the triplets were making a big mistake.

The triplets held a conference to choose positions, while Nicky signed that Matt should bat first. Matt nodded, ready for business.

Jordan was the pitcher. Adam and Byron were combination outfielders and basemen. Jordan stared at Matt. He shuffled his feet around and adjusted the brim of his cap, trying to look professional. Then—*zoom!* He threw a fastball.

Matt was ready. His eyes on the ball, he swung and connected. The ball sailed over Jordan's head.

"I've got it! I've got it!" shouted Adam. And he did have it—but not on the fly. He didn't get it to third base until just after Matt had slid in.

"Yea!" cheered Vanessa and Haley from the sidelines.

"All *right!*" shouted Nicky. "See what the Krushers can do?"

Matt grinned and waved his fist over his head in a silent cheer.

"I see what *Matt* can do," said Jordan, getting set to pitch. "Now I want to see what *you* can do, little brother."

What Nicky could do was miss. He handed the bat to Margo. Margo took it, positioned herself in the batter's box and kept her eyes on Jordan. She concentrated so hard that she didn't even blink when Adam called out, "Hey Margo, you're going to miss!"

Or when Nicky retorted, "You guys must be pretty worried if you have to try to scare us."

Claud and Mal looked at Jessi and smiled.

The triplets shut up. And Margo kept her batting stance.

Jordan pitched.

Margo fouled the ball.

Jordan pitched again. Then seven more times.

Finally Jordan shrugged. Enough was enough. He let Margo walk to first base.

Claire's turn.

"It's the strike-out queen!" shouted Byron. But the Krushers didn't react, and Byron shut up.

"Come on, Claire," Nicky said seriously to his sister. "One out. Runners at first and third. I know you've never hit the ball, but if you hit it now you could send Matt home."

Claire nodded.

"Good. I know you can do it," said Nicky.

On the sidelines, the babysitters smiled at each other again. Nicky was rarely so nice to his sisters. Usually he teased them with rude songs or played tricks on them or tried to wind them up.

"The Krushers stick together," Claudia commented.

And then Claire missed.

60

"Whoa. Two misses. Tantrum time," muttered Mallory.

But nothing happened.

Nicky was up again. He swung and missed. Then he slammed the ball deep into the left field. Matt ran home. Margo ran home. And Nicky reached second base before he realized he had better not go any further.

The Krushers looked at each other proudly. Claudia told me later that the triplets seemed a bit overawed. (And maybe just the teeniest bit proud.) To the Krushers' credit, they didn't gloat. I wish I'd been there. I would have been proud of them, too.

I would have been proud right up until what happened next.

Matt missed, the triplets ran off the field—and Claire threw a tantrum. I'd never seen Claire throw a tantrum. I didn't even know she threw tantrums until Mallory mentioned it over the phone. But sure enough, as soon as her team had missed three times, Claire clenched her fists, screwed up her face, and began screeching, "No fair! No fair! No fair!" until, according to Claudia, who had the job of calming her down, it sounded more like she was saying, "Nofe-air! Nofe-air! Nofe-air!"

"She only throws baseball tantrums," Mallory informed me later. "She does it with ball games on TV, too."

However, Claire got over her tantrum and Matt pitched to the triplets. They scored four runs in the first innings. In the second innings the Krushers scored no runs and the triplets scored three more. By the end of the fifth innings, when Mrs Pike came home, the triplets were ahead, sixteen to five.

But, with the exception of Claire's tantrum, the Krushers never once lost their patience or their courage. They did lose their concentration a few times, but what can you expect from 5.8-year-old kids?

When the game was over, Jordan actually said to Nicky and his sisters, "Good game, you guys." Then he remembered to sign for Matt. Matt grinned.

Haley, who had watched the entire game with Claudia, Mallory, Jessi, and Vanessa, just said, "Whew. That was amazing. There was no way they could beat the triplets—but they never gave up."

"Never," agreed the others.

When Mal and Claudia told me about the game later, I felt terrific. My team, my Krushers, had real spirit.

8th
CHAPTER

"Claire, can you please get out of that tree? And Karen, stop teasing your broth—Jamie, what are you doing? Leave that bat alone. You're supposed to hit balls with it, not walk on it."

"I'm a tightrope walker, Coach." Jamie replied, but he stepped off the bat.

It was the beginning of another practice with the Krushers. I seemed to be having a little trouble getting everyone organized. Claudia was there, and she was supposed to be helping me, but she'd found some sweets in the pocket of her jeans and was concentrating on unwrapping one. You could tell that the sweets were much more interesting to her than softball.

I clapped my hands. Suddenly I felt like Mr Redmont, my old teacher from seventh grade. He was always clapping his hands to get kids' attention.

"Hey, you guys!" I called. "Would you come here, please. . . . PLEASE? . . . *Claudia*. I need help."

What was wrong with everybody? I thought these kids wanted to play softball so badly.

Claudia popped a sweet into her mouth and wandered over to me. "What do you want me to do?" she asked.

I could have been sarcastic, but I kept my temper. After all, the kids were nearby. I didn't want them to think I was an ogre.

"Just help me get them together. We need some practice time first."

"Come on guys!" I called again. "Where's your Krushers spirit?"

Immediately, the kids ran over to me—except for Claire. She was stuck in the tree. Claudia had to lift her down.

Boy, all I had to say was "Krushers" and the kids jumped to attention.

I began assigning tasks. "Jamie," I said, "I know you're a little afraid of the ball. Can you *throw* it, though?"

He nodded.

"Great. I want you to pitch to Claire for a while. She needs practise hitting the ball." And, I thought, if she actually did hit it, Jamie might try to catch it. (Either that, or he would duck it.)

"Okay," said Claire and Jamie.

"David Michael and Nicky, I want you to work on your pitching. You guys just toss the ball to each other, okay?"

"Yup," they replied.

This time I was prepared with more equipment. I'd asked the kids to bring along some of their own things so they would have enough to practise with.

Our afternoon got underway. I'd assigned each Krusher something to work on, and I walked around and gave the kids hints.

"Hannie, run towards the ball," I shouted. "Don't wait for it to come to you. You have to go after it. . . . Claire, keep your eye on that ball. . . ."

I almost shouted Matt's instructions to him, too, before I remembered that he wouldn't hear me. I signed to him instead, and he looked confused. I'd probably just told him to go and buy an elephant or something. I wished Haley or Mrs Braddock or Jessi were there to help.

Claudia looked bored. She sat down in the grass and ate another sweet. Then she examined her fingernails.

"Time for a manicure?" I asked her.

Claud jumped. "Oh, sorry," she said.

"Listen, could you toss the ball to Jamie for a while?" I asked her. "You're good with him," (it never hurts to flatter people) "and I'll work with Claire. They're not getting much accomplished together."

Claire was singing "I'm a Little Teapot" to Jamie, and every time she got to the part about "tip me over and pour me out" she released the softball from her underarm, which Jamie thought was hysterical.

I let the practice go on for about ten more minutes. Then I called, "Game time!"

What a reaction! The kids jammed themselves around me. I made them pair off again, and as soon as the sides were organized, we got a game going. The kids immediately went to work. Karen was the catcher for her side. She crouched behind home plate, wearing her mask and slamming one hand into her glove. "Attaboy! Attaboy!" she kept shouting, no matter what was going on.

I let David Michael pitch. First to bat was Matt Braddock. He swung the bat and fouled. David Michael, who barely knows any sign language, signed something that looked like "monkey." Then he remembered a softball sign, but it was the one for "safe." It took ages to get everything sorted out.

When the first half of the innings was over, which was pretty soon (as after Matt batted, the next three hitters each missed), I let our walking disaster go to bat first. He hit the ball and ran to second! While Linny Papadakis was batting, Jackie reached third base. Then Myriah Perkins got in a single, Jackie ran for home, tripped over his feet, and was stumped out, just inches from the base.

"Darn, darn, double, double darn!" he shouted.

The other kids laughed, but not rudely.

At the start of the second innings, I let Jackie be the catcher. Like Karen, he loved wearing the mask and glove. You could tell he felt professional.

Buddy Barrett was pitching now. He pitched to Jamie. Jamie concentrated, tried not to look scared, and ducked at the last minute. The ball slammed into Jackie's mouth.

"Jackie!" I cried. "What happened to the mask? You were just wearing it."

"I had to take it off, Coach," he replied. "I got my gum stuck on it. I wanted to see if I could make it look like a waffle by pressing it against the mask. You know, like you can do with Silly Put—Uh-oh!"

"What?" I asked.

"My mouth's bleeding! I think I knocked out my tooth. . . . No, it's just loose. Very loose."

I may make comments about food to wind up my friends, but I'll tell you one thing that winds *me* up: very loose teeth. Especially bloody ones.

Claudia knows that. She stepped over to look in Jackie's mouth. "It's so loose it could practically fall out," she said. "Do you want me to pull it out for you, Jackie? I've got a Kleenex right here."

Oh, oh, ew.

"All right," agreed Jackie.

The entire team crowded around to watch

the proceedings. Not me, though. I stood as far away as possible. I pretended to check on our equipment.

A few minutes later, I saw the kids disperse. Jackie held up a tissue. "My tooth's in here, Coach!" he announced. He ran over to me and smiled a gap-toothed, slightly bloody smile. "I just love losing teeth."

Ew. I never liked losing teeth. I'm glad I'm past that stage. "Put the Kleenex and your tooth in your pocket," I told Jackie.

We played another innings, and I must say that everybody played harder than before. The kids *tried* hard, too, just as Mallory and Claudia said the four Krushers had done in the game against the triplets.

But it was getting late.

"I think this game is over," I said at the end of the innings. "How many of you guys have bought T-shirts and iron-on letters?"

Most of the kids raised their hands.

"Good," I told them. "Try to wear your shirts to our next practice. Then we'll really look like a team, and everyone will know we're the Krushers."

The kids began to leave. Charlie arrived to pick up Karen, Andrew, David Michael, and me, and take us to our homes. (Karen and Andrew were going to their mum's house.) After they'd been dropped off, I began to daydream. I daydreamed about Bart. I'd been doing that a lot lately.

An idea came to me.

"Hey, David Michael," I said, "do you want me to walk Shannon for you tonight?"

David Michael loves Shannon, but he also loves getting out of his chores.

"You bet!" he replied. Then he narrowed his eyes. "What do I have to do for you?" he asked suspiciously.

Do for me? I hadn't thought about that, but what an opportunity.

"Umm . . ." I replied slowly, "learn five signs you need to know to play softball with Matt Braddock. Ring Nicky Pike and ask him for help, okay?"

"Okay!"

David Michael thought he'd got the best part of the deal, but I knew that (with any luck) *I* had.

When supper was over that night, I found Shannon in the study, chewing on a rubber toy that looked like a steak.

"Do you want to go for a *W-A-L-K*?" I asked her.

We started spelling *walk* so Shannon wouldn't get all excited and think she was going out every time she heard the word. But we spelled it so often that Shannon has figured out what *W-A-L-K* means.

She abandoned the toy, leapt to her feet, and bounded to the back door, where I clipped on her lead. Then I told Mum and Watson that I was going to walk Shannon, and I set off. I wasn't *just* walking Shannon, though. I was walking Shannon past Bart Taylor's house. Pretty clever, huh?

I thought so. So I was totally surprised when, only halfway there, who should I see coming towards me, but Bart! He was walking a rottweiler on a chain which could have tethered a lion. (In case you don't know, a rottweiler is a really fierce dog. Next to Bart's dog, Shannon looked like a mouse.)

Bart and I spotted each other at the same time and called, "Hi!" Then we both slowed down. We weren't sure how our dogs would behave.

"This is Twinkle," Bart said. "He looks fierce, but he wouldn't hurt a flea."

"And Shannon," I replied, "won't believe that Twinkle wouldn't hurt a flea . . . but let's see what happens."

Poor Shannon approached Twinkle with her tail tucked between her legs. The dogs circled each other and sniffed, and Shannon discovered she was so little she could walk right under Twinkle, which Bart and I thought was pretty funny. When we realized that the dogs were going to be okay, we stood there on the pavement as night fell, and began to talk.

I told Bart how the Krushers were doing. Bart laughed.

"What?" I asked.

"I don't believe it. My team's called the

Bashers. The Bashers and the Krushers."

It *was* funny.

Then I said, "Have you ever run into a kid who's afraid of balls and ducks them?"

Bart looked thoughtful. "I don't think so. But most of my kids are a little older than yours. They're about seven to nine. They're pretty much past being afraid of the ball and things. They're not great players, but they aren't babies."

"The Krushers aren't babies!" I cried.

Bart flushed. "Relax," he said. "I didn't really mean that. I was just pointing out that the Bashers are older."

"Sorry," I said, and then practically melted as the streetlights came on and caught Bart's hair, giving it a sort of glow.

Bart was the cutest guy I had ever seen.

"Hey," said Bart, "I've got an idea. Just to show you that I think your team is as good as mine, even if the kids are younger, how about a game? Bart's Bashers challenge Kristy's Krushers."

A game? A real game? Against Bart's team? I didn't know if the Krushers were ready for something like that, but I wasn't about to say no. I couldn't let Bart think I was afraid of his team. Besides, if we arranged a game, I'd be sure to see him again—soon.

"Fine," I replied. "How about two weeks from Saturday? Is that enough time for the Bashers to get ready?"

"Of course! But what about the Krushers?"

"Oh, they'll be ready."

I grinned at Bart and he grinned back.

As I walked Shannon home a few minutes later, I felt as if there were cotton balls under my feet instead of concrete. And I'm sure my eyes were shining.

9th
CHAPTER

                          Saturday
Wow! The Krushers are something else, Kristy. I'm really glad
I got to sit for the Barretts on
a practise day. Buddy and Suzi
were so excited. They loved everything about being in the team,
especially their T-shirts. They
didn't even mind that it was
on the chilly side today and
they had to wear their team
shirts over other shirts.
    What can I say about this
afternoon? It was great. Easiest
sitting job I ever had. All I
had to do was walk the kids
to practise and back, and entertain
Marnie while practise was
going on. Marnie was in a

good mood, so entertaining her was no problem. Plus she fell asleep for awhile. It's too bad about what Jackie did, but Buddy and Suzi were still excited as we walked back home later ....

Boy. Thanks to me, Jessi really did have an easy sitting job. But I'm not complaining. After all, coaching a softball team was my idea. Jessi couldn't help it if Buddy and Suzie were in the team.

I have to admit that Jessi saw an unusual practice, though. I mean, a more exciting one than most. The kids gathered at the playground on time—and every last one of them was wearing a Kristy's Krushers T-shirt, even the kids who hadn't yet bought shirts and letters when I'd asked about that before. I was wearing a Krushers shirt, too. After all, I was the coach.

You could almost *taste* the excitement in the air.

I got to the playground early. Watson had driven David Michael and me over and was going to stay to watch the practice. He headed for the stands, saying he would keep out of our way.

74

David Michael beamed as he helped me check the equipment. "We're a *real* team now," he said at least three times. "And everyone will know you're our coach. I like that. Red letters."

It was true that my shirt was lettered in red while the kids' shirts were lettered in black, but I was hoping a few other things might be clues that I was coach—for instance, I was thirteen instead of 5.8, and taller than the players.

The kids began to turn up, all wearing T-shirts over sweat shirts or other shirts since it was a cold day.

"Hi-hi!" called Jamie, arriving with Gabbie, Myriah, and Mr Perkins.

"Look at us, Coach!" shouted Suzi, as she and Buddy ran onto the playground, followed by Jessi pushing Marnie in her push chair.

Five more Kristy's Krushers T-shirts.

"We're here!" cried Karen as she and Andrew climbed out of their mother's car and their mum drove off. (This was not one of their weekends at our house.)

Andrew was wearing his Kristy's Krushers shirt.

Karen was wearing her shirt, too. It said Kristy's Crushers.

"Whoa, Karen!" I exclaimed. "How did that happen? Did your mum iron the letters on your shirts?"

Karen nodded.

"Well, she spelled our team name wrong on your shirt."

"*My* shirt is spelled correctly," said Karen. "It'll be the only one, too. Crushers. C-R-U-S-H-E-R-S. Crushers."

Karen sounded as if she was taking a spelling test. I knew there was no changing her mind. She takes her spelling very seriously. Anyway, I didn't see why I should discourage that.

Kids kept pouring onto the playground. Soon all the Krushers had arrived, as well as some more onlookers. There were Jessi and Marnie, of course. And Mr Perkins. He was sitting in the stands with Watson. Haley Braddock, Vanessa Pike, and Charlotte Johanssen (another kid our club sits for) had turned up, too. I suppose they came just just to watch the action. Also, a couple of little boys I didn't recognize were hanging around.

I looked over at Jessi and she waved to me. She was giving Marnie crisps from a bag. When you go places with a two-year-old, you have to bring along an awful lot of equipment—toys, sweets, baby wipes, extra clothes, you name it.

"Okay, Krushers!" I shouted. "Everybody over here! I've got news!"

Watson and I decided that I should tell the kids about our game against the Bashers as soon as possible. Since I wasn't sure how some of them were going to react, I wanted

76

to make the whole thing sound as exciting as possible. I called Haley over to sign for Matt.

"You guys look great!" I exclaimed when we were all sitting down.

"A real team, like I said before," added David Michael.

I'd never seen so many happy faces in one place.

"What's the news, Coach?" Jake Kuhn wanted to know.

"The news," I said, dragging the surprise out tantalizingly, "is that we . . . the Krushers . . . are going to play a *real* game . . . against another team."

A murmur ran through the crowd. If it was possible, the kids' faces lit up even more. (A good sign.)

"Who are we playing?" asked Jackie.

"A team called the Bashers."

"*Bart*'s Bashers?" squeaked Max Delaney.

I couldn't tell whether he sounded excited or terrified.

"That's right."

"Are they good?" asked Jackie.

'I've never seen them play," I replied honestly, "but I know that they're a *little* older than you guys. I mean, just on the average, so—"

"But they're not Little Leaguers?" said Nicky Pike.

"Nope."

There was a moment of silence. Then Hannie Papadakis said, "This is going to be so, so cool." I think she got that from me.

And Matt Braddock raised his hand to attract my attention, then signed that he couldn't wait for the game and that the Bashers had better get themselves ready for it.

"When is the game?" Haley asked me, signing for Matt at the same time.

"Two weeks from today," I answered, "so we had better get to work. We need to practise, and I also want to assign positions to some of you. We've got to have a really good pitcher, a really good shortstop, and really good basemen. We won't be switching around so much anymore. The pitcher is the most important position, though, and *everybody* will need to work on hitting, okay?"

"Okay!" yelled the kids.

"Are we ready to get to work?"

"Yes!"

"Are we going to work hard?"

"YES!"

"Are we going to beat the Bashers?"

"*YES!*"

And at that moment, I got another one of my ideas. Cheerleaders! Boy, could we do with them! And I bet the Bashers wouldn't have cheerleaders.

"Haley," I said. "I know you don't want to play softball, but how would you like to be a cheerleader? Maybe Vanessa could cheer, too. And Charlotte."

"Wow!" cried Haley. "Hey, Vanessa! Charlotte! Come here for a sec!"

The girls left the stands and ran to us. I told them my idea.

Vanessa was so excited she practically burst out of her skin, but Charlotte began to look guarded. "I don't know," she said. "All those people watching. . . ." Charlotte is really shy.

"Oh, please?" said Vanessa and Haley at the same time.

"Well, maybe I could help you make up some cheers and you guys could do them," said Charlotte slowly.

"That'd be great," I told her. I didn't want to force her into anything. Once, Claudia had pressurized her a little into being in a beauty contest, and Charlotte had ended up running off the stage in tears.

"Two cheerleaders and one helper would be perfect," I told the girls. Charlotte is very clever and I knew she'd write good cheers.

The girls grinned at each other excitedly.

"Boy!" exclaimed Myriah. "Cheerleaders and everything!"

"Yeah," said Jackie. "If we're going to have a real game with team T-shirts and cheerleaders, maybe we should sell refreshments."

"Mallory could help Nicky and Claire and me bake cakes," said Margo Pike.

"We could sell lemonade," suggested Suzi Barrett.

I thought for a moment. Refreshments sounded like a lot of fun—and a lot of work. "Who's going to sell the refreshments?" I asked. "We'll all be busy playing or cheering or coaching."

"Our brothers and sisters," said Max Delaney. "I bet Amanda would help."

I doubted that, but Charlie and Sam might help. The Pike triplets might, too. "Well, okay. But what are we going to do with the money we earn?" I asked. "Remember, it will be *team* money."

"Buy team hats," Jackie replied immediately. "We really need them. Only some of us have hats, and they don't match."

So *that* was all settled.

"Great," I said. "But now we'd better do the most important thing of all—practise."

I got the kids all worked up again, then divided them into two teams for a game. They really needed to improve their teamwork.

"Nicky," I said, pulling Nicky Pike aside, "I think you're the best pitcher we've got, so from now on I want you and David Michael to pitch at all our practices. But *you'll* pitch in the game against the Bashers."

Nicky looked awed and proud.

The game got underway.

Vanessa and Haley stood on the sidelines shouting, "Bash those Bashers!" and things like that. Watson cheered loudly for Karen, Andrew, David Michael—and the rest of the team.

But not too long into the game, I caught Suzi Barrett turning somersaults in the outfield and Linny Papadakis, an imaginary microphone in his hand, pretending to be a sports commentator, when he was supposed to be playing shortstop. And Claire's batting average was still zero.

I shook my head.

Claire missed and Jackie stepped up to home plate. Nicky pitched the ball, Jackie swung the bat, and *CRACK!* He slammed the ball so hard that everyone knew he'd got a home run. Grinning, Jackie set off for first base. But before he reached it, we heard another sound.

CRASH!

The ball had gone right through a window of Stoneybrook Elementary. And not just any window, the window of the head's office. Thank goodness it was a Saturday. No one would be—

A face appeared in the window. It was the head's secretary. He was out of the side door of the school in three seconds flat. (Maybe he'd want to play in our team.)

"Who threw that ball?" he shouted.

Poor Jackie stepped forward. "Me," he said. "I mean, I hit it. It was a home run," he added hopefully.

The man smiled. But he still told Jackie

that the Rodowskys would have to pay for a new pane of glass.

When he went back inside, I announced that the practice was over. The kids would never be able to concentrate now. I was sure of that.

Even so—despite the accident and sending the kids home early—Jessi told me later that Buddy and Suzi were absolutely jubilant as they walked back to the Barretts' that afternoon. And Watson was so excited about the forthcoming game that he made David Michael, Andrew and Karen excited, too.

T-shirts, cheerleaders, refreshments, a real game coming up. It had been one of the biggest days in Krusher history.

10th CHAPTER

Tuesday

Whoa! Something is going on. And Kristy, it has to do with you and that other team, the Blasters or whoever they are. It doesn't really have anything to do with babysitting, except that I saw this incident while I was sitting. You see, Mrs. Perkins and Mrs. Newton asked me to take Myriah, Gabbie and Jamie to the Tuesday Krushers practise. I was in the stands watching the game when the Blasters came by, and Kristy, you kind of got mad at their coach. But before you got mad, you got, oh... I'd better stop before I get myself in trouble. Just one more thing. The Perkins girls and Jamie

83

*were upset when we walked home
this afternoon. They were really
annoyed with what the Blasters
did, and embarrassed about it,
too, I think....*

Talk about *Whoa!* Dawn doesn't miss a
thing. Her notebook entry was pretty meaty,
if you know what I mean. The only thing
she got wrong was the Blasters. She meant
the Bashers, of course. I wished she hadn't
noticed quite so much about me and Bart.
And I *really* wished she hadn't written
about us in the notebook. I'd have to talk to
her about that.

The thing is, I hadn't mentioned Bart to
any of my friends, even Mary Anne. I mean,
I haven't mentioned how I feel about him.
The club members know that the Krushers
are playing a rival team soon, and some of
them know that the coach of that team is
named Bart, but none of them knows about
my Gigantic Crush on him. Usually, that's
the sort of thing we club members share,
but for some reason, I wanted to keep Bart
private. And after what happened at the
practice, I was glad I'd been doing just that.

The practice got off to a pretty normal
start. The kids arrived on time (Dawn got
her kids to the playground early—she is *so*
organized), and they were all wearing their

T-shirts again. It was a much warmer day, so they didn't have to wear them over other clothes. I looked at my team. Smiling faces, new Kristy's Krushers T-shirts, running shoes with the laces tied or the Velcro straps fastened, neat blue jeans—all twenty kids. . . . No, nineteen of them. Nineteen tidy team members and one mess, our walking disaster. Jackie's jeans were muddy, his shoes were untied, and his shirt was on backwards and already had a hole in it. Even his hair was a mess. Oh, well.

"All right, Krushers!" I called.

To my surprise, I heard a shout: "Krush those Bashers! Crash those Bashers! Bash those Bashers out of sight!"

Our cheerleaders were on hand.

Then I heard another sound. It was a laugh. I turned away from my team members, who were lined up, ready to pair off, and saw—Bart and about ten of his Bashers. Bart was sitting in the stands, gazing intently at our team, but his Bashers were hanging around behind the catcher's cage. I guessed they were his Bashers, anyway. They were sturdy-looking boys wearing matching red baseball caps. But Bart wasn't paying much attention to them.

"Bart!" I cried. I'm sure I blushed. My knees turned to water, but I managed to run over to him. "What are you doing here?" I asked.

"Just checking up on our competition,"

he replied coolly. "That's legal."

"Oh." I said. I felt something like a rock settle in the pit of my stomach. "We—we haven't checked you guys out."

"Come on and check us out then. It's a free country."

Bart tried to smile, but frowned. This didn't seem like the boy I'd talked to under the streetlight. Was this a side of him I didn't know yet? Or was he only like this on the softball field? (Like Claire and her baseball tantrums?) I mean, I would do anything for my Krushers. Maybe Bart felt the same way about his Bashers.

I didn't know what to say to Bart, so I just walked back to my team. I felt crushed. (Krushed.)

As I passed the Bashers I heard a few sniggers from them. And some whispered comments which I know Bart couldn't hear.

"Look at that messy kid. He looks like Pig-Pen from Peanuts!" (Jackie.)

"Look at that baby with the plastic ball! I don't believe it—a plastic ball!" (That was Gabbie, her T-shirt covering her round two-and-a-half-year-old tummy. The only ball I'd allow her to hit was a plastic ball. And in order to throw it, the pitcher had to stand about five feet away from her. How would I handle that in the game against the Bashers? I hadn't even thought about that, but I was determined to put every one of my kids in the game, even Gabbie and Claire, and even if it was only for a few minutes. Watson and I had decided that was important.)

More comments:

"Look at fatso!" (Okay, so Jake Kuhn was a little overweight.)

"But *that* kids looks like a good pitcher." (Nicky. I was relieved to see that the Bashers appeared worried.)

In the stands, Dawn was watching us. She was taking everything in. She'd seen me have my talk with Bart, and she'd seen Bart's kids snigger at the Krushers. She'd worked out that they were Bashers (or Blasters), and she was surprised. She was surprised because she knew Bart's team was from my neighbourhood, which is pretty far away. The Blasters must be awfully curious, thought Dawn, to come all the way across town just to watch a Krushers practice. Either that, or they were nervous.

I decided to ignore Bart and his stupid Bashers. I pretended they weren't even there. At least I tried to. It wasn't easy. I could almost feel Bart's eyes on me.

"Okay, Krushers!" I shouted. "Practise game! Practise game! Pair off! Let's get rolling!"

The Krushers divided up. David Michael and Nicky were the pitchers, and Nicky's side was to bat first.

David Michael pitched to Margo Pike. She hit a pop fly. One out.

It's too bad I have such good hearing because I heard one of the Bashers say, "What can you expect from a *girl*?"

From a girl? Weren't there any girl Bashers? Even though I had decided to ignore our audience, I turned around to look at Bart. He was still sitting in the stands, watching the game.

Myriah Perkins was up next. She hit the ball and ran to second base. She really should only have made it to first, but Jackie was in the outfield and had so much trouble getting hold of the ball, you'd have thought there was margarine on his hands.

I heard a couple of hoots from behind me. "Pig-Pen can't catch to save his life," somebody shouted.

I whirled around to see Bart's reaction to his Basher's behaviour, but two of the other Bashers were talking to him. For just a moment, I wondered if they were actually distracting him so he *couldn't* hear. . . . Nah.

Matt Braddock was next to bat. Good, I thought. Now we'll show those Bashers what we're made of. If only Jackie weren't in the outfield. . . .

Matt missed twice, but whacked the ball hard on the third try. He let out an animal-sounding yell, which he sometimes does when he's excited (of course, he has no idea how he sounds), and he took off. When he reached second base, he paused, seeing that

Myriah had stopped at third. She signed to Matt to stay put.

At that, the laughter behind me was so loud that the only thing I could be glad of was that Matt wasn't able to hear it. The Krushers looked over at the Bashers. I could see the same thing registering on all their faces at the same time: They knew their competition was watching, and they knew they ought to start playing well.

But just then, one kid said loudly, "A dummy! They've even got a dummy on their team!"

Bart, why don't you make your kids shut up? I wondered. But I could see that one of his players had asked him for pitching tips, which Bart was giving out grudgingly. (He wanted to watch our team.) Now why would a kid need pitching tips in the middle of a scouting-out-the-other-team venture? Bart's Bashers *were* distracting him. I felt very angry. Why wasn't Bart picking up on what his team was doing?

Haley charged over to the Basher who had just insulted her brother. She stood inside the catcher's cage, nose-to-nose with the boy on the other side of the wire fence.

"That 'dummy'," she said with clenched teeth, "is my brother, and if you call him a dummy one more time, I will personally rearrange your face."

The kid just stared at Haley, but she stared back until she had stared him down.

89

The Bashers grew silent. They watched Haley walk back to Vanessa and Charlotte, where the three girls held a hurried conference. Then Charlotte returned to the stands, and Vanessa and Haley began jumping around, shouting, "Krushers crush, Bashers bash, but we'll get you Bashers in a flash!"

After Haley's outburst, the Bashers were quiet for two whole innings. They were still hanging around the catcher's cage (actually, four of them were hanging *on* it, several feet off the ground), but they were quiet. They were quiet until Jackie, running home, somehow couldn't stop in time and ran right into the catcher's cage.

Two of the Bashers were knocked to the ground, like flies flicked off a screen door.

"Way to go, Pig-Pen!" yelled one Basher, and I shot a vicious stare at Bart, but he was now bending over, trying to unknot his trainers, which I could see had been tied together, undoubtedly by his stupid Bashers.

If Bart couldn't control his team, I thought, then he really shouldn't be coaching.

Jackie looked at me with tear-filled eyes, and I couldn't blame him. I called an end to the practice.

Dawn told me later that as she walked Myriah, Gabbie, and Jamie home that afternoon, Jamie sulked, Gabbie cried, and Myriah held her sister's hand protectively.

"Those boys were mean," Gabbie commented, and then hiccupped.

"They were," Myriah agreed, "but we won't be mean back, will we? . . . Will we?" she said again when no one answered her.

"No," agreed Gabbie and Jamie at last.

And I knew that was true. My Krushers would not be mean.

11th CHAPTER

I couldn't believe it! How did it get to be Friday already?

It was the day before the Krushers' game against the Bashers. We were holding a special final practice. The Babysitters Club members were even giving up our meeting so we could cheer the Krushers on.

The day was very important. It was my last chance to work with the Krushers. I knew the practice might be a tough one, though. The kids were pretty wound up. But they needed to practise if they wanted to win—and they all wanted to win.

I wanted them to win, too. Not just because I'm competitive, but because I wanted Kristy's Krushers to know what it felt like to be winners—instead of kids who were afraid to be part of Little League, who were afraid of Bart's Bashers, who had zero batting averages, who were called "Pig-

Pen" and "dummy," and who broke windows and ran into catcher's cages.

And by the end of our practice, I truly thought the Krushers had a shot at winning, even though I had never seen the Bashers play. I hadn't done what Bart had done—check out the competition. I was scared to. I was also scared to admit that, even to myself. So I tried not to think about it.

At most of our practices, a few people would be sitting in the stands watching: club members who had brought kids over to play, maybe a couple of interested parents or a brother or sister, and the cheerleaders. But that Friday, twenty people were in the stands!

The Krushers were awed.

I was awed.

Jessi, Mal, Claud, Dawn, and Mary Anne were there, of course. So were Mrs Newton and Lucy, Mrs Perkins and Laura, Watson (taking the afternoon off from work), the triplets, and a few other people. There was no sign of the Bashers, and I breathed a sigh of relief.

Then, just as I was about to start our game, the cheerleaders turned up. Immediately I noticed two things. One, they'd put together outfits for themselves—Kristy's Krushers T-shirts, matching flared blue-jean skirts, white knee socks, and trainers. Two, Charlotte was wearing one of the outfits!

I ran over to the girls. "You look great!" I exclaimed. "The Krushers really appreciate your cheering. . . . And, Char, you're wearing an outfit, too. Does this mean you're going to cheer tomorrow? We'd really like that, but you don't have to, you know."

"I know," Charlotte replied, "and at the moment it just means I'm the head cheerleader because I made up all the cheers. But I *might* cheer tomorrow."

"She's thinking about it," Haley added.

Wow. I knew the Krushers meant a lot to their families and friends, but if they could inspire Charlotte to think about coming out of her shell, they must really be something. More and more, I was feeling that we just might, as Charlotte would say, bash those Bashers the next day!

I walked back to my team. I stood in front of them, ready to give them a pep talk, but for some reason I glanced into the stands first. My eyes met Watson's and he gave me the thumbs-up sign.

I grinned and gave him the sign back.

Then I faced my team. There they were—nineteen Krushers and Jackie. Oh, Jackie was a Krusher, too, all right. Don't get me wrong. It's just that he, well, he *did* look a little like Pig-Pen. He was still the only kid with a hole in his T-shirt. He was the only kid whose shoes were untied. Even the littlest kids were neat and tidy. Jackie was our walking disaster. Although he *had* been playing better lately. His hitting had really improved. It was just that he had so many accidents.

"Okay, Krushers," I began, "you all know what tomorrow is."

"A game," replied Jackie.

"Well, our *big* game," I said. "Against the . . ."

"Bashers!" shouted the Krushers.

"And what are we going to do?" I cried.

"Beat them!"

"What?"

"*Beat them!*"

"Louder!"

"BEAT THEM!"

"And how are we going to do that?" I asked.

Silence.

"By playing our . . ." I prompted my team.

"Best!"

"Right. That's all I can ask of you," I told the Krushers. "That's all you can ask of yourselves."

This was something Watson had told me many times. In fact, it was something he had told Karen and Andrew and my brothers and me many times, and not just about playing softball. About anything. Once, I was giving him the news that I'd got C+ in a maths test. Now, C+ is not a bad grade, but I usually get mostly A's and a few B's.

Watson looked thoughtful and asked, "Did you study for this test? Did you do your best?"

"Yes," I answered. "Honestly. It's just that we're doing pre-algebra and now it's really hard."

"Your best is all you can expect," said Watson. "If you want, I'll give you some extra help, but since you did your best, I'm not disappointed. I'm proud of you."

"I *would* like some help," I'd told him.

Now, standing before the Krushers, I said to them again, "Just do your best." And without even looking into the stands, I knew that Watson was smiling at me.

I divided the Krushers into teams, and our last practice game got underway. Gabbie went to bat first, so David Michael, who was pitching, had to move in pretty close to her. He tossed the plastic ball. Gabbie missed. He tossed it again. Gabbie missed. He tossed it a third time, and Gabbie swung and hit it. She ran as fast as she could (which wasn't nearly as fast as the rest of the kids), and she reached first base.

"Stop! Stop!" I cried. (Sometimes Gabbie would just keep running.)

Jackie was next to bat and hit the ball (a normal one) straight away. He ran to first while Gabbie made it to second. (Everyone tried to ignore the fact that Jackie had tripped over the bat as he tossed it away.)

Third to bat was—Oh, no, it was Claire.

She missed. But she did not throw a tantrum.

Fourth to bat was Andrew. Well, this could be interesting, I thought. Andrew sort of knocked the ball. He ran to first, Jackie ran to second, and Gabbie safely reached third.

The bases were loaded. "Bases are loaded!" I called.

Buddy Barrett went to bat next and, to everyone's surprise, but especially his own, he missed.

Two outs.

Karen's turn.

"Two outs and the bases are loaded!" I announced.

Nothing like pressure.

"Come on, Karen!" yelled Watson from the stands.

Karen concentrated. She stuck her tongue between her teeth, kept her eye on the ball—and hit a home run! The ball sailed into the school parking lot. Four runs batted in!

The rest of the game went just like that. It was exciting. The Krushers played well and hard. The final score was 13–12. I was so pleased I was ready to explode. And the cheerleaders screamed so loudly I had to tell them to calm down. I didn't want them to be hoarse the next day.

At the end of the game, everyone in the stands rushed onto the field. Watson slapped

Karen, Andrew, and David Michael on the back. Then he have me a hug. "You are doing a terrific job, Kristy," he said seriously. "You've really changed these kids. All of them."

"We'll see tomorrow," I replied.

"No," said Watson, "you've already done it. Tomorrow hardly matters—I mean, in the greater scheme of things." I knew what Watson meant, even if he did sound a little stupid at that moment.

"Well, come on kids. I'll drive you home," said Watson.

I was about to walk off with him and Karen and my brothers when someone tapped me on the shoulder.

I turned around.

"Bart!" I exclaimed, feeling more surprised than excited. When had he arrived? "How long have you been here?" I asked.

"Long enough," he replied. I supposed he meant, "Long enough to see how good the Krushers have got."

"Do you want to walk home?" he asked.

"Okay," I said, even though it would be a long walk and I was tired. "Watson, I think I'm walking," I told him. "I'll see you later."

I was curious to see why Bart wanted to walk me home and what he had to say, but that head-over-heels feeling was gone. I felt as if I didn't quite trust him. He had hurt me.

98

Bart and I left the playground, and I just knew the members of the Babysitters Club were staring at me. Their mouths were probably hanging open, and I bet their eyes were popping out of their heads. I'm sure they thought that Bart and I were interested in each other. I wish I could have been so sure of what was going on.

"You guys are getting good," Bart told me when we reached the street and had a little more privacy.

A-*ha!*

"Thanks," I said. I was about to add something about how hard each of the players had worked, but I didn't want to give anything away to Bart. After all, he was the Bashers' coach.

He was the enemy.

So all I said was, "Tomorrow, I'll want to put Gabbie—you know, the little one?—in the game for a while. She has to hit a plastic ball. So your pitcher will have to move in closer. Is that okay?"

"Fine," replied Bart, stuffing his hands in his pockets. I think he started to say something else then, just as I had done a few moments earlier, but he closed his mouth.

After that, neither one of us knew what to say. So we just walked along silently. When we reached my house, Bart said, "'Bye, Kristy," and I replied. "'Bye." Then he added, "Good luck tomorrow," and I said, "You too."

I walked inside feeling confused and disappointed.

12th CHAPTER

"Kristy! Kristy! Hey, Coach! Get up! It's game day!"

Karen was standing about two inches away from me. It was the next morning, and she was trying to wake me up. She had already opened my curtains and turned on my radio.

"Coach!" she called again. You'd have thought it was Christmas morning.

"Okay," I mumbled. "I'm getting up."

"Really?"

"Honestly. But only if you'll leave me a—only if you'll go downstairs and eat a good breakfast. Tell Andrew and David Michael to do the same thing. You guys need plenty of energy today."

"Okay!" Karen bounced out of my room. She already had enough energy for her whole team, and the Bashers, too.

I sat up. I looked out of the window. The

day was sunny, the sky was cloudless. Maybe that was a good omen. Of course, the weather was just the same over at Bart's house. He was probably thinking it was a good omen for the Bashers. So then, what kind of omen was it? (That's why omens are stupid.)

I put on my coaching outfit—my Krushers T-shirt, blue jeans, trainers, and my baseball cap with the collie dog on it. Jackie was right. We needed team hats.

Then I ran downstairs. I found Karen, Andrew, and David Michael at the breakfast table, along with Charlie. The three Krushers were already dressed for the game.

"Good work," I said to Karen. "I'm glad you guys are eating—"

I stopped. I looked at their breakfasts. Waffles, toast, scrambled eggs, fruit, bacon, and fried potatoes. Andrew had a milk moustache, and Karen and David Michael were drinking glasses of orange juice in addition to everything else.

"Karen," I said, "I know I told you to eat a good breakfast, but you don't want to make yourselves sick." I had never seen so much food.

"We're filling ourselves up, Coach," David Michael told me.

"What do you know about filling yourselves up?" I asked. Then I looked at Charlie, who had suddenly made himself very busy over the oven. "Charlie?" I said.

"I didn't know they'd take me seriously," he explained.

"Well, just eat as much as you want," I told the Krushers. "Don't force it. Charlie will eat anything that's left over, since he's the human Hoover."

I buttered a piece of toast. I ate it slowly. I glanced at my watch. "Nine-thirty!" I cried. "Oh, my gosh! I'd better get going! I have a lot to do! Where are Mum and Watson? Where's Sam? Did he bake those cakes? Where are the tables for the refreshments?"

"Kristy! Kristy!" Watson was entering the kitchen. "Calm down, honey," he said. "Your mum ran to the shop for a few minutes and Sam's on his way downstairs. Everything is under control."

"Are the cakes finished?"

"Yes."

"Did someone find those tables in the basement."

"Yes."

"Did the—"

Ring, ring.

"I'll get it!" I shrieked. I dashed for the phone, but Charlie reached it first, the rat.

"Hello?" he said. Then, "For you, Kristy."

I could have told him that.

I took the phone from him. "Hello?"

"Hey, Coach. This is Jake," said Jake Kuhn.

"Hi. What's up?"

"My mum says I have to wash my T-shirt before the game today. Is that true?"

"Well, *I* didn't say you have to wash your shirt, but if your shirt is dirty, then you should probably—"

"Mu-um!" Jake interrupted me, turning away from the phone. "Coach says she didn't say I have to wash my shirt."

"Jake! Jake!" I cried. Oh, brother, the last thing I needed was a parent angry with me.

"What?" said Jake.

"Wash your shirt," I told him.

No sooner had I put the phone down than it rang again. As my hand was still on the receiver, there was no way Charlie could answer it first.

"Hello?" I said, praying it wasn't Jake calling back.

"Is this Kristy Thomas, the coach of the Krushers?" asked a small voice.

"Yes. Who's this?"

"Suzi Barrett."

"Hi, Suzi!" I exclaimed, but I was wondering, *Now* what?

"Buddy was saying," Suzi began, "that when you're playing a *real* game against *another team*, you're allowed to have four misses before you're out."

"Buddy's teasing you," I told Suzi. "The rules are the same in any game."

"Okay. 'Bye."

104

Suzi hung up.

Just then Mum walked in the back door, and I nearly got hysterical over the refreshment-stand business, which I was beginning to be sorry I'd agreed to. Why can't I be cool-headed like Mallory, or calm in an emergency like Mary Anne, or as organized as Dawn?

"Mum!" I burst out, before she had even put the grocery bag on the counter. "I realized we should have paper towels or napkins or something at the refreshment stand—"

Mum pulled an economy-size pack of napkins out of her bag.

"And I forgot to remind you to buy paper cups for the lemon—"

Mum pulled out several packets of cups. Then she crossed the kitchen to me and took my face in her hands. "Don't worry, sweetie," she said. "The refreshment stand is taken care of. Sam and Charlie will run it. If everyone brings the food they promised to prepare, we'll be in good shape. All *you* need to worry about is your team." She glanced at the breakfast table.

David Michael, Andrew, and Karen were watching me nervously.

I smiled at them. "What are you going to do today, you guys?" I whispered.

"Beat the Bashers!" they shouted.

"Good," I said, and the phone rang again. "I'm sure it's for me," I told my mother as I reached for it.

It was. It was Jackie, the walking disaster, with a question about foul balls. He called five more times after that, with other softball questions, and each time he sounded more nervous. When the phone rang *again*, I picked it up and said, "Jackie, don't worry so much. I promise—"

"Kristy? This isn't Jackie."

"Mallory?"

"Yeah." She sounded a bit depressed.

"What's wrong? I know something's wrong."

"It's Nicky," she said. "He woke up this morning with a sore throat and swollen glands and a temperature of a hundred and one."

"Oh, no!" I cried. "That's terrible!"

"There's no way he can play today. Mum's taking him to the doctor."

"Okay," I replied slowly. "Thanks, Mal. Tell Nicky I hope he's feeling better. I'll see you in a couple of hours."

When I put the phone down that time, I left the kitchen. I went up to my bedroom to think. I was upset and I didn't want my Krushers to see that. After a few moments, though, I realized there was only one thing to do. I went back downstairs and pulled David Michael into the utility room for a conference.

"You," I told him, "and Jake Kuhn are going to pitch in the game today."

106

"*Me*?" he cried.

"Yup. Nicky's sick. You'll be the pitcher, Jake will be the relief pitcher. Do you think you can handle it?"

"I don't know. I'm a better pitcher than I used to be, but I'm still no good. And the Bashers call Jake 'Fatso'. It's hard to pitch when people are calling you names."

"Don't worry about Jake," I told him. "And just do your best. Okay?"

David Michael nodded. "Okay, Coach."

The rest of the morning sped by, and before I knew it, my family was loading things into our cars. There were so many people and so much stuff that we had to take two cars to the playground. We reached it an hour before the game was to begin.

Charlie and Sam set up the tables for the refreshments. Mum and Watson sat in the stands, out of our way. It was funny, I almost wished Watson would tell me just one more time, "Do your best, Kristy."

But the Krushers began to arrive, so I had to take care of them. Some of them came with food to sell at the refreshment table. I sent them over to Charlie and Sam. Some of them had problems or worries. I tried to reassure them.

The stands were filling up. Since I didn't recognize a lot of the faces, I thought they must be Bashers supporters. But where were the Bashers themselves?

I gathered my team under a tree for a pep

talk, and to explain our last-minute change in pitchers. "Jake," I said, "you'll be our relief pitcher, okay?"

"Okay," said Jake seriously.

"Now you guys go relax," I told the Krushers, "and Jackie?"

"Yeah?"

"You're looking good."

For once, the walking disaster looked more like a Krusher and less like Pig-Pen. His shoes were tied. His clothes were clean. The hole in his shirt had been mended. But his hair still stuck out in seventeen different directions.

"Hey, Coach," he said, tapping me on the arm, "look!"

The Bashers had arrived. They emerged from around a corner of the school and walked onto the playing field in a neat, straight line, led by Bart. Twenty-one boys. They were wearing Bashers T-shirts *and* matching red caps. They were followed by four girls in snazzy cheerleaders' uniforms.

I looked at my Krushers. Their faces fell.

What an entrance the Bashers had made.

13th
CHAPTER

Before the game started, Bart and I held a conference. We talked about Gabbie and the plastic ball again, and I reminded Bart that we would have to sign to Matt Braddock. Then we decided on a seven-innings game.

"If you want," Bart said, "I'll make an announcement about the innings. After that, we'll toss a coin to see who bats first."

I nodded. Good. I may not be shy, but I didn't really want to make an announcement to all the people who were jamming the stands. And believe me, there were a lot of them. As well as a crowd around the refreshment tables.

I looked over everything as I listened to Bart greet the fans. He said something like, "Welcome to the first official game between Bart's Bashers and Kristy's Krushers." (*First* official game?) Then he explained the rules of the day's game.

Almost everyone was listening. A few kids were clustered around the refreshment stand, though, and Charlie and Sam were busy making money. Our cheerleaders weren't paying any attention to Bart, either. They were eyeing up the Bashers' cheerleaders, whom I'm sure they hadn't expected. *I* hadn't expected them. I bet Bart got the idea for cheerleaders when he was spying on our practice games.

The Krushers were eyeing up the Bashers. If they were feeling at all the way they *looked*, it was not a good sign. My jumbled team of boys and girls, tiny kids and big kids (well, fatsos), and even a handicapped kid, a useless kid, a disaster, were facing a team of sturdy boys—no little kids, no fatsos or deaf kids or useless kids. I suddenly had the feeling that each Krusher was thinking, "We don't stand a chance."

I tried to send the Krushers a message with mental telepathy. *You do stand a chance, you do stand a chance*.

The game began. Bart was acting as umpire. The Krushers were batting, and Max Delaney was going first. He seemed to be there forever, finally, after the fourth ball (and two misses), he walked to first base.

Behind me, the Krushers were getting agitated. And out of the blue, who should appear to help me, but the rest of the Babysitters Club.

"I can't wait to play! I can't wait to play!" Karen cried. So Mary Anne gave her a piggyback ride around the refreshment stand.

Claudia played Simon Says with Gabbie, Myriah, and Jamie.

Dawn and Mal broke up an argument between Jake and Jackie.

And Jessi picked up and soothed a nervous Suzi Barrett.

They kept the Krushers calm and entertained while I kept my eye on the game.

Things weren't going too badly, although nothing exciting was happening. The next batter also walked to first while Max walked to second.

Ho-hum.

Then Jamie was batting. I looked at the kid who was pitching to him. He was about ten, tall for his age, and had a good, strong arm. He threw the ball towards Jamie.

Jamie ducked.

The Bashers sniggered.

That happened two more times.

"Three misses, you're out!" shouted Bart.

Duh.

Claire was on next. Our cheerleaders caught sight of this and decided to give her a little boost.

"Krush those Bashers!" shouted Vanessa and Haley.

Claire missed.

111

The Bashers' cheerleaders stepped forward. In a neat line, pom-poms flying, they belted out a cheer that I bet they hadn't written themselves. It was just too darn good.

Vanessa and Haley looked at each other. Then they looked at Charlotte, who shrugged. Then *every*one looked at Claire Pike. Why?

Because she was throwing a tantrum, that's why.

"Nofe-air! Nofe-air! Nofe-air!" she shrieked. Her face turned so red that her father had to step over a whole lot of people in the stands, run to Claire, take her aside, and calm her down.

From the stands came gentle laughter.

I let Mr Pike handle Claire and looked at my team to see whose turn was next. It was time for a heavy hitter, and sure enough, Matt Braddock was on. I cringed, though, thinking of how the Bashers had laughed and called him a dummy before. They wouldn't dare do that in front of all the parents, would they?

No way! Not when Matt hit a home run! *Crack!* No signing was even needed. Matt just ran round the bases, sending the two Krushers ahead of him home, too.

The score was 3–0, in favour of the Krushers.

"Outta sight! Outta sight! You hit the ball with all your might!" screamed Haley and Vanessa. They were jumping up and down enthusiastically, but somehow they didn't live up to the Bashers' cheering.

It didn't matter. When Matt reached home plate, the Krushers crowded around him, hugging him and signing to him. (Jessi told me one of the kids accidentally gave him the sign for "oven," but Matt didn't notice, and who cared anyway?) The excitement was uproarious. When it died down, Margo Pike stepped in to bat.

The Bashers must have had her marked out as an unreliable hitter, because immediately, their cheerleaders began chanting, "Miss! miss!" which I thought was really mean.

Apparently, I wasn't the only one who thought so. The next thing I knew, the Pike triplets, dressed impressively in their Little League uniforms, joined Vanessa and Haley and began cheering with them. It was hard to understand what they were shouting, but they drowned out the Bashers' cheerleaders, and that was really all that mattered.

Unfortunately, it didn't help.

Margo missed.

"Three outs!" yelled Bart unnecessarily, and the Krushers gave up their bats and trotted onto the field. I'd thought they'd be devastated, but they looked fine. I even overheard Jackie say to David Michael, "*Three* runs. Can you believe it?"

They were proud!

The Krushers stationed themselves at their positions, while the Bashers were organizing their batting line-up. Once, while the kids were getting settled, my eyes met Bart's. We both looked away quickly.

Then I signalled to David Michael, who was already on the pitcher's mound.

He ran to me. "Yeah?" He looked nervous. But he also looked as if he were saying, with his eyes alone, "If you don't let me pitch, I'll kill you."

"David Michael," I said to him seriously, "just do your best."

His face broke into a big smile. "I will, Watson," he teased me.

I punched him on the arm and sent him back to the pitcher's mound, grinning.

David Michael's grin soon turned to gritted teeth. He simply was not as good as the Bashers' pitcher, and the Bashers kept getting runs. By the end of the innings, the score was Bashers 6, Krushers 3.

The teams changed sides again.

I started the second innings by putting Gabbie in the game for a while. It was an easy time to do that, before things really got underway, and I ran out to the Bashers' pitcher with the plastic ball and told him what was going on. I really should have told Bart, but I just couldn't face him.

The pitcher looked at the plastic ball and rolled his eyes.

"She's only two-and-a-half," I snapped,

114

"so walk forward. Now."

The kid obeyed. And to give him credit, I have to say that he tossed the ball very nicely to Gabbie. He didn't try anything funny.

Gabbie hit the ball. The pitcher was so surprised that he fielded it badly, overthrew the base, and Gabbie was safe at first.

The walking disaster was up next and I caught sight of him near the refreshment stand, testing bats for their weight. He picked one up, swung it, put it down. Then he picked up another, swung it— and suddenly he must have had margarine on his hands again, because the bat slipped out of them and flew into the refreshment tables. *Very* luckily, it didn't hurt anyone. But the legs of both tables collapsed and the food began to slide every which way.

"Catch it! Catch it!" yelled Charlie. He and Sam (and Jessi and Dawn, who happened to be standing nearby) dived frantically for the plates of cakes and biscuits and crisps. They caught most things, but an entire cake went—*splat*—on a rock, and twelve cups of lemonade slid on top of it.

Absolutely everybody saw the accident. And everybody laughed.

I wanted to die, and I think Jackie felt the same way, but he marched out to bat instead. If he hadn't, he wouldn't have been able to live with himself. Besides, if he could hit a home run, then maybe everyone would forget about his disaster.

Jackie gripped the bat. He looked determined, but he must have been totally flustered. The first pitch was wild, but Jackie took a giant swing at it anyway, nearly losing his balance. (A few people in the stands couldn't help laughing.) The next pitch was right over home plate, and Jackie tried to get away with knocking it. He missed. The third pitch was also well-placed. Jackie swung again—and his bat went flying. It nearly hit the pitcher, who gave Jackie a dirty look.

"Third miss, you're out!" shouted Bart.

Jackie was the picture of humiliation. You could see that his hopes of showing off had been completely dashed. His face started to crumple—and then he sort of stumbled. He sank to the ground, clutching his left ankle. "Oh!" he cried. "Oh, my ankle! I think I twisted it."

I ran to Jackie. His ankle looked fine to me (and I gave his parents the OK sign, so they wouldn't have to leave their places in the stands), but Jackie said it was killing him. "I'd better not play anymore," he added.

Jackie walked off the field, limping pitifully on his right ankle. . . . Wait a sec. His *right* ankle? No, now it was his left.

A*ha!* I thought. I knew exactly what Jackie was up to.

116

14th CHAPTER

I let Jackie sit on the sidelines until the first half of the second innings was over. Then I told Bart I needed time out. I didn't even really look at him. I just trotted past him, calling, "Time out!"

"Okay," Bart said to my back.

I sat down next to the walking disaster. I didn't waste any words. "Jackie," I said, "I'm putting you back in the game."

Jackie snapped to attention. "But—but I can't play, Coach!" he exclaimed. "I hurt my ankle." He began rubbing his right ankle.

"When you fell, you hurt your other ankle," I pointed out.

"Oops."

"Jackie, I know you're embarrassed. I also know you're a good player. You've turned into one of our best hitters. And at the moment, we need you at first base. It's

117

either you or Jamie Newton, and you know what'll happen if a ball comes towards Jamie."

(Nothing like a little guilt.)

Jackie nodded. But all he said was, "Do I have to play?"

"No," I answered. "The only thing I ask of you Krushers is that you do your best. If you think this is your best, then okay. Personally, I think your best is over there at first base, not here on the sidelines. We really need you. We *want* you."

"You do?" said Jackie.

I nodded.

He sighed. "All right. I'll play."

Jackie stood up, and a few people in the stands clapped. (I think they were his parents and his brothers.) Then he ran onto the field.

Two of the Bashers laughed at him, and a third yelled, "Hit any good refreshment stands lately?" but Jackie ignored them.

David Michael (after losing his balance and tripping over absolutely nothing), pitched a fastball to the first Basher at bat. The Basher hit it, and Matt Braddock fielded it and sent it to Jackie, who caught it seconds before the kid touched the base.

I took great pride in yelling, "Out!" even though I was not the umpire. But I made the mistake of glancing at Bart then, who looked at me murderously. I didn't care. Jackie was grinning like a cheshire cat. His confidence had returned. And he, David Michael, Matt, and Myriah (who was our second basewoman) didn't let the Bashers get a single run during the rest of the innings.

The score was now 6–4. I don't think anyone was more surprised than the Bashers, even though they were ahead.

And no one was more surprised than *I* when our cheerleaders got to their feet and yelled, "Way to go! Way to go! The Krushers' score is sure to grow!" Why was I surprised? Because cheering along with the others was Charlotte—shy Charlotte Johanssen. I expect the Krushers' playing was just too much for her.

It was Charlotte's cheering, more than anything else, that suddenly gave me a surge of hope for my team. Maybe they could win after all.

The game continued. It was a warm day and the sun was beating down. The people in the stands put on sunglasses and took off jackets and sweaters. The icing on the cakes at the refreshment stand began to melt. A few of the Bashers removed their hats because their heads were too hot, then put them back on because the sun was in their eyes.

I stuck a piece of gum in my mouth, chewed it, and followed the game.

In the third innings, Hannie Papadakis hit the ball—hard.

"Oh, my gosh!" she cried disbelievingly.

"Run, run!" I shouted to her.

"Oh, yeah!" she said, suddenly remembering— and managed to get around all the bases, beating the throw home. She even sent Margo home before her.

Two more runs for the Krushers.

The Bashers frowned. They gritted their teeth. They concentrated furiously on the game. When Gabbie was on next, I didn't even have to say anything to the pitcher. He just switched balls and moved forwards.

At the end of the innings, the score was 8–6, still in favour of the Bashers.

At the end of the fourth innings, the Bashers were ahead 10–6, and Bart called for a "fourth-innings stretch". Everyone needed it—players, cheerleaders, fans, and coaches.

I wiped my forehead with the shoulder of my T-shirt (something Mum absolutely *hates* me doing), and met up with the other members of the Babysitters Club.

"The Krushers are doing really well!" cried Claudia.

"We're *losing*," I replied.

"But you're playing a very tough game," said Mary Anne, even though she knows next to nothing about sports. "Don't you see how the Bashers are acting now? You're giving them a run for their money."

"Yeah," agreed Mal. "I bet they thought they'd just walk onto the field, cream you, and leave. But your kids have got home runs and everything. Gabbie is amazing with that plastic ball."

"Oh, but Jackie and the refreshment stand," I moaned.

"Everyone's forgotten about that," Dawn assured me. "He's played so well since then. Anyway, just look at him."

I looked. Jackie was by the stands, talking to his family. He was grinning, and he looked pretty pleased with himself.

As I watched Jackie, I noticed Karen signalling to mc. Well, not exactly signalling; more like waving frantically. Karen just cannot be subtle.

"I'd better go and see what she wants," I said.

I left my friends and trotted over to my family.

"Hi, Coach!" cried Karen. "I am so excited!"

"What a game!" Watson said.

"Yeah, we're winning," Andrew exclaimed.

"Wait a sec. No we're not," I had to tell him.

"Karen says we are."

"Karen, the Bashers are ahead of us. You know that," I said. "They've got ten runs and we've only got six."

"Only!" cried Karen. "Six is a lot. If we got six, we'll get more. I think we're going to beat the Bashers!"

I looked helplessly at Mum and Watson, but Mum shrugged and Watson said something about "hope springing eternal".

"What?" I said.

"The optimism of youth," Watson tried to explain.

I'd been about to ask him for some advice, but I decided not to. Not if he was in a stupid poetic mood.

"I'd better go and check on Sam and Charlie," I said, and rushed off.

It was a good thing I did, too, because what with the fourth-innings stretch, they were over-run with lemonade requests. I grabbed Mary Anne, and she and I helped them out. While we were filling cups, I overheard someone say, in an awed tone, "Those Krushers are really something."

I turned around. It was a Basher!

Ten minutes later, the game began again. An hour and fifteen minutes after that, it was just about over. It was getting to the end of the seventh innings, the Bashers were still ahead, and the Krushers had two misses. Claire Pike went to bat.

Boy, I thought, trying to send her a mind message, if you've ever needed to hit that ball, it's right now.

Claire missed.

The Bashers leapt to their feet and threw their hats in the air. The game was over.

The score was 16–11, and the Bashers had

won. They had crushed the Krushers. I had seen it coming, of course. The Bashers had been ahead all along.

I suppose I'd been hoping for a miracle.

I took off my collie hat and stuffed it in my back pocket. The Krushers were running off the field and the crowd was cheering. The cheerleaders were cheering, too—all of them, even Charlotte. And then I heard a third cheer: "Two, four, six, eight! Who do we appreciate? The Krushers! The Krushers! Yea!"

And an answering cheer: "Two, four, six, eight! Who do *we* appreciate? The Bashers! The Bashers! Yea!"

The Krushers and the Bashers were slapping each other on the backs. The Krushers didn't look too disappointed, not even Karen.

"Hey, you Krushers!" I yelled.

My team separated from the Bashers and straggled over to me.

"Congratulations, you guys," I said. "You played a really good game. I mean it."

"Even though we lost?" Jackie ventured.

"Even though you lost. You were playing against kids who are older and bigger than most of you. And who have been a team longer than the Krushers have. And you got *eleven runs*. Do you know how terrific that is?"

"Yup," said Karen. "We do."

"And the next time we play the Bashers,"

123

said Jackie, "maybe we'll beat them."

I grinned. "Okay, you guys. Time to go home. Find your parents or your brothers and sisters. Andrew, Karen, and David Michael, let's go and help Sam and Charlie."

People began to drift away from the playground. Mary Anne left with Logan. Jessi walked off with Mallory and the Pikes. But Claudia and Dawn stayed and counted the money Sam and Charlie had taken in at the refreshment stand.

"Wow!" said Dawn a few minutes later when the counting was done. "This ought to buy hats for your team."

"I'll say," I agreed. "Thanks, Sam. Thanks, Charlie. The Krushers really appreciate your help."

"No problem," said Charlie, as he folded up the tables.

I checked to make sure that there were no stray cups or napkins on the ground, and then I turned to walk towards Mum's car.

"Hey, Kristy!" called a voice.

I would know that voice anywhere. It was Bart's.

15th CHAPTER

Even though Bart was calling me, I didn't turn around straight away. I stalled just long enough to see all sorts of things happen—Sam and Charlie nudge each other, Dawn and Claudia raise their eyebrows at each other, and Mum and Watson wink at each other.

Oh, brother. Did they all know there was something more (maybe) between Bart and me than just coaching our teams?

"Yeah?" I said, turning around.

Guess what? Bart wanted the two of us to walk home together again. So we did.

"See you later," I said to my family. Then, " 'Bye!" I called to Claud and Dawn. "I'll phone you tonight."

"You better had," Claud replied mischievously, glancing at Bart. "If you don't, I'll ring you."

Bart and I walked off quite quickly. As

soon as we left the playground, Bart said, "Well, congratulations!"

"On what?" I replied.

"On the Krushers' game, what else?"

"Oh, that," I said.

"They were great!"

"Some of them."

"*All* of them."

"Jamie Newton still ducks balls, and Claire Pike still has a zero batting average and throws tantrums."

"Maybe. But I noticed something today. Your team has total dedication."

"What do you mean?" I asked.

"I mean that they would do anything for the team or anyone in it. They may not be excellent players, but being part of a team means a *lot* to them. I could see it in their faces. I saw it every time one of them was batting, especially kids like Jamie and Claire. I could almost hear them saying to themselves, 'This time I'm going to get that ball. I'm going to do it for my team. I know I've never done it before, but I'm going to do it now.' I think your kids realize that they couldn't be in any other team—at least not easily—so they're really fierce about the Krushers."

Bart paused. Then he added, "That's why I got so nervous about them."

"You got nervous about the Krushers?" I said.

"Of course I did. I'll admit that I brought

126

my kids along that day just to show them they really didn't have to worry about the game—that your kids were no threat. But when I saw them play, I got nervous. I could tell they were really going to hang in during the game."

"Wow," I said. Maybe I'd been too hard on myself—and on the Krushers. Or maybe I'd just set my expectations in the wrong places. What was so important about winning?

"Anyway, what's so important about winning?" I said to Bart.

"Yeah. . . ." he answered uncertainly.

Then we laughed.

"I suppose we both like to win," I said.

"I'm pretty competitive," Bart admitted. "My parents say I'm *too* competitive."

"And I like to be in charge, running things," I told him.

"Well, you can do that when you coach."

"I know. But when I'm in charge of something, I like it to work out, too. I like to win, just like you. . . . My friends and I have a club, the Babysitters Club. It's really a business. It was my idea, I'm the chairman, and the club is a big success. We get tons of jobs. If it weren't a success, though, I don't know what I'd do."

"Would you quit?"

I shrugged.

"Are you going to quit coaching the Krushers? I mean, since you lost today?"

127

I thought for a moment—just a moment. "No way!" I cried.

"Then winning probably isn't as important to you as you think it is," said Bart.

"You sound like a psychiatrist or something," I said, laughing.

Bart and I stepped off the curb to cross a street, and a car came zooming around a curve.

"Kristy, look out!" Bart grabbed my hand and pulled me back to the pavement. We were safe—but Bart didn't let go of my hand, even though he certainly could have. Instead, he held onto it until we had crossed the street.

"Nice hat," Bart commented a few minutes later. (I was wearing my baseball cap again.) "Why the collie?"

"Oh, it's my favourite kind of dog. I wear this in remembrance of Louie. He was our collie. We had to have him put to sleep. We got Shannon after Louie died."

"Put to sleep," Bart repeated. "Wow. If we ever had to do that to Twinkle . . . ." Bart's voice trailed away. Then, "Kristy?"

"Yeah?"

"Remember when Jackie—is that his name?—ran into the catcher's cage that time? Well, I apologize for what the Bashers said to him. I apologize for what they said to all your kids. I found out later that they'd been mean, but I was getting too worried about the Krushers to notice it at the time.

All I could think about was our game."

"That's okay," I replied. "Maybe your kids gave my kids a little backbone. Besides, Jackie *is* a walking disaster. I can't tell whether he's just accident-prone, or if he lives in another time zone or something."

Bart laughed.

After that, neither of us could think of anything to say, because we were pretty quiet for a while. I felt embarrassed and began casting around in my mind, trying to dredge up *some* subject to talk about with Bart. But what? My family? My school? Or I could ask him a question. I could say, "So, do you have any pets besides Twinkle?" or "What's your school like?" or "Do you have any brothers or sisters?" or "Do you like me?"

I had just settled on the school question, which seemed like a safe one, when Bart said, sounding very nervous, "Um, Kristy, I have a question to ask you."

"Okay," I replied. Was Bart going to ask if *I* liked *him*?

"I was wondering. . . . I mean, I know the last couple of weeks have been a bit difficult for us, but now we've both admitted that we're competitive, and we have one game behind us and we survived it. . . ." (What was Bart leading up to?) "So . . . how about another game between the Krushers and the Bashers? Say, in two weeks?"

"Okay," I replied, feeling a little let down.

"Wait," Bart went on. "Only on one condition."

"On one condition?"

"Yes. That in between games we act like something other than rival coaches."

"What do you mean?"

"Well, how about like friends? Or . . . maybe we could go out sometime. To a baseball game, or something. Would that be okay with you?"

I didn't pause for even a split second. "Sure!"

"Good," Bart replied. We both smiled.

We had reached our neighbourhood, and fairly soon Bart would leave me at the end of my driveway. I wished our walk home didn't have to end, even though I was dead tired—but probably not as tired as the Krushers. I'd seen Gabbie nearly asleep in her father's arms as the Perkinses left the playground. And Andrew had looked ready for a nap.

"Well?" said Bart.

There we were, at my driveway.

"Well . . . I suppose I'll be seeing you soon," I said.

"Before the game," replied Bart firmly.

"Great! Maybe you'd like to meet my friends sometime. I think you'd like them."

"Okay. . . . Can I come to a meeting of the Babysitters Club?"

"Do you want to be a babysitter?"

"No."

130

"Then I'll introduce you some other time. Meetings are serious."

"Deal," Bart said. Then he grinned. "See ya . . . Coach!" He turned and started home.

I watched Bart walk away. Then I turned around. I saw Watson gardening in the front flower bed and I ran to him.

"Hi!" I called.

Watson looked up from his work. "Hi, there. We didn't get to talk after the game. But I wanted to tell you that it was terrific, of course. I knew it would be, win or lose."

"You did? How'd you know that?" I stood at the edge of the garden and watched Watson turn peat moss into the soil.

"Because you were the Krushers' coach. That's how I knew." Watson straightened up. The gardens are his domain. He's totally happy when he's gardening.

"Thanks, Watson," I said. If he hadn't been covered with peat moss, I think I would have hugged him. Instead I blurted out, "Bart wants me to go to a baseball game with him. He wants us to be friends." Or maybe more than friends, I thought. But it was a pretty scary thought. Was I ready to be more than just friends with a boy?

"Wonderful," said Watson, smiling.

"I'd better go inside," I said. "I have a few calls to make."

I ran into our house. Suddenly, I was bursting with excitement and energy. I found Mum and told her all about Bart.

Then I rang Mary Anne, Dawn, and Claudia and told each of them about Bart.

Then I made a fourth phone call. "Hello?" I said. "Is Jackie there?"

"This is Jackie."

"Hi, it's Kristy Thomas. I just wanted to tell you how proud I am of you. You played well today. And you were very brave to go back in the game after your, um, accident."

"Wow! Thanks, Coach. You called just to tell m—Oops!"

CRASH!

"What was that?" I asked.

"A lamp," replied the walking disaster. "I just broke a lamp."

Some things never change.

MYSTERY THRILLER

Introducing, a new series of hard hitting, action packed thrillers for young adults.

THE SONG OF THE DEAD by Anthony Masters
For the first time in years 'the song of the dead' is heard around the mud flats of Whitstable. But this time is it really the ghostly cries of dead sailors? Or is it something far more sinister? Barney Hampton is sure that something strange is going on – and he's determined to get to the bottom of the mystery . . .

THE FERRYMAN'S SON by Ian Strachan
Rob is convinced that Drewe and Miles are up to no good. Why else would two sleek city whizz-kids want to spend the summer yachting around a sleepy Devonshire village? Where do they go on their frequent night cruises? And why does the lovely Kimberley go with them? Then Kimberley disappears, and Rob finds himself embroiled in a web of deadly intrigue . . .

Further titles to look out for in the Mystery Thriller series:

Treasure of Grey Manor by Terry Deary
The Foggiest by Dave Belbin
Blue Murder by Jay Kelso
Dead Man's Secret by Linda Allen
Crossfire by Peter Beere
The Third Dragon by Garry Kilworth
Vanishing Point by Anthony Masters

JUGGLERS

There are books to suit everyone in Hippo's JUGGLERS series:

Pet Minders	Robina Beckles Willson	£1.75
The Jiggery Pokery Cup	Angela Bull	£1.75
The Ghosts of Batwing Castle	Terry Deary	£1.75
Stan's Galactic Bug	John Emlyn Edwards	£1.75
My Friend Robinson	Anne Forsyth	£1.75
As If By Magic	Jo Furminger	£1.75
Bags Of Trouble	Michael Harrison	£1.75
The Spooks	Elizabeth Lindsay	£1.75
The Secret Of Bone Island	Sam McBratney	£1.75
School Trip To The Stars		£1.75
Horrible Henry and The Headless Ghost		
	Kara May	£1.75
When I Lived Down Cuckoo Lane	Jean Wills	£1.75

You'll find these and many more fun Hippo books at your local bookseller, or you can order them direct. Just send off to Customer Services, Hippo Books, Westfield Road, Southam, Leamington Spa, Warwickshire CV33 0JH, not forgetting to enclose a cheque or postal order for the price of the book(s) plus 30p per book for postage and packing.

STREAMERS

We've got lots of great books for younger readers in Hippo's STREAMERS series:

The Little Yellow Taxi and His Friends
Ruth Ainsworth £1.75
Sally Ann At The Ballet   Terrance Dicks £1.75
Sally Ann – The Picnic   £1.75
Sally Ann Goes To Hospital   £1.75
Sally Ann – On Her Own   £1.75
Sally Ann – The School Play   £1.75
Broomstick Services   Ann Jungman £1.75
Tom   Ruth Silvestre £1.75
Nate The Great   Marjorie Weinman Sharmat £1.75
Nate The Great and The Missing Key   £1.75
Paws: A Panda Full Of Surprises
Joan Stimson £1.75
Aristotle Sludge   Margaret Leroy £1.75
The Old Woman Who Lived In A Roundabout
Ruth Silvestre £1.75

You'll find these and many more fun Hippo books at your local bookseller, or you can order them direct. Just send off to Customer Services, Hippo Books, Westfield Road, Southam, Leamington Spa, Warwickshire CV33 0JH, not forgetting to enclose a cheque or postal order for the price of the book(s) plus 30p per book for postage and packing.

B— lo— he
pain that was inside her today
v s there on his face; the agony
s felt was mirrored in his eyes.

d it wasn't wanton, or bold, or even
ticularly brave—because, looking at him,
nita knew her kiss wasn't about to be
ected.

sses—strange, delicious things, her mind
ught as their lips mingled.

st this delicious sharing, this sweet
nowledgement that was better expressed
hout words. A kiss that wasn't about
aping, more about sustenance. A little
se in a vile day—a kiss that wouldn't go
ther because for now it was absolutely
ugh.

n and I,' Hugh said, as their kiss inevitably
d, 'are going to have to do some serious
ng.'

now.'

Carol Marinelli recently filled in a form where she was asked for her job title, and was thrilled, after all these years, to be able to put down her answer as 'writer'. Then it asked what Carol did for relaxation, and after chewing her pen for a moment Carol put down the truth—'writing'. The third question asked—'What are your hobbies?' Well, not wanting to look obsessed or, worse still, boring, she crossed the fingers on her free hand and answered 'swimming and tennis'. But—given that the chlorine in the pool does terrible things to her highlights, and the closest she's got to a tennis racket in the last couple of years is watching the Australian Open—I'm sure you can guess the real answer!

ENGLISH DOCTOR, ITALIAN BRIDE

BY
CAROL MARINELLI

MILLS & BOON
Pure reading pleasure™

First published in Great Britain 2009
Harlequin Mills & Boon Limited,
Eton House, 18-24 Paradise Road, Richmond, Surrey TW9 1SR

© Carol Marinelli 2009

ISBN: 978 0 263 86830 2

Set in Times Roman 10½ on 12¼ pt
03-0309-44646

Printed and bound in Spain
by Litografia Rosés, S.A., Barcelona

ENGLISH DOCTOR, ITALIAN BRIDE

CHAPTER ONE

'SORRY if this is awkward for you!' Hugh Armstrong flashed a tight smile at his reluctant patient.

'It's not awkward for me.' Bonita managed through pale lips, shaking her head as Deb, the charge nurse, offered her more gas to inhale. Bonita held her arm slightly away from her body, terrified to move it and even more terrified at the thought of anyone touching it. The journey to the hospital had been short but hellish, the makeshift sling her friend had applied had done little to help and certainly hadn't provided a buffer to the pain—she'd felt every jolt. Every movement, anticipated or real, had also been agony as Deb had helped get her out of the car and onto the trolley. 'I'm just in a lot of pain.'

'Good!' Hugh said, as Bonita shivered on the trolley. 'Not good that you're in pain, of course!' He gave her a patronising smile. 'I mean, it's good that it's not awkward for you. Accidents happen after all or we wouldn't have a job!'

He thought he was funny!

Bonita wished she could make light of the fact that

she was sitting bolt upright on a trolley in the accident and emergency department she worked in, dressed in her netball gear, her long brown curls all damp and frizzy, her shoulder hanging out of its socket and her arch-enemy Hugh Bloody Armstrong the only senior doctor available!

Just her luck. But, then again, the whole day had been a series of errors. She wasn't even supposed to have been playing netball today, had actually given it up last year after she'd knocked herself out and then a fortnight later had hurt her knee. But an early morning phone call telling her that the team was short and begging her to fill in had caught her off guard. She should have said no—centre forward wasn't even her position!

And as for Hugh Armstrong treating her—well, he wasn't even supposed to be on duty, Bonita thought, holding onto her arm so carefully that her neck was starting to hurt with the tension of trying to stay still. Andrew Browne was the consultant on duty today, only he was stuck in Resus and Hugh had just happened to call in to drop off the emergency pager, midway between the wedding and reception he was attending today. Dressed in a grey morning suit, knowing damn well that he looked fantastic, reeking of cologne, with Amber, his stunning girlfriend, trotting faithfully behind, he'd seen Bonita being wheeled through the department. Of course, given she was a staff member, and there was no one else available, it was only right that he deal with her, only right that she wasn't left waiting.

She was staff.

And, because today she was also a patient, for once

he'd be nice to her and, in turn, she'd suffer his patronising attempts at humour, if it meant that her shoulder
would get sorted quickly.

It was entirely irrelevant that they loathed each other.

'Take a couple of breaths of this, and then hopefully
you can give me your arm.'

She was making a scene; Bonita knew that, but
bravery was something she was having great difficulty summoning.

Sobbing, crying and red in the face, she'd turned
more than a few heads since her arrival.

Hugh had almost got an IV in when she'd first
arrived, which had been a feat in itself, given she had
useless thready veins, yet he'd somehow managed to
find one on her good arm.

And then she'd suddenly moved.

Which had caused more pain, made her yelp and Hugh
had let out a hiss of frustration as the tiny plastic tube had
kinked beneath his fingers and her vein had collapsed.

'Come on, honey!' Deb soothed. 'You're an Azetti—
you should be used to this!'

Not this Azetti!

Having a girl after three strapping sons, her mother,
it seemed to Bonita, should have wrapped her in cotton
wool, dressed her in pink and enrolled her for ballet.
Instead, until puberty had hit loudly, she had been raised
as one of the boys, brought up in her brothers' cast-offs
and forced to play with their toys. She had proved a
constant source of irritation to her mother because she
hadn't liked roughing it and, horror of horrors, had no
affinity for horses. Sure, her mother and three brothers

might pop out a shoulder or dislocate the odd patella when they took a tumble from a horse, and handle themselves with pained dignity, but it just wasn't Bonita.

Like her Sicilian father, Luigi, emotion was Bonita's forte, and Hugh knew that. He smiled just a touch as Bonita rolled her eyes at Deb's comment and said nothing. Neither correcting nor commenting on the fact that he knew different.

'Can't you just do something for the pain?'

Impatient to get her to X-Ray, Hugh *was* trying to do just that, Bonita knew. He was holding up a mask and trying to be patient, but the rubbery smell, along with the anticipation of pain, was just upsetting her more.

'Come on, now.' He tried again to be nice. 'I know you're upset, I know you're in pain, but if you just take a couple of big breaths of this and give me your arm, we can get an IV in and give you something more substantial for your pain.' Which was the only thing Bonita wanted to hear. Oh, she'd dealt with plenty of dislocated shoulders in the year she'd worked here, knew that it hurt, only she hadn't realised just how much.

'I really think I've done more than just dislocate it…' Bonita shivered. 'It's way worse than a straight dislocation—I think I might have fractured it or maybe done something to the nerves.'

'Let's just get something into you for pain, we'll get some X-rays and then I'll make *my* diagnosis!'

'Oh, sorry, I forgot I was a mere nurse.' Bonita smarted. 'Forgive me for having an opinion!'

'That's quite all right, Nurse!' He winked. Somehow Hugh had always put her in her place. Growing up, he'd made it clear she was an annoyance, had sat bored through her teenage tantrums and had roared with laughter when she'd announced she was going to be a nurse.

Why couldn't he have stayed in England, where he belonged?

At eighteen he had come to Australia on a gap year. He'd intended to head back to England to study medicine, only Hugh had fallen in love with the country and after a year travelling, he'd transferred his course to Australia. At med school he'd met her brother Paul and become something of a regular fixture in the Azetti household during those years of study. Bonita's parents had a sprawling home on the Mornington Peninsular where they ran a winery, growing their own grapes and producing a boutique wine. Along with her mother's riding school, the winery had expanded successfully over the years. Apart from his blond hair, Hugh had slotted right in with her family. He'd come for regular dinners, stayed over sometimes, picked fruit during semester breaks, worked in the cellar door shop, exercised the horses— not that he'd needed to work, the Azettis had later found out. His family background meant he could have spent the six years it had taken to get through medical school concentrating solely on his studies and partying. Hugh, though, had managed to accommodate all three—work, study and partying, in fact he was a master of them all!

He was almost an honorary son in the Azetti household. One of the only times Bonita had actually seen her mother cry had been when Hugh's father had fallen ill and Hugh had headed quickly back to the UK, not for a holiday, but to live.

Oh, he'd kept in touch, witty postcards and letters regularly appeared in their mailbox, and her mother Carmel had happily read them out. Paul often forwarded Hugh's emails, regaling his latest tales of success, promotions, girlfriends, family deaths, engagements and breakups, but there had been no direct contact between Hugh and Bonita. His had just been a name that had cropped up in conversation, or in an email to read second hand that displayed his stunning dry wit. Bonita had watched Hugh grow from young man to mature adult on a third-party basis, only privy to his life by default.

Until six months ago.

Until she'd arrived home to find him at the family's dinner table—a surprise guest, with surprising news.

He was back.

And not just back—he had taken up the position of registrar in the accident and emergency department of her small town. Which, of course, had delighted everyone. Andrew Browne thrilled that such an eminent London doctor was taking up residence, her family delighted that the prodigal son had returned, all the female nurses and ancillary staff finding an excellent reason to apply a second coat of mascara in the morning. Her mother had long since wound down the riding school, so that just a few of the mounts remained, and Hugh had promptly bought one—Ramone, a devil of a horse—which meant to her parents' delight that he was a regular visitor, paying agistment fees and stopping in for coffee after he'd ridden!

Yes, Hugh's return had delighted everyone, except herself…

Woozy with the gas, she stared at his silky blond hair, flopping over his high smooth forehead, the full, sulky mouth that delivered such effortless mocking wit, dark green eyes that crinkled at the edges when he smiled— and never had she hated him more.

'I need your good arm!' Hugh said, his voice kind now, gently leaning her forward, but every movement was agony. 'Just take a couple of breaths on the gas.'

'It's not helping!' Her words were muffled by the mask Deb had clamped over her face.

'It won't if you keep talking instead of breathing. Come on, Bonny!' She hated it that he called her that. That was what her family called her, and it was OK for them to do it, but here at work she was Bonita. She pulled her face away to tell him but he wasn't listening. 'Let the sling take the weight,' Hugh said, trying to prise her good arm away, but she was terrified to let go, terrified of even the tiniest movement, tears stinging in her brown eyes, determined not to let him see her cry again. But it was so hard to be brave.

'I don't like gas.'

'OK!' He gave a tight smile as he gave in, then spoke in his commanding snobby voice and patronised her just a little bit more. 'Let's just take a moment to relax, shall we? I'll be back shortly.' She saw him roll his eyes to Deb, a sort of apology, Bonita decided, that his patient wasn't meekly behaving, before he, no doubt, went to apologise to his girlfriend, Amber, that the five minutes he had promised her she'd have to wait was turning into fifteen.

'Sorry to be such an inconvenience,' Bonita called to

his departing back. She was very close to tears, but managed a dash of sarcasm before he walked out, hating how much it hurt, hating she was being such a baby, hating making a fool of herself, and especially in front of him!

'Don't be daft,' Deb said. 'Nobody thinks you're an inconvenience, do we, Hugh?'

'Not at all…' Hugh attempted, but didn't elaborate. Instead, he stalked out, clearly less than impressed.

'I saw him roll his eyes.'

'He's worried about you!' Deb soothed. 'I told him to go off to the wedding reception, that Andrew would get to you very soon, but he insisted on getting you some pain control.'

Which meant nothing! He was a doctor after all, and would stay and help a colleague just as he would a dog in the street—it didn't mean a thing!

'OK, then!' Hugh breezed back in with a little medicine pot. 'I've got some oral Valium, which will relax you. And we can have another go when it kicks in.'

'Just do it,' Bonita said, refusing the tablet and gritting her teeth, determined it would work this time.

'As you wish.' Hugh put down the medicine cup and picked up his tourniquet. 'Now, it doesn't matter if it's making you feel sick or dizzy, Bonny, I want you to take some deep breaths of the gas and let the sling take the weight…' As Deb clamped the mask over her face, Bonita caught Hugh's dark green eyes. 'Like it or not, you're going to have to trust me!'

Never.

Oh, she didn't say it out loud, couldn't say it really

because Deb was holding the mask over her mouth, but her brown eyes said it all as, for the first time in six years, they actually met and held his. Even though they'd worked together these past months, even though she'd seen him at her parents' and had made idle chit-chat, for the first time in years she looked into his eyes and remembered the last time she had.

The last time his face had been close.

The last time that full, sensual mouth had captured hers, and somehow she'd believed in him.

But not now.

Older, wiser, and a good dash more bitter, she wouldn't trust Hugh Armstrong as far as she could see him, let alone throw him. She had witnessed first hand his treatment of women...his treatment of her.

'Give me your hand, Bonny.' He was prising it away now, and whether it was the gas, or that the sling was taking the weight, or just that his slow movement didn't jolt her, when finally she let him, it didn't hurt that much at all.

OK—so she trusted him as a doctor, Bonita conceded, as she shook off the mask. In the months she'd worked alongside him he had been nothing other than brilliant with the patients and their care—it was the man she had issues with!

'Good girl,' Hugh said, wrapping a tourniquet around her arm.

'Ten years ago, that might have been appropriate,' Bonita snapped.

'Just stay still,' Hugh warned, and then grinned slightly. 'Actually, it wouldn't have been appropriate ten years ago.' He winked, slipping the needle into her flesh. 'You were always getting into trouble!'

He was right. Ten years ago she'd been fourteen—and despite her mother's best attempts to keep her as some androgynous being, hormones, along with a rather spectacular pair of breasts, had emerged, which had meant frequent blistering rows with her mother about make-up, clothes, magazines and boys. Hugh, who had known her since she was a gangly eleven-year-old, had witnessed plenty of those rows and had seen his share of her tears too.

She didn't want to think about it, found that it was easier to focus on the needle than her thoughts, or him, and the little prick he was making in her arm certainly hurt less than examining her past. Needles didn't bother her. Bonita watched as he slipped it into her arm, and Hugh quickly taped it in place. Only, as much as needles and blood didn't bother her, she'd never actually witnessed one going into her own arm, or the little trickle of her own blood that slipped out as he capped the IV.

It was horribly hot, she could feel sweat trickling between her breasts, the air stifling as she tried to drag it in, saliva pouring into her mouth. Bonita's urgent eyes met Deb's as realisation hit, then she retched suddenly—the violent movement causing such a spasm of pain that she didn't even retch again, just sobbed as 500 ml of bright blue sports drink, erupted into a hastily found kidney dish Deb thrust in front of her. Oh, it was an extremely common event in Emergency but it just added to the utter indignity of it all, especially when Hugh, wearing a rather appalled expression at her Technicolor display, stepped back smartly.

'We'll add an anti-emetic to the painkiller, please, Deb,' he drawled, and, oh, how strained his smile was as he dampened a paper wipe and brushed two tiny— in fact, Bonita was sure *imaginary*—spots off his smart morning suit.

'I'm sorry.' Beyond embarrassed, she just sat there as Deb wiped her face, her nose, her mouth, while Hugh delivered the blessed pain relief. 'I'm so sorry. Your lovely suit…'

'Forget it,' Hugh clipped.

But it was *such* a lovely suit, Bonita thought, the horror receding slightly as the medication took over. Dark grey, with a long jacket, rather like a riding coat. And with legs up to his neck, Hugh wore it well. There was a pale grey waistcoat underneath that accentuated his flat stomach, and it was set off with a pale pink tie. A lock of blond hair flopped over his eyebrows as he checked her radial pulse, making sure the circulation in her arm was OK, and she caught a glimpse of manicured nails and a flash of a very expensive watch. 'I'll pay to have it cleaned.'

'Don't give it another thought,' Hugh said magnanimously. 'It's my fault for not putting on a gown when I dealt with you… How's your pain?'

'Terrible…' Bonita started, but on second thoughts it wasn't that bad. In fact, she could lie back just a fraction on the pillow. Oh, she couldn't move it or anything but if she kept very still, it actually felt OK.

'That bad, huh?' Hugh grinned as she promptly closed her eyes. 'OK, let's have a proper look at this shoulder now, please.'

But not even IV painkiller could fully take away the sting of Deb cutting off her netball top to reveal a rather grey sports bra, and the agony of trying to remember, as Hugh so gently probed whether or not she'd shaved her armpits in the shower that morning.

'Sorry, pet, but we need this off for the X-ray,' Deb said as she snipped away at Bonita's bra and carefully peeled it off, keeping the breasts covered with the sling and a towel as best she could. 'Hugh, could you just hold the towel while I feed the drip through the gown?'

'I'll do the drip!' Hugh responded, leaving Deb to hold the towel and hopefully maintain what appeared to be the very last shred of Bonita's dignity.

It was the only saving grace in the entire afternoon.

'At least Bill's not on duty,' Deb said, trying to cheer her up as she covered her friend as best she could with a threadbare gown, and failed miserably. 'No woman wants her ex-boyfriend seeing her like this... Bastard!' she added—just as everyone who worked in Emergency did these days after they said Bill's name.

Only Bill wasn't a bastard—anything but. A charge nurse in Emergency, he was an adorable guy, perceptive too, Bonita thought with a brain that was starting to refuse to think. Bill was the only person out of everyone who would understand just how appalling this afternoon was for her.

Bill was the only one who knew about Hugh.

'Well, it looks straightforward enough!' Hugh scribbled out his request on a pad. 'Let's get her round to X-Ray.'

* * *

'Anterior dislocation.' Hugh snapped the X-rays onto the viewfinder as soon as Bonita returned. 'Just as I thought. And no fracture. Let's get you into Theatre and we can pop it back and soon have you feeling more comfortable.'

It wasn't the word 'theatre' that had her looking aghast. There was a minor theatre in Emergency, which was used mainly for suturing, but procedures such as this one were often performed there. No, it wasn't that that had her reeling—it was that Hugh was going to do it.

'You're supposed to be at a wedding!'

'That's not your problem.'

'No.' Bonita shook her head, the painkillers making her bravely honest. 'I don't want you to be the one putting it back.'

'I'm sure Andrew would prefer it if he could do it,' Hugh said, studying the X-ray as she spoke, 'but he's in with some relatives and he's going to be stuck for some time. You know that the sooner we get it back, the less swollen it will be and the less chance of nerve damage.'

'I know all that! It's just—'

'Look!' As direct as ever, he left off studying the X-rays and came over. 'I can understand that you'd prefer if it was Andrew who did the procedure. I know you and I don't particularly get on, and to be honest, yes, there are many other places I'd prefer to be right now, but, all that aside, you know I'm a bloody good doctor...' Which was so pompous, so backhanded and so utterly Hugh that it really came as no surprise to hear him say it. 'And I know that shoulder needs to be put back just as soon as possible. So...' He forced his haughty face into an attempt at a reassuring smile, giving her a glimpse of very white even teeth and green eyes that were utterly bored and less than impressed. 'If you'll let me do it, you'll be on your way home very soon and I might just make it back to the reception in time for the speeches.'

It would have been childish and stupid in the extreme to refuse, and, Bonita thought glumly as with her good hand and a hefty dose of painkillers she attempted a signature on the consent form, her mother would never forgive her.

It was quiet in the little theatre, away from the hubbub of the department. Even though Bonita knew what was going to happen, there was something quite peaceful about just lying down and listening as Deb and Hugh set up for the procedure. A sort of comfort almost as she heard the little blip of the oxygen saturation machine as it was clipped to her finger and Debbie attached some nasal prongs.

'We'll give you a sedative,' Hugh explained, 'which will send you off into a nice little twilight sleep.

'Deb, let's just check her ID.'

It seemed the most pointless, ridiculous thing to be doing. Everyone in the room knew that this was Bonita Azetti and that she was 24 years old, only maybe it wasn't so pointless because, as it turned out, they didn't know that she was allergic to penicillin, and though it was highly unlikely she might need it, Deb still scuttled off to get a red armband, just in case. Hugh took off his jacket and waistcoat and hung them up. His immaculate shirt had lifted out of his trousers a touch and she was treated to a woozy glimpse of tanned flesh as he tucked himself in. She was too out of it to even bother looking away.

'OK?' Hugh asked when he turned around.

'Fantastic!'

'You will be soon.'

'Aren't you going to take off your shoes?' Bonita almost managed a joke. For one particularly difficult dislocation she'd assisted him with she'd seen him place the ball of his foot in the patient's armpit to provide traction as he pulled on the arm, though admittedly that had been on some vast, muscle-bound farmhand.

'I don't need to for a skinny thing like you. It'll just pop back in.' Still she could see the towel over the trolley that Deb would pull on and nerves started to catch up with her as she remembered the pain she'd been in.

'It's going to hurt!'

'It won't hurt at all. We'll wait till the sedative has taken effect, and anyway,' Hugh reassured her, 'it's a brilliant amnesiac—you won't remember a thing afterwards!'

'Your mum's on her way pet,' Deb added, but that only made things worse. The next batch of tears for the day came pouring out as she thought of her mother on the way.

'She doesn't need this!' Bonita sobbed into the paper towel Hugh ripped off the dispenser and handed her, 'what with dad being so sick and everything… And it's tourist time; the shop's really busy at the moment—'

'Hey!' Hugh cut off the dramatics. 'This could be exactly what she needs. You're going to have a few weeks off with this shoulder—it might help having you around right now.'

'I doubt it.'

'Your dad will love having you home...' Hugh soothed. 'OK...' He dragged a stool over with his foot and carried on chatting away as he connected the syringe to the bung, talking to calm her down as he would to any nervous patient. 'Let's get this medicine into you. Now, just think nice thoughts—it will all work out. I know things are difficult at home right now, but this could end up being the best thing that ever...' His voice was sort of slowing down, his mouth moved at normal speed but the words were starting to sound jumbled. She could see Deb walking over and talking to Rita who had come to the theatre door, could see Hugh staring down at her as he quietly and calmly waited for the sedative to take effect, knew that she was OK, because Deb was still happily chatting to Rita and Hugh didn't look remotely fazed.

He was looking at her again, his eyes holding hers, observing her carefully.

He really did have beautiful eyes, Bonita thought—though green didn't really accurately describe them. Maybe hazel would be a better choice, because just at the inner rim of the iris there was a swirl of gold. He was smiling at her, a sort of soft, gentle smile that she hadn't seen in a long time, a patient, kind smile that she remembered of old.

The one that had always made her tummy curl into itself, Bonita thought dreamily.

And even if he was a bastard at times, even if it had been so hard to work with him in Emergency, to see him with her family, these past few months, it was as if all the mist that had surrounded them was finally clearing and just the simple truth remained.

'I do love you!'

She could see him frown just a touch, see him glance up to where Deb was still chatting, then he gave her a sort of patronising smile. She could feel his hand patting her in a sort of 'there, there' motion, as if she had no idea what she was saying, as if she couldn't possibly know how she felt. She knew she was drifting off and suddenly for Bonita it was imperative that he get it, imperative that she make herself absolutely clear. She tried to lift her head off the pillow, only it was too heavy. All she was able to do was look at him and hopefully the urgency in her eyes might convey this imperative point, as she sensationally elaborated.

'Hugh—I've *always* loved you.'

CHAPTER TWO

'ALL done!' Deb's smiling face was the first thing Bonita saw as she awoke, her voice soothing as she welcomed Bonita back to the world. 'Everything's back where it should be so you should be feeling a lot more comfortable. For now just have a little rest!'

In stages she remembered: the tackle at netball; the journey here; Hugh… She cringed at the scene she'd made when he'd tried to get the IV in and cringed again when she remembered that she'd been sick.

Not that Hugh noticed her cringe now—he barely even glanced at her as he spoke.

'Wiggle your fingers for me!' he snapped, deigning to give her nothing more than a cursory glance as he slipped his fingers into the navy shoulder immobiliser and again checked her radial pulse. 'How does it feel?'

'Fine.' Bonita blinked in surprise, because it actually did feel fine. Staring around the familiar room from where she lay, she carried on wiggling her fingers, even rearranged herself a touch on the pillows, and it didn't hurt a bit! 'Did it go back OK?'

'Easily!' Hugh gave a tight smile. 'It popped straight back.'

'How long was I out for?' Bonita asked, but Hugh wasn't listening. His duties over, he was back to being his usual abrasive, rude self where she was concerned. He didn't even attempt to answer her question, just filled out her notes.

'You were just out for ten minutes or so.' Deb filled in the silence. 'Everything went really well.'

'You've got a visitor!' Rita popped her head around the theatre door, closely followed by Bonita's mother's rather striking head of curls.

'Oh, Bonny! What on earth happened?' Carmel Azetti was one hundred per cent Australian but, having been married to Luigi for forty-four years, some Italianisms had certainly rubbed off. Seeing her daughter, pale, drained and looking wretched, Carmel came marching over with her arms outstretched. In fact, as Bonita, mindful of her newly placed shoulder, cringed on the trolley, she thought it was odd that the one time her mother might just display some affection, she didn't want her to!

'Gently Carmel…' As if Hugh had applied brakes, Carmel came to a stop in the nick of time and Hugh caught Carmel into a hug of his own, which was probably the last thing he wanted to do, given her mother was dressed in grubby jeans and a T-shirt, with even grubbier boots, and she reeked to high heaven of horses! Not that Hugh seemed to mind but, then, he'd always adored her mother—it was the daughter he had issues with!

'Sorry to call you to come to the hospital like that. It must have given you a fright.'

'It did,' Carmel admitted. 'Mind you, you'd think I'd be used to it by now, three sons and then Calamity Jane here...' She gave an exasperated sigh as she stared over at her daughter. 'After you knocked yourself out last year, you said you weren't going to play netball this season.'

'The team were short a player!' Bonita grumbled. 'They'd have had to forfeit the game otherwise.'

'Well, I wish they had!' Carmel sighed, her brief display of affection soon wearing off as she reverted to her rather more usual brusque self. Bonita couldn't blame her. Her mother had a terminally ill husband, a winery to run, horses to exercise and take care of, and now she had an incapacitated daughter to deal with.

'I'm sorry, Mum!' Bonita said. 'I just didn't think—'

'You never do!' Carmel snapped.

'Well, I'm going to have to leave you ladies. I've got one more patient to wrap up and then I really must get going. Andrew will see you tomorrow at ten a.m. at the fracture clinic,' Hugh instructed, 'just to check everything's OK. Then your GP can take over your care.'

'I'll be fine.'

'You need to be reviewed tomorrow!' Hugh clipped.

'It feels OK,' Bonita insisted, knowing how busy Sundays were for her mother, how busy every day was for her right now, but Hugh wasn't having any of it.

'It feels fine because while you were under I injected local anaesthetic into your shoulder to help you through tonight, but you ought to be seen when it's worn off— to make sure there isn't a trapped nerve or anything. Which,' he added, just to make her blush for her carry-on before, 'you yourself were worried about.'

He wasn't even pretending to be nice to her now. He just stalked off with her notes to see his other patient.

Of course he wouldn't have sat twiddling his thumbs waiting for her to come back from X-Ray. The place was busy so naturally he'd help out, Bonita thought as Carmel tried to help her into jeans that felt way too small. Bonita didn't even attempt to put on the T-shirt.

'I'm in an arm immobilizer, Mum!' Bonita grumbled. 'How would I even get it on? I'm just going to have to wear the gown home.'

"Well, excuse me for trying,' Carmel snapped back as she did up Bonita's netball runners. 'I'm a farmer's wife, not a nurse!'

'I need another gown,' Bonita said, 'to cover my bottom—'

'Just hold it!' Carmel said briskly. 'We're not borrowing two! I'll wash it and you can give it back tomorrow when I bring you for your appointment.'

'I can get a taxi tomorrow,' Bonita offered, chewing her bottom lip. 'You've got church.'

'I'll just have to go to evening Mass,' Carmel said, trying, but not that hard, to make out that it didn't matter, that Bonita wasn't this massive inconvenience that had suddenly landed on her.

'I'm sorry, Mum.'

'Stop it!' Carmel said firmly. 'I can deal with anything except your tears! Let's just get you home.'

Home!

Bonita knew Carmel didn't mean the little flat she shared with Emily. She shuffled along the corridor, clutching the gap in the hospital gown for dear life. It really didn't help that all her colleagues came out to say goodbye and Carmel seized the opportunity for a quick word with Hugh, who was on his way out with Amber.

'You are coming to the barbeque, I hope?' Bonita's heart skipped a beat as she walked into the end of the conversation. 'You too,' Carmel added to the surly face standing beside him. 'Nothing fancy, just the annual Azetti barbeque, too much food, too much wine…'

'I'm actually working that weekend Carmel,' Hugh politely declined, 'though I'll see what I can do.'

'Well, please, do!' A straight shooter, it would never have entered her mother's head to read between the lines, Bonita realized. She wouldn't even guess that Hugh was trying to politely wriggle out of it. And why would he want to come? It may be a tradition but it had been years since Hugh had been here. He'd been in London, had spent a year in France, for goodness' sake. As if he and Amber were hankering for a sausage in bread and the whole circus of her family. 'We'd like to see you there—especially with Luigi not being well.' For a second so fleeting it was barely there, Bonita could have sworn she saw her mother falter, knew, because they all knew, that this would be the last Azetti barbeque with Luigi—not that she wavered long. 'You wait in the foyer,' Carmel instructed Bonita. 'I'll bring the ute round.'

Why would she expect anything less that the ute today? Bonita thought with a sigh as she sat on the little bench in the foyer and awaited her chariot. The whole day had been a complete embarrassment from start to bitter end, so why would her mother spare her blushes by bringing the car? Oh, no, bring out the shabby ute with the dog tied in the back and spades and Eskies and goodness knows what else piled up high. She could almost hear the banjo playing as she climbed on in, could see the slight smirk on Amber's lips as they drove past in Hugh's sleek silver sports car on their way to a sumptuous dinner and endless champagne.

'A nice cup of tea.' Carmel jerked the Ute into first gear. 'That will soon fix you up.'

Home.

Seeing the cellar door sales sign and the endless rows of vines catching the sun as they drove up the driveway, Bonita felt her stomach turn over. Oh, she'd come home almost every other day since her father's condition had worsened, which was more than her brothers did. Ricky and Marco were partners in an equine veterinary practice out near Bendigo, which was a good couple of hours away, and with their busy schedules they couldn't get away that often. Her brother Paul, a surgical registrar at the same hospital where Bonita worked, seemed permanently busy these days—only managing a whirlwind visit to his parents once or twice a week. This left the everyday things like doctors' appointments and shopping for Bonita to deal with, and though she didn't mind in the least, was glad to help out her parents as much as she could, living here again was going to be an entirely different matter.

As she gingerly lowered herself from the ute, sniffed at the familiar scent of fermenting grapes, heard the horses whinnying, saw the endless rows of vines—

despite the abundance of space, she could almost feel the walls closing in around her, a nervous thud of recognition as her mother scolded her to hurry up, and not for the first time since they'd commenced the journey home, Bonita wondered if she was up to it.

Dinner she could handle.

Living here she wasn't so sure about.

'Hi, Dad!' He looked so small in the chair, her big strapping dad just this shadow now. His hair was still as black as hers, but it was limp and brushed back from his hollow face. Making her way over, she kissed him hello and with her good arm cuddled him, horrified at his frailty, that even in the couple of days since she'd seen him he seemed to have lost yet more weight. His cheeks were sunken, his wide shoulders rounded now, and she could feel tears welling in her eyes. But catching her mother's warning look, Bonita blinked them back. 'I'm sorry about all this, Dad.'

'Never be sorry! It's good you are home.'

He was so delighted to see her, delighted even that she'd had an accident if it meant that it brought her home, and it felt good to sit down, to sink into her regular spot on the comfy sofa, all the drama of the day catching up with her as the drugs wore off. Her shoulder was starting to hurt a bit now, and Bonita was touched when her mother made a bit of a fuss, brought her a mug of tea and insisted that she put her feet up, even helped her when it proved a bit difficult, nudging a few cushions behind Bonita, before giving her the brew.

Maybe it wouldn't be so bad, Bonita mused, relaxing into familiar surroundings. The cat jumped onto her lap and purred loudly. Surely this was way better than trying to recuperate at the flat and feeling like an unwelcome guest as Emily's new boyfriend helped himself to the contents of the fridge. They'd shared a flat for a couple of years now and it had worked well till Emily had broken up with her long-term partner and Bonita had broken up with Bill.

No, a few weeks at home might be just the tonic she needed.

'Hugh looked after her!" Carmel said proudly, wrapping a rug around Luigi's knees and pouring out his medicine. With Bonita in her immobilizer, the front room resembled the dayroom at an old people's home.

'As he should!' Luigi nodded.

'No, he was off duty,' Carmel explained. 'On his way to a wedding reception and he stayed to make sure Bonita was OK. By the looks of things he's back with that girl he used to date before he left Australia, that pretty radiographer...what's her name, Bonny?'

'Amber.' Bonita tried to keep her voice light, but the single word seemed to catch in her throat.

'That's the one.' Carmel nodded. 'Maybe she's the reason he came back.'

'Maybe he just likes living here!' Bonita retorted. 'It's not as if he's got any family back in the UK.'

'Poor pet!' Carmel always fussed over Hugh, in a way she never did over Bonita. 'We should ask him to eat with us more often—he can come and have a nice meal when he exercises Ramone.'

'I'm sure he's got other things to be getting on with,' Bonita snapped as her mother shot her yet another warning look, but Bonita wasn't about to be deflected, her own disappointment slipping out as she stated the obvious. 'He didn't even want to come to the barbeque.'

'Hugh's not coming?' Her father frowned and instantly Bonita felt guilty for upsetting him, but, hell, what did they expect? As if Hugh was going to bring Amber to one of their get-togethers.

'He's working, darling,' Carmel said, smiling at her husband while simultaneously freezing Bonita with a look! 'You know how busy he is, but he did say he'd try to come.'

Why did they constantly make excuses for him? Bonita thought, more than a little rattled now.

It was as if the fact his mother had died when he was young and he'd been raised in a boarding school was excuse enough for Hugh to pick and choose when he turned up, excuse enough to bed half his fellow medical students and then work his way through the rest of the hospital personnel.

Every exploit, every broken heart, every late or non-arrival had been brushed off and forgiven by her brothers and parents.

Well, all bar one, Bonita thought, closing her eyes on the beginning of a thumping headache. She wondered how forgiving her father would be if he knew how badly the fabulous Hugh had treated his own daughter.

'How long did Hugh say you'd be off work for?' Carmel asked despite Bonita's closed eyes.

'I've got two weeks in this contraption, and then it all depends. Another two to four weeks...' Bonita let out a weary sigh and opened her eyes as an impossible thought dawned. 'After my knee last year and everything, I've only got five days' sick leave left.'

'Well, you can't go back before you're ready—they'll understand that!'

'I know,' Bonita replied, 'it's just…'

'And you don't need to worry about money. It's not as if you're not going to be going out much or anything.'

'I know!' Bonita said, irritated, because her mother didn't get it, thinking of the rent that would still have to be paid, half the electricity bill that was tucked behind the fridge, and the fact sick pay didn't give shift allowance.

'We'll sort it out a bit later!' Carmel broke into her thoughts, gave Bonita a tired smile that showed maybe she did get it after all, and that they'd talk about it away from her father.

'You can do some work here,' Luigi said later, when after a doze on the sofa they had dinner and, with far less gusto that Bonita, he tried to work his way through some home-made mushroom soup. 'You can work on the till.'

'She's not going to be able to work the till and pack bags with one arm,' Carmel huffed. 'She can't possibly work at the shop.'

'She can answer the phone!' Luigi said.

'What—and tell them to hold while she puts down the receiver to write things down? A one-armed helper in this place is as useless as tits on a bull!' Carmel said, in her usual manner. 'And she can't help with the wine-tasting, because she won't be able to pour.'

'I have got one arm!' Bonita said indignantly. 'I'm sure I can manage the wine-tasting!'

'Are you going to call me down from the stables to pull a cork?' Carmel snapped. 'And, anyway, you don't even like wine! The customers will know you have no idea what you're talking about.'

'So you're basically saying that I'm useless!' Bonita bristled, hoping for a dash of guilt from her mother, not surprised when it never came.

'Pretty much—yes!' Carmel responded, then turned to her husband. 'You'll just have to keep her company, Luigi—stop her moping about the place.'

Taking another gulp of her soup, Bonita was about to give her mother another smart reply, another surly *Sorry* even, but her spoon paused midway, and it was there again, something in her mother's eyes that she'd seen at the hospital.

What was it Hugh had said as she'd been going under?

Dipping buttered bread into the soup, Bonita tried to recall, but it was like chasing a dream, tiny little fragments of conversation, like scooping water with a net, the words slipping away...

'It might help... The best thing that ever...' She could hear those words again, hear his voice lulling her as she had drifted off.

Was her mother, in her no-nonsense way, letting them both off the hook?

Telling them both that there wasn't a thing she could do?

Maybe just her being here with her father would be a help on its own....

'Have you heard from your young man?' Luigi asked, pushing away his nearly full plate.

'He isn't my "young man" any more.' Bonita smiled. 'It's over between Bill and I, Dad.'

'You're sure about that?' Luigi checked. 'You were together a long time. Maybe he'll change his mind.'

'He's not going to change his mind.'

'Then he's a fool,' Luigi said darkly. 'What sort of man would finish with his girlfriend at a time like this?'

'Come on, Gig,' Carmel interrupted, calling him by his pet name, 'have a little bit more soup.'

It was the closest, Bonita realised, they'd ever come to admitting that her father was so ill and, yes, it was a question that plagued her family and colleagues—how could Bill have even thought about breaking up with Bonita now, when she had so much going on in her life? Only Bill wasn't the bastard they all made out. Bill, as it turned out, knew her almost better than she knew herself.

Bill, ending it when he had, had solved a massive dilemma for Bonita—just not one she could ever reveal.

'Bill's a nice guy, Dad. It just didn't work out between us, we weren't right for each other.'

'And it took you three years to work that out!' Luigi huffed. 'He should have done the decent thing by you ages ago.'

'Why don't you have a bath?' Carmel said, and this time Bonita was grateful for the interruption. According to her father's rules she and Bill should have long since been married—that they had been dating for three years and there wasn't even a ring to hurl at Bill was proving impossible for her father to understand. 'I'll give you a hand.'

Her mother bathing her was not an option, and Bonita immediately shook her head.

'I'll have a wash at the sink.'

'Suit yourself,' Carmel said, picking up the plates, trying hard to pretend it didn't matter that Luigi had only managed two spoonfuls of soup. 'But, I'm warning you, I won't have time to help you in the morning. If you want to go for your appointment half-washed, then it's up to you! Oh, and by the way, your hair smells of vomit!'

A farmer's wife she may be, but Carmel would—Bonita realised as they headed to the hallowed sanctum of her parents' room, which was on the other side of the house to the 'children's' bedrooms—actually have made a very good nurse.

'We're all set up for it in here!' Carmel smiled as she flicked on the light in her bathroom. There was a little stool perched in the bath and a hand-rail the occupational therapist had arranged to be inserted, along with a hand-held shower. Even groggy from the day and with one arm out of action, Bonita, could, in fact, have a decent wash.

Carmel would have made a lovely nurse actually because when for the first time she could really remember Bonita had to strip in front of her mother, instead of saying it didn't matter and she'd seen it all before, Carmel held up a towel. Then, once Bonita was seated, Carmel gave her a moment before she dealt with the practical and covered her daughter's arm with a large garbage bag. Then she chatted away, wiping imaginary spots off the shower as her daughter washed.

'Do you want me to wash your hair for you?' Carmel offered.

'It will dry all fluffy!'

'If you rub it dry and don't put some product in, it

will.' Carmel gave a half-smile. Bonita looked at her mum's salt-and-pepper coloured corkscrew curls, as long and as wild as her own dark ones. 'Curly hair *is* something I know about.'

'OK, then,' Bonita said, closing her eyes and letting the wretched day go as her mother massaged shampoo into her scalp.

And it did feel nice to be clean, nice to be wrapped in a big towel as her mother sorted out something for her to wear to bed.

'This will do!'

'It will not!' Bonita baulked at the vast flannelette nightdress her mother held up. 'It's hideous.'

'I know!' Carmel agreed. 'Ricky bought it me for Christmas.'

'Yuk!' Bonita pulled a face, wondering what on earth had possessed her elder brother.

'What about this?' Carmel proffered another creation, and Bonita was about to pull a face but realised it was one of her own gifts that she had given her mother a couple of birthdays ago.

'Wait till you get to my age.' Carmel grinned, popping it over her head and helping her pull through her good arm. 'I've got a drawer full of nightdresses— I don't even wear a nightdress.'

'Mum! Too much information, thanks!'

Hideous nightdress or not, it was nice to sit in her mother's room. Carmel didn't rub her hair dry as she had when Bonita had been a child but instead patted it then put through half a bottle of anti-frizz. It was actually nice to talk to her mother.

'Are you still upset about Bill?'

'No.' Even though she was pleating the nightdress with her good hand, even though she couldn't look her mother in the eye as she spoke, Bonita's answer was honest. 'He was right to end it.'

'Why did he?' For the first time her mother pushed, but Bonita just couldn't answer. 'You two seemed so happy.'

'We were.'

'You still don't want to talk about it?' Carmel said. Then she changed the subject and promptly hit a very sensitive nerve that had nothing to do with Bonita's shoulder!

'How does it feel, seeing Hugh again after all this time?'

'OK,' Bonita said lightly. 'It's a bit weird working with him, though…' She watched her mother's eyes narrow a touch as she worked on her hair. 'I mean, I knew him when he was a medical student—it's strange now that he's a registrar.'

'I always thought that he'd come back,' Carmel mused. 'When he went back to England, of course, I worried, but he always kept in touch and he did love Australia so. I'm surprised he even went back!'

'His father was dying,' Bonita pointed out. Her lips tightened as she swallowed hard for a second, wondering, not for the first time, just how hard it must have been for Hugh—his mother had died when he was very young and he had no brothers and sisters. As much as her family drove Bonita crazy at times, she absolutely adored them. She couldn't, for even a moment, imagine dealing with her father completely on her own.

'I expected him to go back for a holiday perhaps,' Carmel huffed, unmoved. 'Not to live there. I mean, they hardly knew each other—imagine sending a five-year-old to boarding school! I'm sure that's why he's the way he is.'

'What do you mean? Bonita asked, then wished she hadn't, wished she hadn't prolonged the conversation, her heart in her mouth when her mother spoke next.

'With women,' Carmel responded. 'He's good at flirting, good at dating, but he hasn't got much staying power—first sign of commitment and he's gone. I guess it's hard to get close to someone if you've never actually been close to anyone…

'You had a bit of a thing for him once, didn't you?'

'Don't be ridiculous…' Bonita attempted, and then gave in. After all, from the moment puberty had hit she'd blushed every time his name had been mentioned! 'I was a teenager, Mum—hormones raging. I'm not exactly the first girl to have a crush on one of her brother's friends.'

'How about now?'

'Please!' Bonita scoffed. 'I've seen how he goes through women. Good-looking he may be, but he knows it! And he's so scathingly superior at work.'

'Maybe,' Carmel agreed, 'but underneath all that he's still a very nice man. He's always kept in touch, and since he's been back he's been round plenty of times, not just to exercise Ramone but to see your father.'

'I guess.' Bonita attempted a shrug, but it hurt too much, and not just in her shoulder. 'We'll just have to agree to disagree about Hugh.' Grateful for any distraction from this rather difficult subject, her eyes lit up a touch when she saw a heavy framed silver photo on her mother's dressing-table.

'Zia Lucia!'

Fondly Bonita traced the elegant figure of her favourite aunt. 'I miss her.'

'You adored her, didn't you?' Carmel smiled. 'You wanted to be just like her!'

'She was always so glamorous.' Bonita grinned. 'Dashing overseas, sending us lovely gifts…'

'Giving your father an ulcer.'

Oh, and she had. Bonita could remember the tension whenever Zia Lucia had descended. Cooing like a bird of paradise, she'd swoop on the family, showering her favourite niece with shiny dresses and shoes, drinking too much wine with dinner and refusing to help with the dishes. The fact she'd never married had been a constant thorn in Luigi's side, as if somehow he'd failed his sister, as if somehow, by staying single, Lucia also had failed.

'Poor Zia…' Bonita sighed. 'She was just so busy with her career.'

'Career, my foot!' her mother exclaimed. 'She never worked a day in her life.'

'She had a career in sales.'

'Selling herself more like!' Carmel tutted. 'Off with that fancy MP. She was a kept woman—a mistress!'

'Zia Lucia!' Bonita gave a shocked laugh and after a moment Carmel laughed, too. 'Does Dad know?'

'Your dad didn't want to know!' Carmel winked. 'So don't waste any tears crying for your prematurely departed spinster aunt. She packed more into her life than anyone else I've met.'

'Golly!' Bonita blinked at the photo. 'No wonder

you used to get so cross when I said I wanted to grow up and be exactly like her.'

'No wonder!' Carmel rolled her eyes. 'Bed!"

'It's eight o'clock,' Bonita attempted, but she really wasn't up to arguing. She headed to the lounge and kissed her dad goodnight then went happily to her old bedroom, slipped into her little single bed and just lay there.

Thought about Zia Lucia and her fancy man, which made her smile.

Then thought about Hugh, which made it fade.

Bill had been right to end it.

Oh, they had been happy, or at least chugging along, till Hugh had come back—till Hugh had ripped off the sticky plaster she'd applied to her heart when he'd left, and all the old hurt, the anger, the bitterness, the longing had started to seep out. And try as she had to hide it, Bill had sensed the shift, and had eventually ended it…just as she had been about to. How she'd cried, but her friends and family hadn't understood. She hadn't been crying over the ending—instead, she'd been crying at the reason it was over.

That Hugh was back and even though she couldn't stand to admit it, even to herself, her feelings remained.

Hugh had been her first real kiss.

Not her first kiss—oh, there had been plenty of them, half-baked efforts at the local disco.

No, Hugh had been her first *real* kiss.

Real, because he'd been the first one who had truly moved her.

Real, because as he'd held her, as this stunning man had held her in his arms, she'd understood every warning her father had given her, every speech her mother had made that a kiss could lead to other things.

Closing her eyes, she remembered the awful row she'd had with her mother.

She'd been just shy of eighteen, in her last year of high school, studying like crazy for her exams. She had, after a lot of persuading, been allowed to go to her best friend's eighteenth birthday, yet her mother had insisted that she be home from the party by eleven. The first to leave, she hadn't got home till twelve and had stood angrily and defiantly in the kitchen as Carmel had ripped into her. Only that time Bonita hadn't said sorry.

Bonita had known she'd had nothing to be sorry for. She had left all her friends partying the night away, her homework had been up to date, and she'd still worked part time in the shop. Bonita had known she couldn't do it any more, couldn't live like that a moment longer, and she wouldn't. She told her mother she was leaving home, that she was going to share a flat, was going to have a life.

She hadn't even known that Hugh had been there— he'd been trying to sleep in the lounge and had heard every word. But the next morning, when her brother Paul—because it was OK for him to be—had been in bed nursing a hangover and her parents had been at church, no doubt praying for her imagined sins, Hugh had come into the kitchen. He'd found her in her thick candlewick dressing-gown, her eyes swollen from crying, and had tried to say the right thing.

'I hate her,' Bonita snarled.

'She just worries about you!'

'Why?' Angry, hurting, furious, it was all there in her words as she paced the kitchen. 'Because I'm a girl…'

'And because you're the youngest, because you've got three older brothers, because they had you late in life.'

'I'm eighteen in a couple of weeks, I could be married and have children by now, I'm learning to drive, I'll be at university next year. I've had it with her—I'm going to leave. Today, when they get home from church, I'm going to tell them properly. I'm going to get a job, find a flat…'

'Don't leave home, Bonny!' Hugh came over to where she stood. 'Not now.'

'You did!' Bonita pointed out. She was furious now, crying hot, angry tears, hands flailing, blaming him somehow. 'You left the country when you were eighteen—I'm not allowed out the house after eleven! I'm not a child.'

'Come here.' He cuddled her then— and it felt nice. They hadn't ever really got on. Oh, she'd had a crush on him for years, but he'd teased her so mercilessly, had been so downright horrible at times, that it hadn't been hard to dislike him, too. But when he held her, for the first time she felt that someone might just understand. Her brothers didn't, they just told her to toe the line and not upset Mum and Dad, and her parents certainly didn't, and neither did her friends, who told her to just tell her parents where they could stick there rules. But standing in the kitchen Bonita realised two things.

Armstrong was an appropriate surname for him, because being wrapped in his arms was heaven.

And maybe, just maybe, Hugh was the one person on this earth who did understand.

'Your dad's just worried that you're going to—'

'It's not Dad who's the problem,' Bonita interrupted, shaking her head against his chest. 'It's Mum. She's the one who's always having a go—she called me a tart last night before I went out, just for wearing lipstick.'

'If your dad had seen you wearing lipstick you wouldn't have been allowed to even go to the party!' Hugh patiently explained, only she wasn't listening, couldn't see it, refused to get it.

It was her mother who was the problem!

'I just can't stand it here.'

'You don't have to for much longer,' Hugh said. 'Do your exams, get your grades and maybe when you go to university things will settle down, but you can't throw it all away now.'

She nearly had. That morning, replaying the row, three months more at school had seemed endless, way easier to just leave, to get a job, to do *anything* if it meant that she could get away, to be allowed to live. And then he'd held her.

'Don't do anything rash, you could end up regretting it for ever.'

For ever was a lot longer than three months… even her jumbled mind could work that one out. Her head on his chest, she could hear the steady beat of his heart, the hands of time that soothed, only they didn't…

The pendulum paused on the edge of time, dipped into the next second and clattered back into a different rhythm.

His mouth was there, just inches away, talking to her, telling her to hold on, delivering reasonable words that soothed. Only suddenly she was aware of it…and she knew that suddenly he was aware of her, in a way he never had been before. Everything shifted then. A slightly startled look flashed between them as they both caught the other looking in a way they shouldn't. And then he kissed her...or she kissed him.

No matter how many times Bonita replayed it, she could never quite decide who moved first, just lips merging, blending to the most exquisite of tastes. His mouth tender at first, exploring her slowly, her inexperienced lips tentative, savouring each delicious sensation, the feel of him full on her mouth, the tangy fragrance and the soft coolness of his tongue.

And then she found her level, or their level, because suddenly they were equal. Urgency ignited in her, a chain reaction that had every cell flickering to light. Craving contact, she pushed into him as he received her, his fingers knotting in her hair—and she was grateful for the kitchen bench pressing into her back, not because it held her up but because he could push harder. Without breaking contact, his mouth left hers, trailed down her chin, deep kisses on her throat as still he held her hair, deep, deep kisses that stirred her even deeper inside. His hands moved from her hair now, tracing down her back and then around to her front, to breasts that ached to be in his palms. Now, apart from the soft fabric of her dressing-gown, they were. A soft moan from him as still he kissed her, his thumb stroking her nipple, his other hand just holding her waist, and it was like being stroked inside. She could hear their ragged breathing, could feel this growing urgency, this need for more contact, a shameless, wondrous, primal need building to a new target now, a tender kiss tipping into danger.

Oh, her mother had been right. Kisses really could lead to other things,

Wonderful other things like a dressing-gown parting and the soft moan in his throat at the feel of her naked flesh in his palm, soft, soft strokes that made him hard.

Bonita knew that because she could feel him against her, and she wanted more. She wanted his skin on hers. Lifting his T-shirt with urgent hands, she pressed herself against him, kissing him as still he kissed her. She forgot they were in the kitchen, things like time and place were utterly meaningless, until he broke contact, pulled his head away, then peeled his body from hers.

'Bonny…' She could hear him struggle to right himself, his single word an apology almost, only there was no need. She truly didn't want it to end, rained his face with hot, desperate kisses as he pushed her back and again, no matter how many times she replayed it, she still didn't know if it was because he'd heard her parents' car that he'd pulled away. She only knew that moments later her parents were in the kitchen, Bonita, flustered and trying to behave normally, making a drink, trying to remember she was supposed to be angry, while inside her heart was singing as Hugh, for once not so calm and together, sat at the kitchen table and attempted to chat to her father.

Staring at the ceiling now, tears pooling in her eyes then trickling into her hair, it was hard to believe that she'd been so happy—that with just one kiss everything had turned around, everything difficult in her life had been made suddenly more bearable.

Till six hours later when he'd broken her heart.

CHAPTER THREE

'BONNY!' A rather firm rap at the door broke into her dreams, but Bonita chose to ignore it, safe in the knowledge her mother wouldn't come in. Growing up in a house with three older brothers, one of the few productive rows they'd had now assured her a touch of privacy.

"You've got a visitor!"

'Mmm…'

'Bonny!' Her mother rapped harder on the door. 'Wake up, Hugh's here!'

'Oh!'

And given he'd been in her room a moment before, though in her dreams, Bonita flushed in embarrassment as she mumbled her mother to come in. She was grateful that at least he did have the decency to wait outside as Carmel arranged her daughter into suitable doctor-visit order.

'Hugh rang last night after you'd gone to bed,' Carmel explained, 'and said he'd come and check you over, to save us the trip to the hospital.'

'You could have told me!' Bonita muttered, as her mother helped her sit up, which wasn't easy, the local anaesthetic Hugh had injected having long since worn off and she was stiff from sleeping. Her hair, despite a generous dose of product, was no doubt looking spectacularly wild! Not that Hugh would care a jot—he was more than used to seeing people at their absolute worst, Bonita consoled herself as he breezed in. He reeked of his signature cologne and even minus a suit and dressed casually he still cut a dash. Long limbed in black jeans and grey T-shirt, he made her already small bedroom positively tiny as he loomed over her.

'Let me just have a quick look at your shoulder and then you can go back to sleep.'

'What time is it?' Bonita glanced at her bedside clock, glad to see Carmel had placed a mug of tea there. 'It isn't even eight.'

Perhaps realising she couldn't function without at least a sip of tea in her, he handed her her mug. 'Have a drink.'

'Thanks for this, Hugh,' Carmel said. 'It really is a huge help. Do you want to stay and have some breakfast?'

'I'd love to,' Hugh answered easily. 'In fact, why don't you go to church? I don't mind hanging around for a bit.'

'I don't need a babysitter.' Bonita grumbled. 'I've only hurt my shoulder.'

'I'm not here for you!' Hugh drawled. 'I want to have a chat with your dad.'

'Are you sure?' Carmel protested, only not too much—she was already halfway out of the door. 'If I get a move on I can make nine a.m. Mass.'

It was weird being alone with him, weird that her mother had left him with her.

'I can't believe she's actually left me alone with a

man in my bedroom…' Bonita attempted a joke only Hugh didn't smile.

'I'm not a man this morning,' he clipped, 'I'm a doctor!'

It was Hugh's first visit to Bonita's bedroom. The house had been a second home to him during his med-school years, but apart from popping his head around and telling a moody, spotty teenager to finish her homework and that dinner was ready, or her mother wanted her to turn the music down, he'd never once set foot over the threshold of this room.

And it was exquisitely uncomfortable to do so now, especially after yesterday's little revelation!

He thought he'd put that to bed years ago—or, rather, very deliberately *hadn't* put that to bed years ago.

Since his return to Australia, Bonny had made it excep-tionally clear she neither liked nor forgave him—which meant he knew where he stood. Oh, sure, people said strange things when they went under sedation, but it was more the *way* that she'd said it, the note of urgency in her voice, the frantic look in her eyes that had him reeling.

And jokes about him being allowed in her bedroom were certainly not the order of the day, but he felt a touch guilty for his very harsh tone when Bonny's face flushed in embarrassment.

'I was only joking,' she mumbled.

'I know.' He gave a half-smile. 'Hideous nightdress, by the way.'

'Thanks.'

Hideous it may be, but it was also vast, which meant he only had to move it a fraction to expose her shoulder. Hugh swiftly checked it for position and numbness then checked the sensation in each of her fingers before declaring that she'd probably live.

'You've got one helluva bruise there.'

'I know.'

'Which will get worse over the next couple of days.'

'I know that, too.'

'You need to take your painkillers.'

'I promise not to be brave,' she joked, and this time he *did* smile back. 'Was I awful yesterday?'

'You were…' His smile widened. 'Well, the word *stoic* doesn't spring to mind.'

'It never does with me!' Bonita pouted. 'It did *really* hurt, though. I'm going to be much more sympathetic to patients now.'

'You're always lovely to the patients.' It was the first compliment he'd paid her since they'd worked alongside each other, and it must have caught Hugh by surprise because he quickly snapped back to business mode. 'Right, you're your GP's problem now. I've signed you off work for the next four weeks, but make an appointment to see your GP this week. Keep the immobiliser on at all times for a couple of days, but after that you can take it off to have a shower but you must wear a sling or something…you know the drill.

'Here!' He placed a sick certificate and a letter for her GP on her dressing-table. 'Consider yourself discharged!'

'Thanks very much—' Bonita attempted to be gracious '—for yesterday, and for coming out to see me today.'

'Happy to help. I know how busy your mum is at the moment.'

'Well, thanks anyway.'

'Why don't you go back to sleep?'

Fat chance of that! Bonita thought after Hugh had gone downstairs. She'd already been asleep for twelve hours and, listening to the laughter and chatter coming from the kitchen, she wished she could just get up and join in. She wished she could grin and joke and pick up the baton with Hugh the way the rest of her family had—even go back to the teasing and banter they'd once shared when she'd just been Paul's annoying little sister.

One kiss, he'd told her, as he'd broken her heart.

One kiss, that for Hugh had meant absolutely nothing!

But it had been more than a kiss, she *knew* it had been, and had tearfully told him that.

Harshly—extremely harshly—he had made it exceptionally clear that she was wrong!

'Oh, for God's sake, that's what guys do when a girl's there…' His face was as hard and cold and expressionless as granite as he plunged in the knife. 'That's what guys do when it's available. You need to be more careful…and you need to grow up, Bonny. You need to stop embarrassing everyone and get over the stupid crush you've had on me for years and get on with your life.'

Even six years on, his words still hurt, made her blush to her roots, made her want to curl up and die with shame.

How, Bonita thought, gingerly levering herself out of bed, was she supposed to pick up the baton and carry on as before after *that*?

'Oh, you're up! I'll put on some eggs.' Shuffling into the kitchen, she knew she probably looked a fright in her mother's nightdress with her old dressing-gown on her good arm. Her hair was no doubt at all angles, but she was past caring as she joined Hugh and her father at the table where her father, looking a lot brighter this morning, was reading the newspaper.

With some difficulty, her good hand shaking with the weight, Bonita poured herself a cup of tea from the very full pot. She saw the smirk of amusement in Hugh's eyes.

'Ask and you shall receive!'

'I can manage, thanks!' Bonita said, spilling half the pot as she did so.

'Give me your keys, Bonny, and I'll drive into town after church,' Carmel called from the cooker. 'I can drop into the flat and grab a few of your clothes and toiletries and things!'

'I'll come with you!' Bonita croaked.

'There isn't time for you to get ready for church and I'm not going to come all the way back just to pick you up! Just give me your keys and tell me anything you want me to fetch!'

Hugh was grinning like a Cheshire cat at her discomfort. Unseen by her parents, he pulled a look of mock horror as Bonita squirmed in her chair, imagining her mother dressed in her Sunday best bursting in on Emily and heaven knew who else! And... Oh, no, Bonita thought, drenched suddenly with a cold sweat. Her pills were in her bedside drawer...

'Help!' Hating it that she had to, but hating the prospect of her mother's wrath more, she mouthed the word to him, only he wasn't looking at her. Hugh just poured a cup of tea and sort of smiled to himself, then, catching her frantic eyes, his smile widened into a lazy grin.

'Actually, Carmel…' He looked over at Bonita's mother. 'I'm going into town today. Bonny, why don't you ring your flatmate and ask her to pack up some of your things into a case? I can drop it off to you tonight.'

'Are you sure?' Carmel frowned. 'We can't ask you to do that!'

'It's really not a problem.' Hugh shrugged. 'I'm going that way anyway.'

'Well, you must stay for dinner when you bring the case! All the boys will be here,' Carmel said casually, making her way over to the table, as if it was a regular occurrence that her three sons just happened to be coming over this Sunday. 'It will be nice to have everyone together.'

'I don't think so,' Hugh said. 'I'll just drop off the case.'

But her parents couldn't take a hint if it slammed into them at a hundred miles an hour. It wouldn't enter their heads that Hugh might have a million places he'd rather be on a rare weekend off!

'Come for dinner!' Luigi ordered. 'It will be like old times.'

Carmel gave a tight smile, and deposited two boiled eggs with the tops still on and a round of unbuttered toast on the table. Bonita realised that any maternal instinct her mother had displayed last night had seemingly drained away with the bath water as she sped off to get ready for church and left Bonita to deal with her breakfast.

'Did you want some help there, Bonny?' Hugh grinned. 'With your eggs, I mean.'

'Please!' Bonita gave a tight smile back, sitting rigid as he came over. His long fingers held the knife and expertly beheaded her eggs. He even buttered her toast and cut it into soldiers.

'Thank you!' Hugh reminded her as he put down the knife.

'Thank you.'

Carmel took about three minutes to get ready, her usual jodhpurs and T-shirt exchanged for a smart grey dress and sensible black shoes, her hair still pulled back into its usual low ponytail. Bonita buttoned her lip instead of suggesting her mother put a little make-up on—they'd had that argument too many times to repeat it. However, it irked Bonita. Her mother, if she made even a shred of effort, was a stunningly attractive woman. Still, maybe she didn't need lipstick because her husband's face lit up when she came down dressed for church. He could see how beautiful she was without it.

'I'll be back by ten-thirty, eleven at the latest.'

'No rush,' Hugh assured her.

'Why don't you stay for the coffee morning after the service?' Bonita suggested, seeing the lines of tiredness around her mother's eyes and knowing that she needed a break from the house. The social side of the church, Bonita was sure, was one of the main reasons her mother loved to go, but as usual she'd said the wrong thing.

'Why would I want to hang around for coffee and cake?' She kissed Luigi goodbye. 'I'll be back at ten-thirty.'

Which actually suited Bonita just fine!

It was annoying how easily Hugh just slotted back in. She knew he wasn't there for her benefit, that since he'd returned to Australia he had visited regularly, but trying to concentrate on the Sunday papers, as he sat playing cards with her father, as they chatted away like the old friends they were, it hurt how wonderful they all thought he was. Hugh could do no wrong. If only they knew! And Hugh hanging around, when she was perfectly capable of watching her father, just irked. Still, by the time the hand edged past ten-thirty and she saw Hugh pull her father forward to arrange his cushions when Luigi had a coughing fit, and the calm way Hugh put on her father's mask and gave him a nebuliser, Bonita conceded, it was good that he was there.

And, yes, she *was* glad he was around when she rang Emily and asked her to pack a case—anyone would surely be better than her mother dropping in on a Sunday.

'Here.' She handed him her key ring. 'Emily says that she might be out, but she'll leave a case in the hall. She knows what I need, so you don't—'

'Don't worry,' Hugh interrupted, 'I have no desire to snoop around your things.'

Strange, Bonita thought later as she stomped around, helping her mother prepare dinner, that Hugh could both reassure and put her down at the same time.

It was almost like old times.

Ricky, there without his wife Harriet, who had forfeited the two-hour drive to get the kids to bed; Marco, who was Ricky's veterinary partner, had arranged for a locum to cover them both; and Paul, who had for once asked a colleague to cover him for the evening, all arrived as if it had been the easiest thing in the world to get away and drop by for one of Carmel's Sunday roasts.

Yes, almost like old times as the guys argued good-naturedly and Luigi told Bonita to go and give her mother a hand in the kitchen.

'Literally!' Hugh smirked as Bonita duly headed off.

Carmel had made it blazingly clear throughout the afternoon that Bonita was more of a hindrance than a help, but she did let Bonita stir the gravy as she set about serving up.

'Make sure it doesn't go lumpy, like the cheese sauce you made this afternoon.'

So she stood and stirred as Hugh, the *golden one*, came in and offered to carve, while Luigi enjoyed his sons' company in the lounge.

'Bonny!' Carmel barked as for a second Bonita missed a beat.

'It's actually quite hard to stir and turn the gas down at the same time, with—'

'Only one hand!' Carmel snapped. 'Save the sob stories Bonny!'

So she did, gritting her teeth and stirring on, knowing that a row was the last thing everyone needed right now, but the tension was unbearable, the heat in the kitchen rising with every dish Carmel brought out. Carmel hadn't just adopted her husband's religion on marriage, she'd adopted a few other Italian ways too—like making way too much food, a massive piece of beef, glazed carrots, roast potatoes, roast pumpkin, peas, cauliflower, cheese and, of course, just in case anyone might still need something to nibble on while they waited for the apricot crumble dessert, there was a vast lasagne as well!

'Any one would think we had the Royal Family

coming for dinner.' Bonita attempted a joke to lighten the tense mood.

'It's *my* family!' Carmel glared, taking over the gravy, leaving Bonita standing. Bonita glanced at Hugh, who gave her a thin, half-lipped smile. She didn't know if it was in support or disappointment that *again* she had managed to say the wrong thing and upset her mum.

'This looks great, Mum!' Marco said the right thing.

'If there's any lasagne left over, Harriet asked if I could bring some home for her!' From Carmel's smile Ricky had said the right thing as well.

'I want some to take back, too!' Paul added.

Oh, they were all on form tonight, even Hugh!

'What's this rubbish!' Luigi frowned at the bottle of expensive wine Hugh had bought.

'What are you talking about—it's a great drop!' Hugh said in his pompous voice as Bonita's hand clutched the knife and fork. Arrogant Hugh may be, but surely he knew better than to question her father on wine!

Except Luigi was laughing, getting the joke long before the rest of them did. It was, in fact, Luigi's arch-rival's wine that Hugh had brought. Hugh was doing what he so often naturally did, and just winding her father up.

'We drink *my* wine at *my* table!' Luigi said firmly, and of course Hugh did the honours, getting a bottle from the wine rack and filling up everyone's glass. Worryingly for Bonita, given that her father was on a morphine infusion, Hugh filled his to the brim, too.

'Perhaps Dad shouldn't...' Her voice trailed off as Hugh shot her a warning look.

'*Salute.*'

And just as her glass would be filled and she would barely touch it so, too, Bonita realised, her dad would do the same. It was a desperate pretence at normality—everyone pretending it was just any other Sunday night, that this wasn't one of the last Sunday nights that they would sit around the table like this.

But it was.

As everyone laughed and chatted, Bonita joined in, though she struggled with her meat as much as her father struggled with his gravy and mash. She struggled, too, with the knowledge that this was probably the last time they would all be like this. Even the barbeque in a few weeks seemed unattainable.

'Bonny!' Carmel said, for once not scolding her for not eating enough. 'Make yourself useful and clear the table.'

So she did   cleared the plates with one hand—then took grateful refuge in the kitchen for a moment, blowing her nose loudly into the tea-towel.

'Hope you're not going to use that to wipe the dishes.' Carrying plates, Hugh caught her. 'How are you doing?'

'Great!' Bonny forced a bright smile.

'You are!' Hugh answered, which was just about the nicest thing he could have said, letting her know that he knew how hard tonight was. 'Let's get these puddings out.'

'Just custard for your dad…' Carmel marched into her kitchen. 'Come on, Bonny, mash Dad up a bit of apricot from the crumble perhaps.'

Which she did with her good hand while her mum deftly served the crumble onto the other six plates and juggled three as Hugh did the same, leaving Bonita to bring her father's.

It was just another Sunday night—almost. Flopping in front of the television after a huge dinner, for once Bonita didn't have to do the dishes. Perfect Paul, the Surgeon, for the first time where there wasn't blood involved, actually pulled on the rubber gloves, as Ricky and Marco went through the inoculation schedules for the horses with Luigi. Hugh fell asleep in front of the television and, unlike most, managed to look fantastic as he did so—no open-mouthed snoring for Hugh! His long legs stretched out in front of him, his fingers laced behind his blond head. He looked just as he did on the couple of night shifts she'd worked with him and found him in the staffroom, half asleep, yet half ready to jump into action.

Did he ever fully relax? Bonita thought as she curled up on the sofa, her own eyes almost closed, wishing it *was* just another Sunday, wishing nights like these could happen again. Hugh kept a formidable schedule, both professionally and socially. The professional she knew first hand, knew that he was also studying for his FRCS, which would enhance his emergency career. As for the social, well, the hospital grapevine kept her pretty up to date with his regular action there! Amber, the radiographer who he had gone out with towards the end of his time in Australia, was now a regular fixture. As Hugh shifted slightly in his seat, stretching just a touch, Bonita was treated to a glimpse of flat-toned stomach, and from this impressive view it was clear he still managed to find the time to eat well and exercise.

And from the lovely snaky line of hair that dipped below his belly button, she could see he was certainly a natural blond!

He could make her blush with his eyes closed!

Quickly Bonita snapped her eyes closed, absolutely *determined* not to be caught gazing at him from across the room. It took about ten seconds flat to fall asleep and, no doubt, Bonita thought when her mother awoke her later, far less elegantly than Hugh!

'Go and get your bags from Hugh's car!' Carmel ordered. 'He wants to get going.'

'I can bring them in, Carmel!'

'Bonny can help, even with one arm—you're not the bell boy!'

He was just so nice to them, Bonita thought with a sudden twist in her stomach that was surely borne of envy. He thanked her parents and kissed them goodbye, and they were so nice to him, loading him with plates of lasagne and beef, thanking him back, adoring him...

Little did they know the bastard he could be when he chose.

'You're quiet tonight!' Hugh observed as they crunched along the gravel driveway past several Azetti cars and utes till they came to his.

'Better to be quiet than say the wrong thing!' Bonita answered.

'Meaning?' He stopped walking, but Bonita didn't. 'What have I done to offend you now?'

'It doesn't have to always be about you, Hugh!'

'Bonny!' He grabbed her good arm and halted her. 'I'm not good at cryptic crosswords!'

'I'm just tired of watching everyone else say and do the right thing. Paul will go home and then rock over in a few more days for a ten-minute visit and my mum will fall on him, Ricky or Marco will promise to *try* and get down next weekend and Mum will be delighted to see them. You they can't get enough of when you call by. Yet I just seem to get in the way!'

'Your mum's so happy you're here, Bonny! She is,' he insisted as she gave a disbelieving snort. 'It's just the way she is with you and that's not going to change while…'

'While what?' Bonita pushed, but Hugh shook his head. 'Just be patient.'

'I am being patient.'

'I know.'

'She doesn't tell me anything—she hasn't even said that he's dying.'

'I know that too,' he said gently.

'I know he's got bowel cancer, I know it's spread, the rest is guesswork… She asks me to come to all the hospital appointments with them, then she tells me to wait outside.'

'She's just trying to shield you.'

'I'm a nurse!' Bonita growled. 'I'm his daughter. I've tried to speak to Paul about it—he must know more, for goodness' sake, but he just fobs me off! I'm trying to do what's best for Mum and Dad, but without any information.'

And if *that* day hadn't happened all those years ago, if he really was a friend, it would have been entirely appropriate for him to pull her in his arms now and offer a hug of support. But it had happened and they weren't friends, so all he did was stand there and watch as she wiped a couple of tears away with her good hand.

Only she wanted him to take her in his arms so badly,

to just…be held, for some physical acknowledgement as to just how hard this was.

To just rest a while in his embrace.

And it was *that* that confused Bonita as she stood there in the silence of night with him—that she should want comfort from the man who had hurt her most in the world. That and the fact he was so generous with his affection to everyone but her. It left her feeling isolated and confused.

'Let's get your bags.' His voice was harsh as it broke the silence, reminding her just how far apart they were.

There was no relief on offer or in sight as they walked the few more steps to his car.

'Bags!' Bonita gave a small yelp as he opened the boot. 'Did she completely empty my room?'

'Well, you are going to be away a while…'

'How was Emily?' Bonita asked.

'I didn't see her,' Hugh clipped, handing Bonita a vanity case and taking the other case and a couple of bags for himself. 'These were just in the hall.'

'She must have been out.'

Up to that point Bonita had been trying to make idle conversation, but when Hugh gave a shrug, and suddenly busied himself with the complex task of closing the boot, Bonita found herself frowning.

'Hugh?'

'What?'

'Did you see Emily?'

'I told you, no. These were just in the hall.'

He was lying.

As Hugh deposited her bags, said another prolonged

goodbye to her family then waved himself off, Paul lugged
her cases into the bedroom and she set about unpacking,
all Bonita knew was that Hugh had just lied to her.

Only why she couldn't begin to fathom.

CHAPTER FOUR

THE novelty of living at home had soon worn off.

The questions that had incensed her as a teenager were, it seemed, still completely appropriate now she was twenty-four.

'Who was that on the phone?'

'How much did that cost?'

'Who are you going out with?'

'When will you be home?'

Not that she'd exactly been hitting the nightclubs. Last night, in celebration of her immobiliser coming off, a few of the girls from netball had picked Bonita up and taken her to the local pub to celebrate.

It had hardly been a wild night.

A local band, a steak, which Bonita, terrified without the security of the immobiliser, had had to have help cutting, washed down with several fruit juices. But from the curtains twitching when she'd been dropped off and the stony glare and heated words from her mother when she'd stepped inside the house, she might just as well have arrived home drunk after a rave.

Her mother was still sulking the following afternoon when a car pulled up and there was a knock at the door.

'You've got a visitor.'

Over the past couple of weeks Bonita had had several visitors, mainly friends from the netball team and the hospital, but they hadn't caused Carmel's mouth to purse in distaste. And given her mother hadn't invited the visitor in, Bonita could guess who had been left standing at the door.

'Hi, Bill!'

'Hi, there.' He gave her a very nice but apprehensive smile, no doubt worried about the reception he'd receive from her family. 'I heard what happened. I've tried ringing your mobile a few times…'

'Emily didn't pack my charger so I'm a bit marooned.'

'I didn't want to ring the house and I didn't know whether or not I should come over, but it's been weeks and I haven't heard. I just wanted to make sure that you were OK.'

'I'm fine.' Bonita grinned, about to invite him in, but not wanting to make things even more awkward she thought better of it. 'Fancy a walk?'

They walked up through the vines towards the stables, a familiar route that they'd taken many, many times, only today they weren't holding hands.

'I didn't know whether to stay away,' Bill admitted. 'I know I'm not exactly popular at the moment. Your mum just about closed the door on me.'

'I'm sorry.' Bonita gulped. 'How are things at work?'

'Not great,' Bill admitted. 'So it's been hard to find out how you're doing. Everyone still thinks I'm an utter bastard for ending it with you. Saying that there must have been someone else involved...'

'Bill.' Bonita halted him. 'You were right to end things. And...I guess there was someone else involved. They just don't know that it was on my side.'

'Should I have waited? I mean, with your dad so ill....'

She thought about it, really tried to picture these past few weeks with Bill in her life, and she couldn't. Hugh, even though there was nothing between them, *was* a factor in her life. His return had her reeling....

She tried to fathom dealing with her father's impending death and Hugh's return, while all the time lying to Bill—and she had been lying, Bonita acknowledged. While not technically unfaithful, her mind hadn't been on the man she'd been with. Though there was nothing between herself and Hugh, it was he who consumed her thoughts.

Standing there, facing Bill, there was her answer. His arms weren't the ones she wanted around her. Oh, she wanted his friendship, missed him at times, but his embrace wasn't the one that could soothe.

And if there was any relief to be had at the moment, it was in being alone.

To close the door at night and be honest—at least with herself.

'You were right to end it when you did.' Bonita gave him a sad smile. 'I don't have anything left to give at the moment, Bill.'

'I know.' He actually looked her in the eye and for the first time Bonita didn't look away. 'You were going to end it, weren't you? I mean, if I hadn't.'

'I think so.' She gave a confused shake of her head. 'I just need to deal with losing Dad...'

'I understand that,' Bill said. 'I want you to know that, not once, while we were together...' He swallowed hard. 'Bonita, I was devastated when we broke up, but it was the right thing to do, and I know now because—'

'Bill...' She put her hand up to stop him. She was not up to hearing about her faults, to hearing how she'd thrown away a good relationship in this strange, unwitting quest for the glimpse of perfection she'd had all those years ago. 'I don't want to talk about it now.'

'We have to.'

'Have to?' Bonita frowned.

'I need to tell you something before someone else does.' Bill, *Bill*, who had looked her in the eye and demanded the truth a couple of months ago, couldn't look at her now. 'Did Hugh speak to you?'

'Hugh?'

'When he came to Emily's...' Bill swallowed uncomfortably 'He saw me there when he came to collect your things.'

Funny, that when there was so much going on in your own life, when you were struggling to stay afloat, you just assumed the world was on pause, waiting patiently till you were ready to resume living. But standing there, Bonita realised the world carried right on turning, people carried on laughing and living and falling in love—even as your own world eroded.

'Hugh didn't say anything,' Bonita said—embarrassed all of a sudden that Hugh had known first.

That Hugh must now feel sorry for her.

'I thought he was going to hit me,' Bill admitted. 'He didn't. He just stomped about, grabbing your things.'

'*Hugh* got my things!'

'Emily meant to pack. Like I said, we never planned...' So Hugh had walked in the morning after a night of passion. Cold shivers of embarrassment swept down her spine. Ridiculous that it should matter, given the circumstances—except that it did. The thought of Hugh fumbling around in her knickers drawer, through her toiletries, had Bonita breaking out in a cold sweat. She added a quick prayer of thanks that she didn't keep a diary.

OK, there was one photo of him on her bedside table—it had been put up after she'd broken up with Bill—but that same photo had been taken by her and included her parents and brothers and was, because she was paranoid that anyone might guess, nestled in without about five other family photos. Even if Hugh had seen it, he wouldn't have given it a thought.

Still, she had more important things to worry about right now, walking slowly alongside Bill as she tried to process what he was telling her.

Trying to fathom how she felt.

'I've been working up to tell you—I just didn't know how. Emily's the same.'

'I thought I hadn't seen her much since my accident.' Bonita frowned, one question vital all of a sudden. 'When?' Bonita swallowed. 'When did you two start seeing each other?'

'Then,' Bill said. 'The day you had your accident.' Which had been a good month after they had broken up, but she couldn't keep the dash of bitterness and doubt out of her voice when she spoke next.

'Very convenient, Bill—you mean, you were *caught*, then!'

'I'm telling the truth, Bonita…' And he did look at her then and she knew he wasn't lying—knew because Bill was a good guy, and Emily was actually a really nice girl—even if, as Bonita had privately thought on occasion, she wasn't exactly famed for the strength of her knicker elastic. 'It was the last thing I expected to happen. In fact, it would be easier all around if it hadn't happened. I've already got everyone at work out to get me, calling me a louse for leaving you. Wait till they find out this. I went round that Saturday to get the last of my things and Emily told me what had happened with your arm. I had a beer… Emily was going on, saying she couldn't believe we'd broken up. I didn't tell her about Hugh, of course.' He'd registered Bonita's anxious eyes. 'I still haven't. I never would. What I did say, though, was that you weren't happy, that it wasn't that straight-forward, that you'd just gone off me. And the next thing she was trying to boost my ego a bit, and…'

'One thing led to another?' Bonita offered.

'There was nothing, *nothing* between us till then. I really need you to know that.' Bill voice was urgent and as much as he really needed her to know that, she, Bonita realised, needed to know it too. 'I didn't know how to tell you, what with your dad and every-thing…I'm so sorry.'

'You've got nothing to be sorry for, Bill.'

'Try telling that to everyone when it gets out.'

'I will tell them.' Bonita looked at him squarely. 'I'm pleased, pleased for both of you, I can honestly say that. Though it feels a bit...' Bonita fumbled for the right word. 'It's going to take a bit of time to get my head around it, I suppose.' An appalling thought suddenly occurred to her. 'I can't imagine moving back.'

'I haven't moved in.' Bill gave a half-smile. 'Please, don't move out on my account. I don't even like going there particularly. It just seems wrong.'

'Well, it isn't.'

And it wasn't, Bonita realised as they walked slowly back to the house. You don't choose who you fall in love with—if only life were that kind, she thought pensively. She hadn't chosen to still have feelings for Hugh, just as Bill hadn't chosen to develop feelings for Emily.

Life and love didn't always come with a guaranteed set of choices.

'Hugh's here.' Bill nodded at the silver car that had appeared in their driveway since they'd gone on their walk.

'Hugh's always here...' Bonita gave a small half-smile. 'He's either riding Ramone at the crack of dawn or chatting to Dad, he's like a son to them.'

'But not like a brother to you...' Bill gave her a sympathetic smile.

'I saw him less when I was working with him. Still...' Bonita faltered for a second. 'I guess everyone's coming around more these days.'

'How is he doing?'

'Great! Well, according to Mum he is...' Tears pricked her eyes. 'The weight's just falling off him, though. The palliative care nurse wants to put down an

NG tube and give him supplementary feeds, but he's refusing. Still, he has actually got a bit of a second wind, organising the barbeque and everything.'

'It's on Saturday, isn't it?' Bill checked. 'It will be weird, not being here for it. How are things with you and your mum?'

'The same.' Bonita shrugged. 'Everything I do at the moment seems to confirm Hugh's opinion of me: that I'm just the immature little Azetti girl.'

'You immature?' Bill frowned. 'That doesn't sound like you.'

'That's a matter of opinion.' Bonita gave a tight smile. 'Things are a bit strained at home at the moment. You know what Mum and Dad are like—mature to them means settled down and married. Not walking through the vines with my ex and hearing he's on with my friend…'

She smiled at his wince.

'Joking.' She gave a wince of her own. 'Sort of. They seem to think my life is chaotic, whereas actually it's boringly normal. Hugh just seems to catch every row I have with Mum at the moment. Living back here, I feel like I'm teenager again.'

'Well you're not.'

'I know! If I'd followed their rules we'd either be stuck together and as miserable as all hell or heading for divorce courts now. I'll stick with my game plan.'

'Which is?'

'I haven't got one,' Bonita admitted with a smile. 'I'm happy with my life and seeing where it will take me…' Her smile widened a touch. 'I always hated that your name was Bill. Bill and Bonita—it sounded like a nursery rhyme, there were just too many Bs for it to be perfect!'

'It nearly was.'

'Thank you.' Bonita said. 'For having the guts to come over. I know how hard it would have been.'

'When will you be back at work?'

'A couple of weeks.' Bonita shrugged. 'Just light duties. Really, I don't know what I'm going to do about the flat. I'm going to have to see how things go with Dad for now. I don't know if I'm helping Mum much, but I might stay on a bit. I just don't know. I'll give Emily a ring soon—but tell her I'm OK.'

It was right to accept a hug goodbye.

Right because when he held her in his arms and it couldn't even vaguely be described as awkward, it confirmed what they both knew.

There was just nothing more than friendship there.

'He's got a nerve,' Carmel snapped as Bonita walked back into the house.

'Leave it, Mum.'

'Walking up to the front door, as bold as brass, after all he put you through…'

'Bill's a nice guy.' And seeing Hugh playing cards with her dad, it incensed her when she saw the slight rise of his eyebrow as she defended Bill to her mother. That Hugh thought he knew better than her what was going on had Bonita boiling.

'Nice!' Carmel snorted. 'I can think of a lot of other words for him…' And as she opened her mouth to deliver a few, to ram home yet another point, it was all

too much for Bonita. The tears, the emotion that her
mother hated so much all bubbled to the surface as
Bonita promptly burst into tears, loud angry tears that
disturbed the quiet afternoon her mother had striven to
create—raw, emotion-charged tears that in the Azetti
house just mustn't happen.

'Look what he's done,' Carmel shouted. 'Look at
how he's upset you.'

'If he comes here again…' Luigi attempted, coughing
before he continued, 'he'll have me to deal with!'

'You don't know what you're talking about,' Bonita
sobbed. 'None of you!' she added angrily in Hugh's di-
rection, and then fled to her room.

CHAPTER FIVE

SHE wasn't sure which of the lesser of two evils it would be as someone knocked on her bedroom door an hour or so later—whether it would be Hugh or her mother. She knew it *would* be one of them, telling her to hold it together, that her dad didn't need the stress right now. And all Bonita knew was that she didn't need to be made to feel young and stupid merely for *feeling*.

This time in her life hurt, hurt so much she could barely breathe—living here, being here, watching her dad fading away and pretending not to notice, losing her relationship with Bill to a man who would never love her, then hearing people blame Bill for something that truly wasn't his fault. It was almost more than she could bear.

'Hey!' It was Hugh. Her arm was over her eyes but she could hear him plonking down a mug of tea and standing over the bed where she lay. It didn't even merit comment this time that he'd been allowed into her bedroom. He wasn't a man or even a doctor today— more a big brother, coming in to give her a lecture. 'How do you feel?'

'Great!' Her covered eyes and swollen lips just added

to the irony of her surly word. 'I suppose you've been sent to talk some sense into me.'

'Your mother was going to—then your father thought that he should...' Hugh peeled her arm away and smiled at her tear-streaked face. 'They were even talking about ringing Paul to come home from the hospital.'

'Well, they'd have a job getting him. He hasn't been round for a week.'

'He doesn't know how to deal with your dad. It upsets him.'

'Poor Paul!' Bonita gave a twisted smile.

'And with the other two out at Bendigo, I know a lot of this is landing on you.'

'And you!' Bonita said. She had not realized this before: the regular visits despite Hugh's schedule; his patience with her father as he became harder and harder to understand. Luigi's mind had started wandering in mid-conversation, and Hugh had sat through endless rounds of reminiscing.

'You're living with it,' he said gently.

'And I really don't think I can,' Bonita admitted. 'You know we never really got on. I love them and everything, but I left home at eighteen because of the way they were. Now I'm back, they're carrying on as if I'm still fourteen.'

'It's just their way—and your mum's just trying to be supportive about Bill.'

'By being horrible about him! How does that help? And now she'll be angry with me for crying.'

'She just wants things kept as calm as possible.'

'I don't need a lecture, Hugh. I really don't need to

be told how sick my dad is, how they don't need the drama, because, believe it or not, I'm not being child-ish—all I'm being is me…' She bit back a scream almost, then covered her eyes again as he looked on. 'I'm fed up with being told it's because I'm the youngest or because I'm immature when I'm actually being more mature than I've ever been in my life. I'm hurting and I'm not allowed to show it and it doesn't help when they speak like that about Bill.'

'OK…' He took a deep breath. 'I know you think the world of Bill, I know it hurt like hell when you broke up, and you're probably hoping that he'll change his mind, but you do need to move forward, Bonny.' She could hear the patronising tone in his voice, the grown-up who knew better. Mr—or rather Dr—Mature, who knew that poor little Bonny's boyfriend was cheating on her, that poor blind Bonny didn't have a clue, when actually Bonita Azetti had handled today's turn of events with more dignity than most women could have mustered. 'There's something you ought to know…' Hugh said gently, and ever the doctor he gave a grim smile, as if he was about to deliver a fatal diagnosis, but Bonita beat him to it.

'I know about Bill and Emily.'

'You know?' He couldn't disguise the shock in his voice.

'And, for your information, I'm fine with it.' She gave a small shake of her head. 'Well, not *fine*, but I'm OK with it. Emily's not the reason we broke up.'

'What was?'

'Does there have to be a reason, Hugh?' Pulling down

her arm again, he could see her eyes well with fresh tears. 'We weren't married, we weren't engaged, we didn't have kids—why does everyone keep waiting for me to come up with this neatly defined *reason* as to why we broke up? It wasn't working.'

'But even so…'

'Why did you call off your engagement?' Bonita challenged. 'Or rather *engagements*? You've had more girlfriends than I can remember, Paul too and Ricky and Marco in their time, yet not once do I remember any of you being held to account for them not working.'

She could feel panic building, a horrible, horrible panic because all she was doing was hurting. All of it was unfair, and every road out was a dead end because there was nowhere to go to escape—she didn't even have the flat to fall back on, thanks to *bloody* Bill and Emily.

'I know this is hard for you.' He sat down on the edge of the bed. 'This is all hard for you…'

'I want to help Mum.'

'You are just by being here.'

'I make her so cross.'

'Bonny… Bonny,' he repeated, waiting till her eyes met his to convey the importance of his words. 'She adores you—you scare her…'

'Scare her!' Of all the ridiculous things to say! 'How could I possibly scare her?'

'You say what she feels.' Hugh's explanation just added to her confusion. 'You open so many lids, and she walks frantically behind, closing them.'

'No…' He didn't understand. Cross, Bonita shook

her head on the pillow, because Hugh was talking nonsense. 'You don't know what you're talking about.'

'But I do.'

'Maybe I should just go back to the flat,' Bonita said frantically.

'You can't.'

'Why not?' Her chocolate-brown eyes snapped wide open. 'If it makes Bill and Emily feel awkward, tough! They should have thought of that. They can stay at Bill's if they can't stand to be around me!'

'You can't,' Hugh said again.

'Well, I can't stay here. I went out for the first time in weeks last night. The first time,' Bonita emphasized. 'Just with the girls, just to hear a band. I was home by ten-thirty and she's *still* furious with me.'

'Then don't make waves.'

'Are you suggesting I don't go out?' Bonita said.

She waited for him to laugh, to say, 'Of course not!' Instead, she was left stunned and disbelieving when Hugh gave a tight shrug.

'Maybe you could meet your friends for lunch instead?'

'I do not believe this!' She sat up so hard it hurt her shoulder. 'You! You of all people! Would you say this to Paul?' she demanded to his grim face. 'No wonder people say I'm immature—I'm not allowed to grow up.'

'Bonny—'

'Thanks for the pep talk.' She sneered as he hopelessly closed his eyes. 'Oh, sorry to disappoint you. Were you expecting to swagger downstairs and say that everything's fine now—that I'll be down to mop the floor in ten minutes and that I'll only see my friends during the days—?'

'Bonny, please!'

'It really would be better for everyone if I move out,' Bonita said, only more calmly now. 'Dad doesn't need the tension right now and Mum and I aren't getting on—it will be easier on everyone!'

'None of this is easy,' Hugh said, grabbing her wrist as she made to get off the bed. 'Just listen to me for a minute, Bonny.'

'I've heard enough.'

'Please.' There was a slightly imperative note to his voice that stilled her—had her change her mind in mid-flight off the bed. Hugh's free hand dragged through his hair as he blew out a long breath.

For Hugh, he felt as if he were about to skydive for the first time!

He was standing on the line between getting involved and staying the hell out.

He'd known Bonny since she'd been eleven—had buttoned his lip on so many occasions, but he could feel things coming undone now.

The Azettis were his first glimpse at a real family in action. The strange dynamics that had at first intrigued him. The shifts of power that, to Hugh, had seemed like a science experiment. An objective observer, he'd watched with wry amusement. He'd smothered a smile as a fiery little girl had challenged what, in this house, was considered the norm. Then there had been no smiles to smother, just the genuine pull of seeing a problem from all sides—and adoring them all.

'Can I trust you?'

'Meaning?' He watched as her eyes narrowed.

'I just don't want you to repeat what's said….'

'I never have to date!'

He gave a grim smile at her inference.

'Paul's struggling.'

'We're all struggling!'

'He's a surgeon, Bonny—' those dark green eyes held hers '—and this isn't a "you're merely a nurse" lecture. I need you to listen.'

And for the first time she was, watching him swallow, registering the hesitation in his voice, the careful choice of his words as he tried to reveal something without breaking his friend's confidence.

Without possibly pulling a family apart.

'He feels…' Hugh closed his eyes.

'That he should have known?' She knew there was more when he nodded, knew he didn't want to say it.

So she thought about it.

Sat on the bed and thought how it must be for a surgeon—a surgeon who operated on bowel-cancer patients every week, a surgeon whose own father's cancer had been too advanced by the time it had been discovered.

'Dad had symptoms for everything,' Bonita whispered. 'If Mum put too much butter on his toast, he thought he was having a heart attack. If we took every complaint seriously, he'd have spent his life undergoing investigations. And the one time he did have symptoms, the one time he did have something really wrong—well, he was too scared to say anything.' Bonita gulped. 'Too scared to do anything about it. It's not Paul's fault.'

'That's what he needs to hear.'

'He will.' Bonita nodded. 'I know how difficult Mum and Dad can be…'

'Which brings me to you.'

He stared at her questioning face and could almost feel the axe in his hand as he prepared to wield it.

'You ought to stay at home.'

'I can't, Hugh.' Tears plopped down her cheeks. 'I'm not going to storm downstairs with a suitcase, but I do have to go. I can't stay indefinitely. Dad could have months left…' She hated the tiny shake of his head. 'And I can't just walk out on Mum straight afterwards.'

'Stay, Bonny.'

'How? You said yourself I shouldn't go out, just stay home to keep the peace. For how long, though? Mum and I…'

'It isn't your mum.' He almost braced himself for the impact of his words, watched her frown as she tried to understand. 'Your mum's on your side here, Bonny, she's *always* been on your side. It's your dad that's the problem—your dad who gets upset if you go out.'

'You've got it wrong! Dad was asleep when I got home last night.'

'Because she told him you were fine—the same way you told him your mum was fine when she was five minutes late back from church the other week.'

'You've got it wrong!' Bonny insisted, only with less conviction this time.

'Bonny, do you remember that party you went to, the time we…' She screwed her eyes closed, couldn't believe he could bring that up now. It was a no-go area, something never to be discussed, the most raw painful part of her, yet here he was, bringing it up, on today of all days. 'You remember how desperate you were to go…' Her heart was hammering in her chest, the murky past suddenly being uncovered, and she was scared to go there, especially with Hugh, but he spoke on. 'Your dad wasn't going to let you go.'

'It was Mum!' Like a scared kitten she struggled to escape, didn't want to hear this, only somehow she knew she had to, knew that there was no escape. Six feet two of Hugh bloody Armstrong was on her bed and blocking all exits!

'Your dad refused point blank to let you go. I know because I heard the row. She begged him, pleaded with him to just let you be, to trust you.'

'And then I was late home.'

'I heard that row, too,' Hugh said. 'Your dad wanted the address, he was all set to go and get you and *bring* you home. Your mum refused to give it, insisted that you'd be home soon. He went to bed furious, told her that it was on her head if anything happened to you.

'She knew,' Hugh continued, 'how mortified you'd be if your parents showed up. Bonny, she spent all those years trying to let you be you, while somehow reeling you in so as not to upset your dad. You and your mother are far more alike than you realize—'

'Alike!' Bonny shot out the incredulous word. 'She's nothing like me.'

'But she was,' Hugh said softly. 'When your dad met her, by all accounts, she was this young, impetuous thing…'

'Well we're not alike now!'

'Your mum would no doubt love a break, would love to stay on at the church for coffee and cake, but she knows it would upset your dad. It would have been the same last night when you went out.'

'So I shouldn't go out?'

'No,' he said simply. And it was so unfair, except now she was starting to see why. 'You're not going to change your dad now.'

'No.'

'Whether he's right or wrong, that's how he is. And if you want to make these last few days...'

'Days!'

'Weeks perhaps...' Hugh shook his head helplessly. 'But he doesn't have long—I'm not telling you anything you don't know.'

Oh, but he had.

Hugh had told her so much that she hadn't known, and she was very glad that he had because, somehow, hearing the truth shifted everything. Took the wind right out of her angry sails as she relaxed back on the bed. Somehow hearing the truth, *seeing* the truth, didn't make her love her father less, it just let her love her mother more.

'Just go easy on her now. Don't try and change things.'

'I won't.'

'It's her way with you,' Hugh continued. 'She doesn't want fuss and drama. She needs your dad to see that you're OK. And it's not about being the youngest or immature, it's about being you...and trying to let you be you with an old-fashioned Italian dad.'

'You think?'

'I know.' He smiled down at her. 'I love your dad, Bonny, he's been more of a father to me than my own ever was. There's no man I admire more, *but* he is a supremely difficult man.'

'Dad!'

'Yep.'

'Dad?' she asked again, and he confirmed it with a nod.

'And your mum's doing what she always has—trying to let you be and somehow keep the peace. She gets you, Bonny.'

Which made even less sense! And Bonita pulled away, resumed her usual sulky position these days of lying on the pillow, staring at the ceiling, only she lay back a touch too heavily and winced as she did so.

'How's your shoulder?' Hugh asked.

'Sore,' Bonita admitted, 'but only because I had physio yesterday—light duties at work are going to be a picnic after the army drills she puts me through.' He was still smiling down at her but she just wanted him to go, wanted to think about what he had said, without the distraction of him in her room. 'Thanks for the pep talk. You can go now—tell them I'm fine...'

'Are you?'

'I will be.'

'You're a tough little thing really...' he smiled '...underneath it all.'

'Underneath what?'

'The tears and the drama!'

'I am half-Italian!'

And so rarely was Hugh nice that when he was, well,

it was easy to forget just how mean he could be at times. Very, very easy to forget when his fingers were on her sore shoulder, gently soothing her hurt.

He caught her by surprise.

He was doing nothing except idly stroking her shoulder, yet he caught her by surprise. He wasn't a doctor in her room and he wasn't a brother either—he was Hugh, staring down at her, still stroking her shoulder and making it suddenly impossible to breathe.

'You'll come out and talk to them?' Hugh asked, as if the conversation was continuing normally, as if the crackling charge in the air wasn't present. Only his voice was just a touch gruffer now, and Bonita's, when it came, was a teensy bit breathless.

'Soon!'

'OK,' Hugh nodded. 'I'm going to go soon—I'm working tonight.'

'OK.'

It was just a normal conversation, except he was kissing her.

Oh, he *didn't* kiss her, and she *didn't* kiss him, but they *were* kissing, each tracing the memory as they stared, remembering again that morning when last he'd comforted her—forgetting just how badly it had ended.

'I'll drop in tomorrow after I wake up…' His fingers worked in deep, firm strokes, and it was like the electricity returning after a power cut, her whole body thrumming back into sudden life. She felt the flood of energy in her body, awareness drenching her as still he stared down at her, still his fingers worked their gentle magic. 'And see if things are better.'

His blond hair was dark from riding, the mingled scent of man and beast and cologne made her feel faint. She wanted him to lie down beside her, could almost see the frantic knot of denim-clad legs on the bed, could taste him on her mouth, wanted his hand to move lower. She wanted to burrow into him for refuge so badly, only she didn't dare.

'We'll be fine,' she said instead.

'Then I'll go.'

And then came his arms, and it was bliss, not the antidote to her pain but a comfort. The still, strong silence that he wrapped her in stopped the panic for a little while, halted the frantic running of her mind, and she did burrow into him, dragged in his scent as he held her, listened to the lovely thud of his heart in the shell of her ear.

Hugh, the man who could soothe her.

His arms, the ones that could do it.

And there, in his arms, there was an unspoken, un-fathomable, confirmation taking place, that whatever was between them, there was something. That beneath the jibes, the banter and the teasing, somehow *they* re-mained, until he pulled back.

Until he stood up and did the right thing.

'You're doing great.' He ruffled her hair in a sort of brotherly way, normal services resuming. Bonita blinked as if she'd woken from a dream. 'You'll get through this.'

And she did.

She went downstairs after she heard his car leave and apologised to her parents for upsetting them.

'We're sorry, too!' Carmel's eyes darted to Luigi, who sat with a face like thunder. 'We'll keep our opinions of Bill to ourselves.'

'Thank you,' Bonita said, looking at her mother through different eyes now.

The rose-coloured glasses she'd worn for her father lifted a touch, only it didn't hurt to see, to witness the very real love that was between her parents. The give and take that actually came from both sides.

And Bonita stopped trying to make things easier for her mother by suggesting she go out, because now she realised that it only made things harder for her.

That as much as her mother might need a break and a rest, here at home was where her father wanted Carmel to be.

And that it was actually Luigi who worried if the sauce wasn't perfect or there were lumps in the gravy— worried that if Bonny couldn't get that right then, heaven forbid, she might end up a sad old spinster like Zia Lucia!

Somehow, Hugh's wise words had defused the impending explosion. A calm descending on the family, a gentle, womb-like calm as they battened down the hatches and huddled together to greet the storm. And Bonita tried not to examine her feelings too much, refused to dwell on what had, but hadn't, taken place with Hugh. She just couldn't bring herself to look ahead because if she looked to the future it was without her dad and she truly wasn't ready to go there, so she just dealt with the present, dealt with what she could.

Held it together as one life slowly neared its end.

Bonita held back the tears as day by day her father

faded. She crawled into bed at night and breathed in Hugh's scent on her pillow, imagined his arms around her and drew from his strength. She woke every morning and opened the curtains brave and scared and wondering if this day was her dad's last.

CHAPTER SIX

THE Azetti family barbeque was so much more than a barbeque.

A lamb spit would hold centre stage, but Carmel had been cooking for days. Vast tomato and ham lasagnes, hand-made gnocchi that would be offered with carbonara or meat sauce, cannolli and tiramisu for dessert—and to her father's delight there was absolutely no excuse for Bonita not to learn how to make a million Azetti arancini balls—a vital rite of passage that Bonita had, till now, managed to avoid!

And though she didn't exactly squeal in delight at the prospect of a day in the kitchen, being scolded by her mother, it was surprisingly nice—rolling balls of rice with bacon and basil and adding a knob of mozzarella cheese, then dipping little balls in breadcrumbs—and, most importantly, her father was delighted, even coming into the kitchen at one point to watch *his* women at work.

'This needs more basil!' Luigi said, tasting the rice. 'But very good.' And there was something in his expression Bonita couldn't read at first…pride…? Satisfaction?

It was actually relief, Bonita realised as he shuffled out and Carmel gave her a small eye-roll.

'Now you know how to feed a man you won't end up like poor Zia Lucia—jetting around the world and staying in five-star hotels!'

'Lucky me, then!' Bonita said, smiling at her mother. Inexplicable tears trickled at the back of her nose as Carmel smiled back, in this moment they both seemed to say without saying anything, that they understood the other.

Yes, lucky me, Bonita thought, when two hundred little balls that had been painstakingly deep-fried and drained on layers of kitchen paper were being carried out to the trestle tables the next day, because it so nearly hadn't happened. Without Hugh's intervention, these gentle days spent with her family could have been mired in pointless bickering.

Hugh's candour had actually given her a glimpse of her real parents, while there was still time to witness them, and for that at least she was grateful to him.

'Hope there's enough food!'

He *had* to be joking! Looking disgustingly handsome and utterly at ease on Ramone, who was a beast of a horse by anyone's standards, Hugh left the pack that were preparing to set off and towered over her as she carried trays over to the already laden tables. He'd clearly managed to juggle his shifts to accommodate Carmel's request that he attend, and, given Luigi's increasing frailty, Bonita wasn't surprised, but she was also more than a little relieved that Amber wasn't there.

She wasn't sure she could handle Amber's usually

cool greeting, or meet her eye after what had taken place. The fact Amber appeared off Hugh's list spared Bonita more than a few blushes.

Oh, nothing had happened *technically*. In fact, the more Bonita thought about it—and, boy, had she thought about it—the more she had convinced herself that she was imagining things, that Hugh had been patting her shoulder, just as her mother would, that the thick sizzle of sex in the air had been but a product of her over-active imagination. Especially because he'd bounced straight back to his usual scathing self. In fact, as he eyed the arancini rather than her, Bonita realized with a thud of disappointment that he'd only come over looking for a quick feed!

'What have you got there?'

'Arancini,' Bonita said. 'But lunch isn't till after the ride!'

It was a loose family tradition at the barbeque that the guys all galloped off at breakneck speed as the women set up and, in truth, it was the one time Bonita didn't mind the blatant sexism that existed in her family—she far preferred her feet on solid ground. And as this year her dad wasn't going riding she was only too happy to stay behind and spend a couple more precious hours with him.

'So you're not joining us?' Hugh asked, tongue firmly in cheek—Bonita would do anything to avoid saddling up!

'You know I'd love to.' Bonita smiled sweetly. 'But, given my shoulder and everything...'

'You're not still using that as an excuse!' He grinned,

because since the sling had come off there were *no* excuses, according to her mother, and Bonita was seriously wondering if going back to work early might be easier than resting at home. 'Come on, Bonny,' Hugh said, eyeing the little arancini balls in the bowl she was carrying. 'Give me a handful...I'm starving.'

'You'll have to wait, like anyone else!" Bonita's smile stayed in place.

'Give Hugh something to eat!' Carmel snapped, catching Bonita by surprise as she wheeled Luigi across the grass.

'Thanks, Carmel,' Hugh said, grabbing a handful and taking a greedy bite. 'You've excelled yourself, as always!'

'Bonny made them!'

'Really?'

'She can cook and she is beautiful,' Luigi said, as Carmel wheeled him off, leaving Bonita blushing to her roots.

'Well, that's all right, then!' Hugh grinned.

'I feel like he's auctioning me off!' Bonita sighed. 'He fails to mention that I'm intelligent and that I have a career.'

'Ah, but can you keep a clean house?' Hugh laughed, turning Ramone with thigh power alone. 'Anyway...' he winked over his shoulder '...with a body like that, you'll soon be sold off.'

She almost swallowed a fly!

Open-mouthed, Bonita stood there as he kicked Ramone into an impressive trot, and went to join the gang. And even though she chatted and laughed easily with friends and relatives as she helped set up, her heart

was banging in her rib cage at the impossibility of what
had just taken place.

Oh, it was tiny!

Maybe it shouldn't merit a thought, given it had come
from the lips of a guy like Hugh *and* that her parents
weren't actually *that* far off, but he'd definitely been
flirting. Which meant, Bonita realised, striding towards
the tables, that she hadn't imagined the other day after all!

'*Stop it!*' Bonita scolded herself, joining her mother
and aunts, making small talk as she prepared the
drinks—immersing herself in what was important.

Making today the best it could possibly be.

Carmel's military-style preparations paid off.

The Azetti barbeque was held in early autumn. The
grapes were generally in, or the last of the fruit hung
plump and ready on the vines, and Carmel and Luigi had
for as long as anyone could remember held this celebration for family, their regular workers and the seasonal
staff who descended between January to April to pick the
fruit. Despite his failing health, despite the fact the winery
employed its own winemaker now, Luigi had still assisted
in the important decision as to when to harvest the grapes.
And this year's vintage would, Bonita knew, for so many
be an extra-precious one in the years that followed.

Everyone Luigi loved was there on his land, eating,
milling around, chatting, eating, drinking, oh, and
eating, and the smile on her father's face, the pride in
his eyes as he watched the people he adored all together,
all enjoying themselves, was, Bonita realised, surely
the best medicine of them all.

Even the weather behaved.

Early autumn, it could have gone *any* way, yet the sun was out, but not too hot, and seeing her father laugh and joke with his sons, Bonita wondered for a moment if she was worrying about nothing—that the frail man she had kissed goodnight to last night might actually be around for a good while longer yet.

'He's had a great day.' She and Hugh were washing up, Bonita staring out beyond the dark window to the pergola. She watched her father sitting on the cane couch with his family, heard the laughter and chatter drift back into the home. 'He doesn't even seem tired.'

'He's been looking forward to this.' Hugh's eyes followed her gaze.

'Maybe it was what he needed,' Bonita said. 'Maybe this will give him a bit of a second wind...' Her voice trailed off, waiting, hoping, desperate for Hugh agree, for him to ignore the fact that despite the copious food, despite Luigi making a token effort at carving the lamb, he hadn't eaten a single thing. 'Maybe he'll pick up a bit! Now that he's—'

'Bonny.' Hugh stopped her there. 'Your dad's not going to get better.'

'You don't know that.'

'I do know that,' Hugh said firmly, 'and so do you.'

'Can't I just have one nice day?'

'You've had a nice day,' Hugh pointed out. 'Have you told him?'

'Told him what?'

'Everything you want to.'

'Such as?'

'That you love him?'

Clutching the stem of the wineglass she was washing, for a moment she thought she might snap it. 'I don't have to tell him. Dad knows that I love him.'

'Have you told him, though?' Hugh pushed.

'I think so.' She was washing up quickly now, sloshing the glasses in the soapy water and trying very hard not to think about it—trying very hard indeed. It was easier in many ways to focus instead on Hugh. 'Did you?' She watched his hand pause as he picked up a draining plate. 'Your dad was dying when you went back to England. Did you tell him you loved him?'

'I tried.' Hugh shrugged. 'You know, when I went back home, I really wanted things to be different. I'd seen how your family worked and I had this idea that if we just…' He shook his head. 'I tried to tell him, but it was way too late, we just didn't have those sort of conversations, we had never had them.'

'Never?' He gave a brief shake of his head, and for the first time Bonita delved. So many times she'd wondered about his past, had heard bits and pieces from her brothers and parents, but it had never seemed appropriate to ask…

Till now.

'What about when your mum was alive?' She held her breath after she'd voiced her question—this was one of the first conversations they'd had without barbs and she was loath to end it by probing too deep, yet it felt right to ask. It felt right to know a little more about the man who consumed her. And instead of holding back, as he usually did, Hugh actually opened up.

'I guess.' He gave a sort of half-laugh. 'It's funny you ask because before I came back here I was boxing things up, sorting things out, and I came across some photos. I actually recognised Mum. It was my father who looked completely different from the man I remember.'

'In what way?' Bonita asked. 'Younger?'

'Happier.' Hugh shrugged. 'Just a completely different person really. When Mum died I went to boarding school so I only ever saw him during term breaks and even then he was always working. There'd be an aunt or a nanny looking after me.' He said it without a trace of pity, just stated the facts.

'Did you get lonely?'

'Nope!' He shook his head, made heavy work of drying a plate as he thought about it for a moment. 'It wasn't lonely, it was just the way it was. And not just for me—most of my schoolmates came from similar families. It wasn't until I came to Australia and met your family that I realised how different it should be.'

'Should be?' Bonita checked.

'Do you remember the row I had with your parents?' He registered Bonita's frown. 'You were probably too busy slamming doors of your own to notice. I was staying here over the summer break and I'd gone away for a weekend with some girl...' He frowned as he tried to remember the name, then quickly gave up. 'We were having a great time and ended up staying on an extra day—I swear it didn't even enter my head to ring and tell your parents. I was twenty-two, I'd never had to ring in to anyone before! I came back here and your mum was crying, your dad was shouting at me and telling me how inconsiderate I'd been...' Suddenly he laughed. 'It was great! You know, till that point I'd sometimes thought that I could disappear for six months and no one would actually notice.'

I'd notice, Bonita thought as he spoke on.

Had noticed.

In those hellish months after he'd gone back to the UK, Bonita had missed him so much it had actually hurt. She'd cried so hard sometimes at night it had felt as if she hadn't been able to breathe.

'You should tell him.' Hugh broke into her thoughts. 'You should say it while you have the chance.'

'I guess!'

'I've told your dad what he's meant to me,' Hugh said, by way of convincing her.

'You told him!' Bonita blinked. 'How? I mean, if you start talking like that then you're saying that...'

'He's dying,' Hugh finished what she couldn't. 'He knows, Bonny. Is there anything you wish you had said?'

'Maybe.'

'Like what?'

'That even when he was cross, even when he was angry...' tears plopped into the soapy water '...that even when I was cross, when I was angry, I always knew he was only looking out for me...'

'Tell him.' Dishes done, he threw down the teatowel.

'I'll think about it.' She closed her eyes at his raised eyebrow, knew that maybe she didn't actually have time to *think about* it, and wasn't particularly grateful to Hugh for pointing that out.

'I'm going to go and say goodbye and then I'm going home.'

'You're not staying?'

'Nope.' He shook his head. 'I'm on at seven tomorrow morning. You think about what I said, Bonny, but don't think about it for too long.'

And because her parents weren't there, because he didn't have to pretend to be polite, he didn't give her a friendly kiss on the cheek, just offered a quick 'Goodnight'. And as suddenly as that he was gone. She watched him walk over and kiss her mother, shake hands with her brothers and then hug her father.

Watched him lavish the affection he gave so generously to everyone except her—only that wasn't what was hurting right now.

Seeing her father hug him back, seeing the open affection between the two men she adored, brought a huge lump to her throat.

He'd told her dad just how much he meant, had managed what she could hardly bear to attempt…but knew somehow that she had to.

So later when Hugh had long since gone and her brothers' cars were a noise on the drive, Bonita walked out to where Carmel was tidying up, and helped. Luigi was sitting on the recliner, just as he always had, and she waited till her mother had stacked the last of the plates and was carrying them inside.

'It's been a wonderful day,' Bonita started.

'It's been the best day.' Luigi smiled.

'Thank you.'

It felt like a speech—the worst sort of speech as she approached him, as he patted the cushion beside him.

'For what?'

'For loving me.'

'You are so easy to love.'

'Even when I was horrible.' Bonita gulped. 'Even when...'

'Always.' He pulled her towards him, held her so close she could feel the thud of a heart winding down. As she resisted, he cuddled her in, held her closer.

'Born angry!' Still he held her. 'The midwife said we must be pleased to have a daughter. I was, till I held you...' And she couldn't help but smile as her father spoke. 'You were this angry little thing and nothing I tried calmed you. Born feet first and defiant. "We have trouble," I told your mother.

'You changed our world.'

He lifted her chin and the same hazel eyes that greeted her each morning in the mirror held hers—except the fading colour told Bonita he'd soon be gone.

'We were too old for a baby—your mother was forty, I was fifty. The boys were all at school, everything was sorted, and then you came along.' His hand cupped her cheek. 'You—the best accident that ever happened.

'Sometimes when I was cross, when your mother was cross...'

'I'm so sorry—'

'I am sorry,' Luigi interrupted, apologising when he had nothing to apologise for. 'I was scared to let you grow up, scared to let you go, scared of the mistakes you might make, and I wanted to prevent every last bit of pain for you. And yet I see now I tried too hard. You were not careless or about to make a big mistake, you already knew your mind. You really were a good girl...'

'Not always!'

'Good!' Luigi smiled. 'It means you have lived!'

Oh, she'd miss him for ever, couldn't bear to be in his arms and know that it wouldn't last, that every day they enjoyed was one day nearer to being without him. Daddy's girl wouldn't be a daddy's girl soon. She could see her mother looking over through the kitchen window. The trestle tables had all been cleared and she still tried to look busy, tried to let a moment that just couldn't last, last for just as long as it could.

'I love you, Dad.'

It was the only thing left to say.

CHAPTER SEVEN

'BONNY!'

Snapping open her eyes, Bonita forced herself to alertness.

She recognised that urgent summons for help, because she'd heard it so many times at work and had been dreading it in the last week. Luigi had faded since the barbeque, that last stab at living utterly depleting him. Bonita was sleeping in shifts with her mother, the palliative nurse was coming in twice a day to help with meds and to turn her father, the family GP was visiting daily, oxygen tanks were being delivered, family, friends all descending—the house a hive of activity.

Except for this morning when it was the three of them alone, and as she ran through the house Bonita prepared herself for the worst, determined to be strong.

But it was hard to be strong when the scene she faced was worse than the worst-case scenario she'd predicted.

'He can't breathe…' Carmel was frantic as she hugged her husband, her eyes urgent, as Bonita raced into the room.

'It's OK…' Sitting him up, Bonita grabbed at

pillows, thrust them behind his head, listening to horrible gurgling noises from his chest, feeling his clammy skin covered in sweat. Yet her hands were remarkably steady, fiddling with the flow on the oxygen tank that was by the bed then feeling again her father's thready pulse. 'Mum, call an ambulance!'

'No.' Carmel shook her head. 'That's not what he wanted. He wants to die here —we planned—'

'Mum, he can't breathe, it's his heart…' She was dialling for the ambulance herself, but Carmel stopped her. 'No!'

'He needs treatment.' Bonny tried to keep her voice even. 'This isn't how it should be—he needs something to get that fluid off his chest…' He was literally drowning in it, Bonita could hear it.

'Please, Bonny, ring the doctor, tell him to come here!'

What to do, what to do… Her head was whirring, every ingrained response depleted by love. He wanted to be here, Bonita knew that, and that thought alone had her dialling one of the many numbers on the list by the phone.

'It's his paging service,' Bonita said, leaving a frantic garbled message, begging the doctor to come. 'We'll have to call an ambulance.'

'Paul!' Carmel urged. 'Ring Paul! He'll know what to do.'

But Paul was in Theatre, the calm voice of the switchboard operator just increasing Bonita's agitation as, for the second time, she was put through to the second on call.

'Put me through to the nursing station in Emergency.'

'Charge Nurse Baxter…'

'Bill!' Just to hear his kind efficient voice helped so much. She closed her eyes and pictured the emergency department, knew that if she couldn't get hold of Paul, then that's where they would soon be. 'Dad can't breathe—they won't put me through to Paul.'

'Have you rung an ambulance?'

'Mum doesn't want that. He wants to be home. Please, Bill, can you just tell Paul?'

'Your dad needs to come here.' Bill wasn't debating the point—especially when Bonita described the symptoms and, no doubt, Bill could hear for himself the horrible sounds Luigi was making in the background. 'Andrew's here now—he'll be waiting for him, Bonita. I can call an ambulance for you... Just hold on a second...' There was a low murmur of talk, and then for Bonita a flood of relief as a clipped English voice came onto the phone.

'I'm on my way!"

He'd cut himself shaving that morning—tiny details were just so much easier to deal with as she prepared the diuretic for Hugh. And his hair was still wet from his shower... He probably hadn't even had a coffee...

Yet he was so focussed, so completely together and assured he might just as well have been in the emergency room as in her parents' bedroom. He'd strode into the house, told Carmel to wait outside for a few moments and was now snapping his fingers impatiently as Bonita struggled to pull up a large bolus dose of diuretic from the card of 2 ml ampoules he must have grabbed as he'd run out to help.

'Morphine,' Hugh said, only he must have seen her shaking hand with the diuretic and instead drew it up himself, delivering Luigi an IV bolus and talking to him at the same time. He whipped out his stethoscope again and listened to the flooded chest.

'That's better, Luigi. The medicine will work quickly now and you'll be able to breathe much more easily.'

Funny that he sounded like a doctor, Bonita thought, just the way he had when he'd come in to her room that morning and checked her arm. The cool detachment she had hated so much that day suddenly made more sense. Because cool detachment *was* needed—especially on a day like today when you were dealing with someone you cared for deeply.

'What's that?' Bonita asked as he pulled up another drug.

'Atropine,' Hugh answered. 'It will help dry up secretions.'

'And what are you doing now?' Bonita asked as he pulled out a large white pack.

'Could you wait outside with your mum now?'

That didn't make sense—she was a nurse, his daughter. What right did Hugh have to tell her to leave?

'I'd rather stay with Dad.'

'I'll come and get you soon,' Hugh said firmly, and it was then that she realised he was opening a catheter pack.

'The diuretic should start taking effect soon.' He was talking to her like a relative, showing her outside, ushering her out as he would a crowd of onlookers. And so she stood in the hall and gulped in air while he quickly fitted a catheter. And Bonita realised he was looking after his patient, as well looking after her.

Her dad wouldn't want her there now.

She didn't need to be in there either.

Because Hugh was.

'He couldn't breathe…' Carmel just sat at the table as Bonita walked into the kitchen on shaky legs. 'I never thought I would panic—they told me what to expect and I thought I was ready…'

'This *was* an emergency, Mum.'

'I nearly called an ambulance—your father had made me promise that I never would, that he'd be able to die at home.' It was the first time her mother had acknowledged to Bonita he was dying. Not 'not good' or 'not so well today'. Perhaps, Bonita realised, this was the first time they'd been truly honest. 'I so nearly let him down.'

'You've never let him down, Mum,' Bonita said, taking Carmel's cold hand and holding it. It felt right, especially when Carmel gripped Bonita's hand back.

'Acute on chronic.' Bonita looked over to her mum. 'That's what it's called—an acute event on top of a chronic illness.'

'It makes sense, I suppose.' Stoic, practical, Carmel nodded. 'I mean, when everything else is failing, you'd expect his heart to suffer. So what happens now?' For the first time her mother asked her opinion and it was the one time Bonita wasn't able to give it. 'How long do you think he's got?'

'I don't know, Mum.'

She just didn't know what to say. She couldn't be a nurse and a daughter today and do justice to them both.

* * *

'He's a lot more comfortable.' Hugh walked into the kitchen where they sat on tenterhooks. 'Did you ring the boys?'

Hugh's words as he came into the kitchen and joined them gave Bonita comfort, and his question gave her the answer she'd been dreading—this was it.

'They should be here in a couple of hours, depending on the traffic,' Bonita answered in an unusually high voice.

'Good.'

'Bonny explained about acute on chronic.' Ever the good hostess, Carmel poured Hugh a cup of tea. 'Did he have a heart attack?'

"It would seem that Luigi had a cardiac event.' Hugh nodded. 'But I'm not going to put him through tests. His lungs were filled with fluid— that was why he couldn't breathe and was making so much noise. I've given him a large dose of diuretic that will get the fluid off, and some more morphine to help with pain, as well as a nebuliser to open up his airways. He's also got a catheter in because he'll be having a large diuresis. I mean, he'll be getting rid of a lot of fluid and I didn't want him having to worry about a bottle.'

'So he's comfortable,' Carmel said.

'Very,' Hugh replied. 'However…'

'It won't be the cancer that kills him.' Carmel stood up. 'Will it be today?'

'I don't know, Carmel,' Hugh said gently. 'But I think so.'

'His GP should be here soon. I know you have to get

back to work but would you mind staying until he gets here? I want to sit with my husband.'

'Of course.'

'Can I see him?' It was the first time Bonita had spoken since he'd come in the room. 'Just for a moment.'

Hugh had done a wonderful job. Her father who had been so breathless and agitated now lay peacefully, propped up on a mountain of pillows, his breathing shallow but not laboured. Bonita gave him a kiss, told him she loved him again, but she couldn't sit by his bed, and just wait. She also sensed that her mother wanted to be alone with him.

'I'll wait in the lounge till his GP or Paul gets here, so call if you need anything,' Hugh said kindly to Carmel. 'But once they're here I'm going to have to get back to work.'

'Thank you, Hugh.' Carmel accepted his hug with one of her own. 'You've been marvellous.'

'You, too.' Hugh smiled, and Bonita watched, her throat thick with tears as Hugh said goodbye to her dad, not as his doctor but as his friend. He leant over the bed, his strong arms hugged Luigi's frail body, and thanked him, too—for everything.

'Will you be OK to go back?' Bonita asked as they stood in the lounge.

'No choice but to be,' Hugh answered, rubbing his forehead with his hand, looking as tired and as wretched as Bonita felt.

'I'll go and ring the boys on their mobiles,' Bonita said. 'Tell them that he's more settled. Paul should be here soon—apparently he was in the middle of an operation. He's waiting for someone to come in and take over from him.'

'Bill asked if you can ring.' Hugh's lips pursed just a touch '...when you get a chance. He's worried about you.'

'I'll ring him.' Bonny gave a pale nod.

'Your mum wants the priest,' Hugh said gently.

'I'll ring him, too.'

Hugh sat quietly on the sofa while she made the round of phone calls. A strange sort of silence had descended on the house and Bonita knew that it wouldn't last, knew that in a hour or two the place would be full. For the first time since her mother had woken her, Bonita realised she was wearing nothing more than a flimsy nightdress. She padded upstairs and dragged on some jeans and a T-shirt, but didn't even bother with a comb through her hair, just pulled it back into a low ponytail before heading back downstairs.

'How are you?'

'I don't know.'

The adrenaline surge that had rocketed her out of bed and into action had long since abated and all she felt was depleted. She stood there, unsure what to do, where to go, how to be, *how* to feel, until Hugh caught her wrist and pulled her onto his knee.

'Come here.'

And all it felt was safe.

All it felt was right.

And even if he couldn't fix it, then he'd fixed it enough this morning—had turned hell into almost bearable.

For the moment at least.

She didn't actually know who was holding who, his arms as tight around her as hers were around him. It was just a resting place for a moment as they both silently braced themselves for what lay ahead.

'Remember when I was going under…'

'Sorry?' She felt his arms stiffen, the gentle ease in the room faltering for a moment, causing Bonita to pull back and frown. 'When you put back my shoulder, what you said about it being for the best, me spending time with Mum and Dad. You were right.'

'You remember that?'

'I think so.'

'What else do you remember?'

They held each other's gaze.

'Nothing.'

'Nothing?' Hugh checked. 'You can't remember anything else?'

'You telling me to wiggle my fingers.' Bonita smiled. 'But you were right, I am glad I hurt my shoulder, that I've had these last few weeks here. If I'd been at the flat I'd have missed so much.'

'You've done so well.'

And that meant so much—her mother's scolding, even if she could now understand it, her brothers' expectations that she would be there, even if she accepted it, all grated at times. But that Hugh thought she'd done well meant so much.

'This is hard for you, too.' They were still looking at each other, talking like they hardly ever had, and she truly didn't want it end, didn't want him to go.

'Don't worry about me.' His voice was thick, and she could hear his pain, and something else too.

'But I do.'

It was as honest as she could be with him. As close as she could come to revealing to him that he lived in her mind, but it was close enough for now.

'I had this aunt.' Bonita rested her head back on his chest. 'Zia Lucia…'

'The glamorous one!' Hugh said, and Bonita actually smiled.

'How do you know?'

'I've heard your family talking about her. Your dad spoke to me about her just a few days ago.'

'She was my dad's sister and I don't think my mum really approved of her—she'd never been married, was always dressed up in jewels and fancy dresses and flying off to exotic places. I used to love it when she came to visit. She'd always send me something pretty for my birthday—dresses or make-up or costume jewellery. I've been thinking about her a lot lately. When she died I never thought I'd get over it, I honestly thought that I'd never stop crying.'

'But you did.'

'And I will with Dad.' Bonita sniffed. 'I just don't want to do this.'

'I know.'

'What was it like when it was your dad?' Bonita asked, and she felt him stiffen, heard the long weary breath he let out before answering.

'*This* is actually harder.'

She jerked her head up—looked at him again—and

the pain that was inside her today was there on his face, the agony she felt mirrored in his eyes.

And it wasn't wanton, or bold or even particularly brave because, looking at him, Bonita knew her kiss wasn't about to be rejected.

Kisses—strange, delicious things, her mind thought as their lips touched.

A delicious sharing, a sweet acknowledgement that could be expressed better without words. It was a kiss that wasn't about escaping, more about sustenance, a little pause in a vile day—a kiss that wouldn't go further because for now it was absolutely enough.

'You and I,' Hugh said when inevitably it ended, 'are going to have to do some serious talking.'

'I know.' There was a tiny glow inside her on a day she'd never expected to feel it, a tiny window into the future that had been so smudged and fogged up she'd never expected to see through it.

'Just not now, huh?' Hugh said as the first of many cars that day pulled up. 'Let's get through this.'

Hugh did more than talk to the GP. He talked to Ricky and then Paul when he arrived, too. And Bonita was so grateful that Hugh had warned her about Paul, so glad that she knew, because the smart words were long gone from her tongue before she saw Paul's stricken face.

'I couldn't bloody get away.'

'I know.' She put her arm around her brother who sat on the sofa, his head in his hands. 'My boss was doing surgery at the private hospital—I couldn't get anyone in to take over.'

'It must have been hell!'

'My own dad needs a doctor and I couldn't even be here.'

'You're here now,' Bonita said kindly, catching Hugh's eye as he patted his friend's shoulder and then went back to work. Oh, he popped back later on a manufactured lunch-break. For Bonita, his was the most welcome face of them all as visitors came and went, as everyone waited for something nobody wanted. Carmel came out now and then, but the whole day was a long silent blur—an unsustainable pain. But Hugh had been right. Luigi was comfortable, in his own bed, surrounded by the people who loved him most.

'I'm going to bed.' It was Carmel who ended the day for everyone. 'You all should, too.'

Hugh was on call at the hospital and had long since gone, Paul was in charge now and the GP had been in and out, and the palliative care nurse had helped Carmel to wash Luigi.

Kissing her father goodnight was almost more than Bonita could bear. She didn't want to go to bed but was too exhausted not to—and, anyway, her mother wanted to be alone.

So she told her father she loved him, which, thanks to Hugh, she knew he already knew.

Slipping between the cool sheets, she lay in a hyper-vigilant state, waiting for what she didn't know, scared not of going to sleep but of what she would surely wake up to.

'Here…' A mug of tea beside her bed was so normal, so what always happened in her house, that for a tiny second Bonita was soothed. Only her mother hadn't knocked, Bonita realized. She was actually sitting on the bed beside her now and playing with her daughter's hair.

'He's gone, Bonny.'

How she wanted to argue the point, but she knew it was hopeless. Bonita stared at her mother's tired face and wished she knew what to say. She felt something shrivel up inside her, a horrible vacuum as her mind tried to fathom that he had gone, that while she had slept her father had left.

'When?'

'An hour or so ago,' Carmel said. 'He was asleep, he just slipped away.'

To where? she wanted to scream.

'And you didn't tell me!' That she hadn't told her, that her brothers, the doctor, everyone knew was almost too much, but again she'd misread her mother.

'I'm going to tell your brothers now and then I'll ring the doctor.'

'You haven't told anyone?'

'I wanted some time with your dad,' Carmel said, 'before it all starts.'

And start it did.

Friends, family, visitors, funeral directors, priests and flowers, the house was a flurry of activity as Bonita curled up inside, wanted her dad to be dealing with it, wanted her dad to be in charge, as he always was.

Hugh was marvellous, stepping in, giving lifts, taking the brunt of Carmel's temper when a grief-stricken Paul disappeared for a day of horse riding, Ricky had to get back to the kids and Marco had to see to a prize horse in Bendigo that was about to foal.

Hugh was the lynchpin. He blended in yet stood apart—family, only not quite. Someone they could all lean on because it wasn't as painful for him.

'OK?' He checked on the morning of the funeral.

'I think so.' She didn't know how to behave, didn't know how she was expected to be today. Her new black shoes were already hurting, the new linen black dress she was wearing was already as crumpled as the tissue in her hand. Little Italy was sitting wailing in the lounge as her mother sat pale and tight-lipped upstairs, her brothers made small talk with uncles and Bonita just didn't know where in this she belonged. The tears she shed so easily were a slow constant trickle today.

'I don't know what to do.'

'Just be there for your mum. How is she?'

'Getting ready...' Bonita's voice trailed off as her mother appeared, and Bonita felt her already full eyes brim over as she saw, perhaps for the first time, how beautiful her mother really was. Rarely, so rarely did Carmel make an effort with her appearance, but she had today. Her salt-and-pepper curls were piled on top of her head, she was wearing a smart black suit with black suede shoes— a picture of understated elegance. And for the first time in ages she'd put on make-up, her dark eyes accentuated with mascara, a smudge of lipstick on her full mouth.

'You look wonderful, Mum.' Bonita squeezed Carmel's hand as they stood waiting for the cars.

'I wanted to look nice for him, this last time...' Carmel gave a small nod and then she smiled and squeezed Bonita's hand back. 'Anyway, he can't tell me off for wearing lipstick any more!'

It all passed in a daze.

The congregation was a strange blur of familiar faces—the Azettis were well thought of and the church was full, but Bonita, even when they arrived home, couldn't really place who had been there or remember words that had been said. She held her mother's hand again as her brothers, along with Hugh, the honorary son, carried her father on his final journey.

There was this hollow loneliness and piercing sadness as she did what her father would have expected her to do—served drinks and food—all the time wishing everyone would just leave. Though part of her didn't want them to. She wanted the day to end, but at the same time didn't want it to be over.

But it had to be.

'Thank you, darling!' Bonita watched as her mother kissed Ricky, his wife and kids goodbye. The last of the guests had thankfully gone, Marco had gone to bed about an hour ago and Paul had worked his way down a bottle of wine and was about to go to bed as well.

'I'd better ring a taxi!' Hugh pulled out his phone, but Carmel shook her head

'Since when did you ring a taxi, Hugh?'

'You need your family with you now.'

'You are family.' Carmel gave a tired smile. 'So much so that you won't mind if I don't change the sheets in Ricky's room. Stay,' Carmel said. 'Actually, I will go and do the sheets.'

'Don't worry about the sheets, for goodness' sake.' Hugh stood up and Bonita noticed her mother, who had been so strong all day, suddenly looked small, confused and bewildered and, Bonita realised, lost. 'You sit down.' Hugh guided Carmel to a chair. 'It's been a long day.'

'Actually…' changing her mind the second she sat down, Carmel stood again. 'If you two don't mind, I might just go to bed.'

'Have a cup of tea first…' Bonita dragged her bone-tired body from the sofa and frowned in concern as her mother declined. Bonita kissed her goodnight, could feel her mother's tired shoulders as she hugged her. 'Go to bed and I'll bring one in to you.'

'No.' Firmly Carmel shook her head. 'I want to be on my own now.'

'Just leave her,' Hugh said gently as Carmel dazedly wandered off.

'She hasn't even cried…she just looks so lost…'

'You haven't cried either.'

'I have…' Bonita gave a half-shrug. 'I'm like a leaking tap.'

'I meant—' He never finished. A wail ripped through the quiet house, Carmel's keening wail that shot Bonita across the room towards her parents' bedroom, but Hugh caught her hands.

'Leave her.'

'Listen to her!' Bonita sobbed, hardly able to stand her mother's lament. 'How can I leave her?'

'What the…?' Marco was in the hall now, Paul staggering behind. 'Are you just going to stand there?' Paul demanded of Bonita, but Hugh stepped in.

'What do you want her to do, Paul? Go in and calm her down, or maybe tell her to pull herself together and stop crying? Your mum specifically said that she wanted to be alone.'

There was anger in the air, only no one was at fault. There was the horrible sound of their mother's tears and not a single thing that any of them could do to take her pain away.

'I can't do this.' Marco headed back to the bedroom and Paul sat with Hugh and Bonita, waiting till it abated, till low, anguished sobs were all that remained.

'You're right.' Paul's head was in his hands, and Bonita could see his tears. 'She just needed to get it out.'

'She'll be OK!' Bonita said.

'You know, I thought I was helping, being here for a few days and everything,' Paul said, wine and grief making him maudlin. 'Maybe we should leave her on her own for a bit...'

'See how it is in the morning,' Hugh said to his friend. 'Go to bed now, Paul.'

And Bonita was so glad that Hugh had stayed, so glad that even if he was considered family, the bit of him that *wasn't* family had been there when needed tonight.

'Thank you.' White, shaken, still reeling from her mother's pain, from the grief of the day, Bonita sat stunned. 'She needed that.'

'What do you need, Bonny?' Hugh asked, watching her brown eyes jerk to his, watching her as he had through the day as she'd tried to find her role, her place, to stay strong while bewildered.

'You've done enough,' Bonita gulped. 'Helping Dad at the end, being there this week, all you've done today...'

'I'm not talking about that. I meant for you. Is there

anything I can do?' He watched a dull flush spread on her pale cheeks and he felt as if he was cheating. It was like doing yesterday's crossword with today's answers. But if she had meant what she'd said, if she did love him, then surely this was one of the nights in her life that she needed him. One night she really shouldn't have to face alone.

And, Hugh realised as a fist of pain tightened in his stomach, he needed her, too. He couldn't stand the thought of sleeping alone tonight, of lying alone with his thoughts when he could be lying with her.

'I'm fine.' Her two words slapped him to his senses— this was not what was expected of him tonight.

'You're more like your mother than you realize.' Hugh smiled, standing up and kissing her on the cheek. 'Holding everything in.'

'Me?' She gave a short incredulous laugh.

'Because, if you do need anything…' He stopped himself then, now not the time to push things. ''Night, Bonita.'

She didn't answer, just sat stock still as he headed to the door.

'Stay with me tonight.' Her voice was the most assured he'd heard it all week. Turning around, he saw not a flicker of doubt on her face, her wishes exceptionally clear. 'You asked if there was something you can do, and there is— I don't want to be alone.'

And it would be impossible to say no to her, to walk away from her pain—which made it incredibly easy to walk towards her.

'Then you don't have to be.'

It was the simplest of decisions, the hows and whys

didn't matter. She was in pain, and needed him. For Hugh, for that moment, it made utter sense to take her hand, to turn out the light and take her to her room.

Perfect sense to undress, because this wasn't about a kiss that might lead somewhere else, this was about being together, about being as close as they could be, about lying with her in her single bed and holding her. A little shy and awkward as she was, Bonita relaxed as his body spooned behind her, strong arms wrapped around her, and he didn't say anything at all when she started to weep, just carried on holding her.

It felt so good to be held, the agony still there, so painful to unload, but it was a relief to visit scary places in her head with the safety net of Hugh holding her, to know it was OK to cry now, which she did, till respite was needed.

A sweet, sweet respite.

Turning round to face him in her bed, it was hard to fathom Hugh was there, that it was his skin beneath her fingers, his long, toned, warm body next to hers. Once, twice in her life she'd tasted heaven, and she was tasting it again now—breathing in the reckless, dizzying scent of him. And this wasn't Hugh in his twenties and some frantic kitchen kiss getting out of control, this was Hugh in his thirties, pushing her face back on the pillow and kissing her so deeply she didn't even want to breathe. It was Hugh who found the emergency exit to her soul and dragged her outside herself for a little while, chased away her fears, her terror, her grief till his mouth, his scent, his embrace took her to a still silent place for a moment, where all there was was them, and nothing else existed.

And when she started crying again, it didn't matter, when the sun of his kiss dipped behind the cloud of grief, he just held her, letting her sample the necessary pain, diluted it by being there as she took it in small measured doses. His lips were still waiting, his body still patient when she didn't want to face it again.

She found out that that first kiss *had* meant something, knew because his hands went to her breasts, just as they had then, heard his moan of pleasure as finally he held her the way he had wanted to, his lips tracing her neck, as they had once before, only he was utterly unhurried this time, relishing each lick, each taste.

'Do you know how much I've wanted this?' His mouth was on her nipple now, his tongue sliding around her areola, then sucking, his body taut and aroused beside her yet somehow languorous and lazy, this night theirs. She could feel his erection on her thigh, could feel the comfort of his kiss on her breast, the warmth of his long legs wrapped loosely around hers. And when it seemed wrong to feel right tonight, and she sobbed her regret as it took over, all he did was hold her, all he did was tell her that he wasn't going anywhere.

'I can't stop thinking…'

'You don't have to do anything.'

'I want to…' Her need was suddenly urgent. She wanted this escape so badly, but for entirely selfish reasons.

'So, when you're ready we will…'

He was so infinitely patient, it bemused her, so slow

and unhurried, content to kiss her. Content to let her explore him at her leisure. Her fingers marvelling at the velvet skin, the thick, fierce heat of his arousal that she had kept at bay for so long now.

'You must want—'

'Hey.' He smiled as he kissed her, his voice low in her ear, making her stomach curl deep inside. 'I've been thinking about you a *lot* recently, so take as long as you like.'

She didn't know what he meant at first, her eyes locking with his and seeking clarification. Then she understood that her image had been used in quiet, urgent moments, and that made the curl in her stomach tighten to a hot ball. She imagined that their frantic thoughts might have met at times, and all she wanted now was *them*. Wanted the heavy weight of him above her, wanted him consuming her. The nudge of his thigh between hers met her need, her throat constricted with delicious anticipation, then the luscious stab as he entered, the sheer heady bliss as her body acclimatised to the feel of him, locking eyes with his as he moved inside her.

'The bed!' she could hear the rhythmic squeaking, and giggled into his chest as they shifted over. The frantic noise continued, only ceasing when they barely moved, but even if their bodies were almost still, there was frenzy within. They faced each other again, but with only the other on their minds... And now she wasn't smiling, just staring at the man she'd adored since the age of eleven and had hated since eighteen and loved for a whole lot longer, and now she knew why.

Every question she'd ever asked was answered as he moved deep within her.

Because *they* were right.

'Shh…' His mouthed hushed hers. She hadn't even been aware that she was crying, but they were a different sort of tears now, she was almost scared of the reaction in her body. They weren't kissing, just exchanging breaths. She could feel the rip of tension in him leashing then unleashing as she held him intimately tight, the involuntary paroxysm of her own body as her orgasm shuddered on, dragging him deeper, dredging his reserves as he sated her.

'Bonny…' Gasping, breathless, exhausted, oblivion was the antidote to pain, and he had given her that. Hugh had shared this long lonely night, had actually taken her pain and divided it. Still he divided it further, hooking her into his arm, kissing the thick curls on the back of her head, his hot, tender hand stroking her stomach in tiny wavy circles. Bonita closed her eyes, able finally to relax now, knowing that he'd stay awake till she was safely asleep.

CHAPTER EIGHT

'BONNY.' Her mother's voice at the door woke them both up. They lay there absolutely still, a knot of arms and legs. Their frantic eyes stared in horror at the doorhandle.

'I won't be a moment!' Bonita attempted a normal voice, climbing out of the warm bed as Hugh lay there, his face and his body utterly rigid.

She hadn't drunk a drop yesterday, scared at the emotions it might unleash, yet she almost felt as if she was tripping over champagne bottles as she walked to the bedroom door, as if she was in the grip of some vile hangover after the most careless, reckless of nights.

'Don't get up,' Carmel called through the door. 'I'm just going down to the stables. I didn't want you worrying where I was…' Her voice was already trailing off as she walked down the hallway. Bonita turned to where Hugh lay, and every fear she might have had, had there been time to think about it, was confirmed in his taut features.

Horror and regret at what had taken place were visible on his strained face as he lay there unable to look her in the eye.

'She had no idea that you're in here.'

'I know…' He climbed out of the bed, pulled on his trousers. She could see the muscles straining in his shoulders, his neck as he quickly dressed then dragged a hand through his hair before he could even face her. 'Bonny, I'm sorry, we should never have risked it…I should never have…' He gave an appalled shake of his head.

'Hugh, it's fine,' Bonita said, because to her it was. Yes, there were better places for it to have happened, but last night hadn't been one for sensible thought processes. Last night had been about survival, about need, about being with the one you loved.

'No, it's not all right. Your father…' He didn't finish, his whole body filled with tension. 'Look, check the hall, I'll go into Ricky's room. It will look strange if we appear together. I'll get up in a bit…we'll talk later…'

'Sure.'

She knew he felt awful, knew emotion had carried them to bed last night, but for Bonita nothing had changed. As upset as she'd been, her thought process had been crystal clear—everything she had felt last night she still felt in the cold light of morning. Her only regret was his.

'Later.' Briefly he kissed her worried mouth. 'We'll talk later.'

A shower couldn't wash away her doubts. Pulling a comb through her hair, Bonita dressed then braced herself to go down to the kitchen. And though everything looked the same it felt new and different, her mother out, her father not there, just Paul, boiling the kettle, giving her a grim smile as she joined him.

'Have you seen Mum?' he asked as soon as Bonita appeared.

'No—she just knocked on my door. She's gone down to the stables.'

'How did she seem?'

'I don't know. She just knocked on the door and said not to worry—she was going for a walk or something. She sounded OK.'

'I'm sorry, Bonny.' Paul gave a tight smile. 'I told you off last night. You were right to leave her alone.'

'Don't be sorry.' Bonita accepted his apology with a half-smile. 'To be honest, I didn't know what to do either—it was Hugh who said to leave her.'

'He's been great, hasn't he?' Paul joined her at the table. 'Look Bonny, I was talking to Ricky and Marco yesterday... When do you go back to work?'

'Monday,' Bonita answered. 'They offered me another week for compassionate leave, but I'm going back on Monday.'

'So will you be moving back to the flat at the weekend?'

'I don't know, Paul,' Bonita answered carefully. In many ways she'd seen this coming—with her shoulder and everything, the last few weeks had fallen pretty much on her, but decisions had to be made now, and Bonita could guess what was coming.

'Well, as I said, we were talking... The thing is, we don't feel Mum should be left on her own at the moment—'

'So you move in, then,' Bonita interrupted.

'I have to be close to the hospital—I've got a lot of on calls coming up. And Ricky and Marco are out in Bendigo.'

She'd sort of expected this, but it still hurt. A doctor and two vets they may be, but what right did they have to assume that her life, her job was so much less important than theirs?

'Can you stay on here for a couple more weeks?'

'I've already been away for a month!'

'I know that,' Paul said. 'Look, don't take this the wrong way…' A very embarrassed Paul slid a cheque over the table towards her and as he spoke on, she realised that she almost *had* taken it the wrong way.

'We know you're not getting shift allowance, we know that the bills are still coming in. Take this to tide you over, give Emily some rent, pay some bills. I've spoken to my boss and I'm taking a fortnight's leave in two weeks, Marco's going to do the same after that and Ricky's trying to swing it, though the practice is new, but if he can't, Harriet will come down with the kids. We all know it's asking a helluva lot of you, but if we can just have two weeks to organise things, it will mean Mum won't be on her own for a couple of months.'

She'd never felt closer to them.

Oh, it wasn't the money—just the thought behind it, and that they had seen how much she had done.

'Put it in your pocket,' Paul said, handing her the cheque. "Don't let Mum see—she'll think she's a bloody charity case or something.'

'I *can* manage.'

'Well, you're doing better than me, then.'

She felt guilty how relieved she felt. Not just that she wouldn't have to hang out now till payday to give Emily the rent but that she had some time to decide what to do.

She'd been back to the flat a couple of times, but it was like going back to school after the summer holidays and finding that all your friends had changed—or rather that you'd grown up and changed. And it wasn't just about Bill. The girls' nights in, and girls' nights out and the jumble of flat sharing just didn't appeal to her right now.

Maybe a couple weeks at home, to adjust to going back to work, might be the answer for everyone.

'Did Hugh end up staying last night?'

'Sorry?' Bonita asked, jumping to embarrassed attention as Paul broke into her thoughts.

'Hugh. He was talking about getting a taxi—I just wondered if he stayed.'

'Not sure.' Bonita blushed, covering her flaming cheeks with her hair as she concentrated on stirring her tea. 'I think so.'

'He's usually up first.' Paul yawned, glancing at his watch. 'Mind you, if he did stay, he's no doubt already gone home. Amber's probably sick of our family's dramas pulling him away from her all the time.'

'Amber?' Adding another unnecessary and unwanted teaspoon of sugar, Bonita could hear the high note in her voice and fought to check it. 'I didn't know he was still seeing her.'

'Oh, yes!' Paul affirmed. 'They're the talk of the hospital. Lucky man—she's stunning.'

'I didn't think they were that serious.' Bonita offered, as if she were privy to information, as if the hospital grapevine had personally delivered her that vital piece of news.

'You've been out of the loop with your shoulder, remember!' Paul smiled. 'He's besotted with her—that's why he came back to Australia apparently. It would seem Hugh's finally found the first Mrs Armstrong—well, for a little while at least…'

'Meaning?' She could feel bile churning inside her, took a massive gulp of tea in the hope of calming it down and almost threw up.

'Well, the novelty of being faithful might appeal for five minutes or so, but I'm sure it will soon wear off. Can you really imagine Hugh committing to one person for life?' He laughed, actually laughed at the very thought of it, and Bonita was too thrown and confused to even pretend to join in. 'From what I hear, he's intending to propose to her soon. He's bought the ring and everything. It's massive.

'Hey, Marco!' Bonita was glad when Marco joined them, because she was starting to hyperventilate, could feel her breath coming in short, tight bursts. 'I was just telling Bonny the news about Hugh!' Paul said.

'Lucky guy,' Marco grumbled. 'The ring's stunning by all accounts… Who'd have thought?'

Who didn't think?

No wonder Hugh had been so appalled when he had awoken this morning. Even a man with the morals of an alley cat would be struggling a touch. Or maybe he was just worried how she was going to be. If she'd be making demands, telling people…telling Amber!

'Bonny?' Paul frowned at her pale features. 'Hey we're sorry, chatting away about nonsense. It's just our way of dealing with it.'

'Morning!' Her eyes swollen and a touch shaky, but very together, Carmel walked into the kitchen and for the first time in living memory she didn't head to the fridge and start fixing breakfast, just came and joined them all at the kitchen table.

'How are you, Mum?' Paul asked, and Carmel took a moment or two to think about it before answering.

'I'll get there, darling. How about you?'

'I keep forgetting,' Paul admitted. 'Then it nearly kills me when I suddenly remember.'

'How are you doing, Bon—?' Her voice faded as she saw Bonita's pained expression. 'I know it's awful for you, darling. You did so well yesterday, not just yesterday…' Again she didn't finish as Hugh joined them at the table. He kissed Carmel on the cheek and Bonita had no idea if he was looking at her because she was completely avoiding looking at him.

'Breakfast, anyone?' Carmel said, sounding more like the old Carmel, but Paul shook his head.

'I've had some toast. I'm going to go out for a ride—try and clear my head.'

'Well, it worked for me.' Carmel smiled. 'How about you, Hugh? What would you like?'

'Not for me thanks—I'm due at work in half an hour!'

'Have some toast at least.'

But Hugh couldn't…just gulped down a cup of tea, and then headed off to his bedroom to pack.

'He's been such a help!' Carmel smiled as he headed to the bedroom to grab his things. 'He just adored your father…he'd do anything to make this easier on all of us.'

Anything.

Even sleeping with her if that was what she needed—

hell, what was a night of sex to a guy like Hugh? And why hadn't she seen the writing on the wall?

He'd told her.

In this very kitchen he'd stood and told her—and she'd refused to believe it.

That's what guys did, Bonita brutally reminded herself. When it's available.

Well, she'd save him the effort of breaking her heart again.

Heading down the hall, she knocked on Ricky's bedroom door, gave Hugh a thin smile as he turned around from where he was packing his bag.

'Can I call you later?' he asked. 'Maybe we could go out tonight, away from here.'

'I don't think so.'

'It would just be easier to talk, what with your mum around and everything.'

'It didn't stop you last night.'

'About last night…' She watched his hand drag through his hair, his lips purse for a second as carefully he chose different words, and watched the awkward dart of his eyes and the swallow of his Adam's apple. 'I haven't been completely up-front with you, Bonny. There are things we should have spoken about, things you don't know…'

Oh, but she did know. They were humming the same tune—just a different song now.

It was a slightly more mature version that allowed for the years since the first time she'd heard it—then it had been a kiss, now they'd make love. Hey, maybe she could be a diversion now and then, maybe when Amber was pregnant, or things weren't going well with her partner they could be friends with benefits, no-strings sex...

She was hard pushed not to slap his cheek.

She didn't want to hear what he had to say. This time she'd get in first.

'I wanted to thank you for last night actually.' She watched two lines appear above his straight nose at the casual edge to her voice. 'It was great.'

'I know.'

'Just what I needed.'

'Bonny—'

'I don't want it brought up again.' She smiled at his confusion, smiled as she took the wind right out of the bastard's sails by getting in first.

'I'll pick you up tonight—we can go for dinner.'

'Better not.' Bonita shook her head. 'Mum would start getting ideas if we went out and I don't want that.'

'Bonny—'

'Bonita!' she corrected. 'Look, last night was great and everything, but let's face it, I was upset, couldn't sleep, you were there...'

'I'm sorry if you think I took advantage.'

'We both took advantage,' Bonita interrupted.

But Hugh wouldn't have it, refused to buy it. 'We'll talk tonight. I've got to get to work, but I'll call you later. We can meet somewhere if it makes it easier.'

'I don't want to meet somewhere, because we've got nothing to talk about. Let's just forget it happened.'

'But it did.'

'Well, it shouldn't have,' she clipped. 'I don't want to make a big deal of it, because it wasn't a big deal!'

'I don't believe you, Bonny. I know how much you like me.'

'Oh, you *know*, do you?'

'Yes!' Adamant, pompous and refusing to let her get out gracefully, he confronted her with the truth. 'You told me so yourself, when I was putting you under for your shoulder. Look, I don't know what's going on in that head of yours, I know you're upset this morning, but I also know the truth!'

'The truth!' An incredulous laugh shot out of her lips—and if she'd rued having three brothers, for the first time in twenty-four years she was actually grateful for the fact. Grateful that she knew how their minds worked, grateful for Marco—or was it Paul?—telling her that no matter what, she should never let a man know just how much she cared about him. Grateful too that she could hold it together while inside she fell apart. 'I had my wisdom teeth out last year and I told Dr Lau that I was in love, too. She's married with three children, by the way.'

'You're a liar, Bonny—and not a very good one. I know what I heard and I know that last night wasn't some fling because you were upset and I happened to be there.'

'Oh, but you were there,' Bonita pointed out, and revenge certainly did taste better served cold, because her voice was like ice as she echoed the very words he'd knifed her with all those years ago. 'That's what people do when it's available...'

'How long did you wait to use that line?' Hugh's eyes were two slits, his face as white as chalk, his voice harsh as he spoke through strained lips.

'Six bloody years!'

'How wrong can a guy be?' Hugh strode off but at the last moment changed his mind and tossed his parting shot at her. 'You know, for a little while there I actually thought you'd grown up. Well, I was wrong—you're still the self-centred little brat I remember so well.'

CHAPTER NINE

ON LEGS as shaky as those of a newborn foal, four days after her father's funeral, Bonita walked through the doors of Emergency, praying she'd get through the shift without breaking down. Everything that had been so familiar seemed different and new—even her colleagues, though friendly and clearly pleased to see her, were just a touch awkward as they welcomed her back. And not just about her father, with Bill in charge today and Emily on duty tomorrow, exquisite discomfort was guaranteed at every turn.

Still, she knew it was just a matter of time till things settled and Bonita was grateful when Bill told her they'd start her off gradually—and not just because of her shoulder.

'Stay out of Resus and Triage for a while,' Bill said kindly. 'Normally I'd give you the walking wounded in section B, but we're a couple of nurses down with this flu that's hit, so we're seeing all the patients up here— just take the straightforward ones. Do you want to do the clinics this morning or the trolleys in section A?'

'Flu!' Bonita frowned. 'It's a bit early in the year for that, isn't it?'

'Not according to the staff that rang in!' Bill said. 'The vaccinations are here, though, so make an appointment at staff health—then you'll have no excuse.'

'Oh, I won't be ringing in sick.' Bonita gave a pale smile. 'I haven't got any sick days left!'

'So where do you want to go?'

'I'll take section A,' Bonita said, glancing at the chalkboard Bill was updating and seeing Hugh was down for two clinics. Oh, she knew she'd have to face him, but would avoid it for a little while longer if she could. Over and over she'd wondered how she'd deal with working with him, how she'd react on seeing him. She had decided to attempt cool and professional and just hoped that he'd manage to do the same.

Her first few patients were all straightforward enough. There was an eight-year-old with epistaxis, or nosebleed, who, after a brief examination from the emergency intern, was accepted by the ENT team. Bonita chatted away with him and his mother as they wheeled him up the ward to be examined by the specialist. Then there was a fourteen-year-old with abdominal pain who, according to the GP letter, was expected by Paul, who Bonita duly paged.

'Hi, Paul. Malcolm Lewis, your abdo pain, is here.'

'How is he?'

'A bit uncomfortable—his obs are all OK, though,' Bonita answered. 'How long will you be?'

'I'm just about to start a ward round. Could you arrange an abdo X-ray for me?'

'You're supposed to see him first,' Bonita reminded

him, though it was pointless. If the surgeons were doing rounds then Paul would be a good hour or so away, and one of the first things he would order when he arrived in the department was an abdo X-ray! It really was silly just to keep the patient lying there till then.

'Just ask Hugh to write up the slip.'

Fat chance!

'How are you doing,' Paul asked when Bonita didn't respond, 'being back at work?'

'OK so far! They're breaking me in gently.'

'How was Mum this morning?'

'Glad to get rid of me,' Bonita said, hanging up. Then she duly got the X-ray request slip signed by Andrew and arranged for a porter to take her patient round to X-Ray. Given his mum was obviously pregnant and Malcolm was fretful, Bonita told Bill she was going with the patient.

'It won't take long,' Bonita assured her tearful patient, handing over the slip to the receptionist. Because he had a nurse escort, he was pushed up the list and after only ten minutes or so of waiting Malcolm was being wheeled into X-Ray Two. It was Bonita who was the anxious one now, and desperately trying not to show it.

In her head she'd gone through scenario after scenario—how she'd be when she saw Hugh, how Hugh might be when he saw her. She'd consoled herself that, given they'd pretty much never got on well at work, no one would notice much difference. Yet, with all her planning, and all her angst, she hadn't actually factored in facing Amber.

"'Erect and supine abdo.'" Amber read the slip without glancing at Bonita, who was purple she was blushing so fiercely. But Amber didn't notice, just checked the paperwork then gave a very nice smile to the patient.

'I know these machines look scary, but they're really just big cameras.' Amber chatted kindly to Malcolm as Bonita pulled on a lead gown, glad that her blush was fading, determined to act normally. Amber sat the patient up and asked him to hold the cold film holder over his stomach, even making him laugh when she asked him if there was any chance he might be pregnant. But the pain was too much for him. He kept dropping the film and wriggling about and after a couple of attempts at positioning him Bonita suggested she hold the card and stay with him while the X-ray was taken.

Amber was an appropriate name, Bonita realised as amber eyes turned to hers and voiced the very same, very necessary question, only minus a glint of a smile.

'Is there any chance that you might be pregnant?'

And in that instant Bonita thought she surely knew, could have sworn she could see the challenge in Amber's eyes as she tossed the question.

'None,' Bonita croaked, holding the film against Malcolm's chest, the weight of the lead apron hurting her shoulder. Shame, guilt, wretchedness swept over her as she averted her eyes and did her best not to face Amber.

'Hold your breath now,' Amber called, after she had slipped behind the screen and prepared for the shot, and though her words was surely aimed at Malcolm, Bonita's own breath was bursting in her lungs.

'You OK?' Bill checked, running a worried glance over her as Bonita returned Malcolm to his cubicle. His

pain had worsened and Bonita was heading off to call
the surgeons as she spoke to Bill.

'I'm not sure…' Bonita admitted, biting down on her
lip and realising that Bill was perhaps the one person she
could actually talk to about things. 'I can't discuss it
here. Is there any chance we can go to lunch together…?'
Her voice trailed off as she realised Hugh had joined
them at the nursing station. She hadn't seen him at work
yet, hadn't seen him since the morning after the funeral,
and he looked, at least by Hugh's usually impeccable
standards, awful! His suit was perfect, his shirt fresh and
white, but his tie didn't match and it looked as if it was
choking him, as if it had been knotted by a five-year-old.
It was such a tiny detail, but she processed it in seconds.
His face was grey, that usually immaculate blond hair was
less so now—tousled and had just tipped into needing a
cut. Lines she'd never seen before seemed grooved
around his eyes and, even though she'd rehearsed over
and over how she'd be when she saw him, even though
to anyone else, he undoubtedly looked divine, instinct
kicked in and overrode her planned greeting.

'Are you OK?' Bonita frowned at his taut features,
and though she was more than used to him treating her
coolly at work, the contempt in his voice, when it came,
shot her straight back to their last bitter exchange.

'When you've finished discussing your lunch plans,
would you mind telling me why that patient has not been
seen by a doctor when he's been in the department for
an hour?' Hugh's surly manner when he addressed her
was, by now, familiar to all. Back from Outpatients, he
set the unfriendly tone instantly. He frowned at the

patient card that only had nursing obs recorded and no doctor's notes.

'He's a surgical patient,' Bonita answered tartly. 'That's why there's a sign saying "Surgeons" above his cubicle.'

'So who ordered the X-ray?'

'Andrew,' Bonita answered. 'The surgeons are doing rounds and Paul asked if we could get an abdo X-ray before he came down.' Given Andrew Browne was Hugh's boss, she was confident that would stop him, but yet again she'd misread him.

'So the patient's been in pain for all that time.'

'He's only just become distressed,' Bonita patiently explained. 'I was just about to ring the team to come down.'

'Well, do that!' Hugh clipped, standing there unmoving as Bonita called Paul. Her face burned as Paul told her he'd be there as soon as he could, but things weren't looking good for a quick getaway.

'You need to send someone down to see him now,' Bonita pushed, wishing Paul would take her seriously for five minutes.

'The kid's constipated, Bonny. I'll send someone as soon as I can.'

'Can I have the phone?' Hugh interrupted, taking the receiver and curtly addressing his best friend.

'Paul, I appreciate that your team's busy—but so are we. We're not running a babysitting service here. You have a patient that needs a doctor to see him! If one of your team isn't down here in five minutes, I'll take over the patient, examine him and give him analgesia, which will make your diagnosis, when you do get here, a lot harder to make.'

Hanging up the phone, he turned to go, then changed his mind. 'In future, can we please follow procedure? A doctor is supposed to examine the patient before he goes to X-Ray.'

'Can you speak to me first if you have a problem with the nursing staff?' Bill asserted.

Hugh's head deliberately lowered as he looked down at Bill in a curiously insolent gesture.

And two bulls certainly shouldn't share the same paddock, Bonita realised as she awaited Hugh's curt response.

'I don't have a problem with the nursing *staff*.' Hugh's voice dripped with derision. 'I have a problem with certain *departmental procedures not* being adhered to.'

'Your consultant ordered the X-ray,' Bill bravely pointed out.

'As a favour,' Hugh responded. 'A favour that has resulted in a fourteen-year-old boy crying in pain. Rest assured, I'll be discussing it with Andrew! Procedures are in place for a reason!'

'Whoa!' Bill gave a shocked grin as Hugh stalked off. 'What's upsetting him?'

'Lunch?' Bonita winced.

'Definitely!' Bill nodded.

'No way!' Over a sad excuse for chicken and avocado foccacia, which Bonita took one bite of and discarded, and a sip the canteen's attempt at cappuccino, she told Bill the sorry tale. He immediately shook his head. 'No way would he have told her.'

It would seem strange to many, Bonita realised, that

she could have this conversation with Bill, that she could even trust him after all that had happened, but she did. If three years together had taught her anything, it was what a decent guy Bill was—and she knew in her heart that he wouldn't breathe a word, knew because he'd had her heart once and had treated it with care.

'You didn't see how she looked at me.'

'She's probably picked up on the fact that you two like each other.'

'We don't!'

'Oh, come on, Bonita, I picked up on it! Amber's probably feeling how I did a few months ago. He's hardly going to have gone back home and told her…' Bill shook his head. 'They're getting married, you say?'

'He's bought the ring apparently!' Bonita sniffed. 'He's working his way up to asking her. It's common knowledge.'

'Not to me,' Bill mused. 'Mind you, Emily and I aren't exactly top of the social scene—hardly anyone's talking to us. Did you not think to ask if he was still seeing her?'

'I didn't think about anything!' Bonita crumpled at his criticism. 'He'd been around so many times, and never with her. But, no, that night I wasn't thinking…'

'I'm sorry.' Bill squeezed her hand. 'That was harsh. Don't beat yourself up.'

'They're getting married. Have you any idea how bad I feel?'

'He should be the one feeling bad!' Bill insisted, then promptly let go of her hand. 'Speak of the devil.'

Grey in the face and looking stunning but awful, Hugh stalked past with his tray.

It came as no surprise when he didn't ask to join them. The day was unbearable.

At two p.m. Andrew announced that Hugh had come down with flu and they were a doctor short. Bill gave her a small nudge.

'Maybe there really is flu going around.'

'I guess.'

'He did look shocking,' Bill said. 'And it more than explains his vile mood.'

Only Bonita wasn't convinced.

Her first day back was uncomfortable and long, but the night was even longer. Staring at the ceiling, remembering what had taken place in her bedroom, the task she'd avoided since her bitter exchange with Hugh had to be done now. She had to take an honest appraisal of herself and what she had done.

She'd assumed there had been no more Amber.

Assumed Hugh was operating by the same code of conduct as her.

What a fool! What a stupid, blind and very much in the wrong fool.

Maybe that was Hugh's way, Bonita reflected—affection, intimacy his prescription for pain—maybe he had comforted her in the only way he knew how. Delivered a shot of temporary relief in the same way he'd numbed her shoulder, a quick fix to see her through.

Bonita had thought nothing could come close to the pain of losing her father, only this was actually worse.

She felt as if she'd lost herself.

CHAPTER TEN

'You've lost weight.' Carmel observed, looking up from the thank-you cards she was writing, as Bonita came in the door after a long, boring shift in Outpatients.

'I haven't lost any weight,' Bonita lied. Not that she'd weighed herself, but her uniform was hanging off her and food was the last thing on her mind at the moment. Still on light duties, she was climbing the walls working in section B and Outpatients, but not for much longer. After a discussion with Deb, it had been agreed that tomorrow she could venture back down to section A and test her shoulder and mental state on some sick patients! And Bonita was beyond relieved. Mind-numbing tasks didn't exactly help take her mind off her troubles, and, even though Hugh was due back from sick leave soon, she was over worrying how she'd react to him. In fact, she was way past the embarrassed stage and had moved on to fury.

A restless fury that needed unleashing.

And opportunity came when she least expected it.

'You're not eating properly!" Carmel insisted. 'You didn't have any breakfast before you left this morning.'

'Because I was running late.'

'And you left the lunch I made you in the fridge!'

'Mum, please.' Bonita took a banana out of the fruit bowl and ate it just to *prove* to her mother she hadn't suddenly developed anorexia. 'See!' Bonita swallowed the last of it and opening her mouth poked out her tongue to prove it was all gone. 'Now, stop worrying.'

'I'm not worried.' Carmel gave a tired smile. 'Well, a bit. You just don't seem yourself, moping around here each evening. You've only had one night out since you've been at home.'

'I've been off sick!' Bonita pointed out. 'And what with Dad, I just don't feel in the mood for a girls' night out.'

'You haven't even made a move to go back to the flat.'

Oh, that!

'Actually…' Bonita gave a nervous swallow '…I'm thinking of moving out.'

'To where?' Carmel asked slowly.

'Back here.'

'No!' Carmel shook her head. 'Absolutely not—I do *not* want a babysitter.'

'It's not about that…' Bonita attempted, only how could she tell her mother? Sure, it would be the easy option. Her mum would understand in an instant if she found out Emily was seeing Bill. But Bonita couldn't go for the sympathy vote here. She couldn't taint Emily with the very brush that should be colouring herself. 'We'll talk about it later. Is there anything you want me to do?'

'Actually, yes!' Carmel stood up and headed to the kitchen, returning a moment later with two vast casseroles. 'Can you drop these round at Hugh's?'

'Hugh's?'

'He's had that flu…'

'He'll be back at work in a couple of days,' Bonita quickly interrupted.

'Which means he won't feel like cooking and will need a good meal when he gets home. Come on, Bonita, he's done a lot for us these past few weeks, and I've got more casseroles and dinners in the freezer than I know what to do with.'

'I'll give them to him at work when he's back.'

'Fine!' Carmel said in the martyred voice she did so very well. 'I'll take them to him myself, though I *did* want to get these thank-you cards from your father's funeral finished today.'

How did she do it?

Wild dogs couldn't drag her to Hugh's, yet one pained sigh from her mother and she was grinding the car's gears, two casseroles bouncing on the back seat, as she headed towards Hugh's plush bayside apartment.

Well, she assumed it was plush from the address her mother had given her, and the glittering bay views that swept into vision as she hit the beach road.

It was a sign, Bonita decided, parking the car and marching towards his apartment. A sign that she should do something about the appalling awkwardness that would descend again when he was back at work. An opportunity, in fact, Bonita told herself as she took the lift up to his floor, to get things out in the open—to find out how they were supposed to deal with the fact that, like it or not, their lives merged at times.

She could do this! Taking a calming breath, Bonita

attempted a brisk knock, which was rather difficult, considering she was balancing two casseroles.

Maybe the fact that he wasn't home was also a sign, Bonita decided a couple of moments later. She placed the casseroles on the floor and scrabbled in her bag for a pen and paper, relief flooding her at the prospect of leaving a note.

Dear Hugh, she started, then screwed it up.

Hugh, Mum wanted…

'Can I help you, Bonita?'

There were certain people who could wear white shorts and a skimpy white T-shirt and look stunning, and though Bonita wasn't one of them, Amber certainly was! Smooth long brown legs greeted Bonita as she was crouched down to write. She retrieved the casseroles and stood, noticing Amber's equally smooth brown crossed arms.

'Sorry, I thought no one was home.'

'Hugh's asleep—I was out on the balcony.'

'My mum wanted me to drop off these…' Bonita gave her the two dishes, hoping, *hoping* the lids were on properly and a massive smear of tomato sauce wouldn't taint that lovely top, but Amber's arms were still folded. 'Just a couple of casseroles for Hugh—given that he's been unwell.'

'From your mum?' Amber asked, taking the two dishes and, thankfully, smiling.

'Yep, she worries about him.'

'Hugh thinks the world of her. I'll see he gets them,' Amber said. Bonita gave a relieved nod and turned to go, but Amber halted her. 'If you ever come here again,

Bonita—' and there was something in Amber's voice that told Bonita she should not turn around '—then you'll be wearing this casserole!'

Unsustainable.

It was a word frequently bandied about in the emergency department. When a situation—because of staffing levels, or patient influx, or a patient with calamitous injuries or vital signs—just *had* to be dealt with before the consequences became dire.

And over the next couple of days Bonita came to the unpalatable conclusion that her situation was just that—unsustainable.

Whether or not Hugh had had a moment of guilt and confessed what had happened, Amber clearly knew there was something between them—or had been.

And though her night with Hugh would never be repeated, though there wasn't a thing Bonita could do to erase what had happened, there was one thing she could do for Amber—take herself out of the equation.

She could do it for herself, too.

At the tender age of eleven she had fallen in love. Yes, at first it had seemed a silly girl's crush but, as immature as her parents might have considered her, Bonita was actually very astute. The love that had breezed into her life the first day Hugh had appeared at the Azetti dinner table had been a love that had endured more than a decade. A love that, despite what had taken place, for Bonita at least still endured.

But reckless choices made for bitter consequences— and now she had to face them. A move to the city would, as she had told her mother, be good for her career and a major teaching hospital had vacancies in Emergency. And it was only an hour or so's drive away, so she could come home on her days off. Now, at twenty four, it was time to lug her broken heart to new surroundings.

She waited for a lull in the department and asked Deb if she might have a word in the office while things were quiet.

Sensible?

Yes.

Agony?

Of course.

'I think you're making a mistake.' Deb gave her a kind smile. 'You shouldn't be making any major decisions now.'

'But I *have* to make some major decisions now,' Bonita pointed out, because she did. Because, aside from Hugh and Amber, despite the fact she was OK with Bill and Emily, she couldn't go back to living at the flat. And even though they were getting on now, staying with her mum was just a temporary solution.

'I could wring Bill's neck.'

'Bill's my friend,' Bonita said firmly. 'No one, apart from Bill and I, knows what went on between us. We went to great lengths to keep our relationship out of work, and now that it's over suddenly everyone thinks they're entitled to an opinion. Well, it's not helping and, given I'm here for another month, I'd really appreciate it if you could call off the firing squad. Bill doesn't deserve it and it's not helping me.'

'Fair enough.' Deb nodded. 'I'll have a word with

everyone. That's the problem with smaller hospitals—everyone knows everyone's business.'

'Or thinks that they do,' Bonita responded, terminating the interview, standing up and taking charge. She headed out to the floor and talked to Emily who was about to go on her coffee-break. Bonita did not really care what anyone thought any more. She was just ready to get on with *her* life.

'How was it with Deb?' Emily fished.

'Fine.'

'Coming for your coffee-break?'

'Not yet,' Bonita said. 'Why?'

'I just want to chat about the flat.' Emily scuffed the floor with her foot. 'About when you're coming back.'

'I'm not.'

'Oh.' Emily flushed, but quickly recovered. 'What about the rent? We agreed one month's notice.'

'You've had your month,' Bonita said, standing tall and just a little bit proud.

'Oh.'

'I'll bring the ute around tomorrow. Pick up the last of my things.' And breezing into the first available cubicle, Bonita got on with the job in hand.

Except Hugh was already in there!

Edna Williams was seventy-four and had collapsed at the shops that morning. She had presented with right-sided weakness. She was already in a hospital gown, but Bonita could tell without looking that the clothes that were bagged under the trolley would be immaculate. Mrs Willliams's hair was carefully cut and her nails were painted, her lovely lined face beautifully made up. Bonita could see she was also beyond embarrassed at being there and very distressed at the difficulty she was having with speaking.

Hugh, though, was lovely with her.

'Try not to get distressed, Mrs Williams,' he soothed, his very English voice clipped yet somehow comforting. He told her to rest back on the pillows and asked Bonita to dim the lights as he carefully looked into Mrs Williams's eyes, telling his patient how well she was doing. When the lights were back on, he performed a comprehensive neurological examination. And when a very worried Mrs Williams attempted to ask questions, her speech slurring, her face anguished at the hopelessness of her lost words, Hugh, just as he had been with Bonita's father, was infinitely patient.

'We're going to give you a CT scan—like an X-ray of your brain,' Hugh calmly explained. 'Now, I know you can't speak very well, but for a moment I want you to listen. When the paramedics first arrived, you had no movement on your right side. Since you've arrived here, that has improved, which is encouraging. So let's get you around to X-Ray and then I'll know more what's going on and I'll come and talk to you properly then.'

'Will you go with her?' Hugh asked Bonita.

'Of course.'

Once they were left alone Mrs Williams gave a crooked smile and Bonita introduced herself properly. The older woman looked at her name badge, smiled, nodded and relaxed a touch.

"Do you know my mum?' Bonita asked, not in the least surprised when Mrs Williams nodded again. 'Then

I'd better take extra good care of you or I'll have my mum to answer to.'

The CT area of X-Ray was routine for Bonita, but she knew how terrifying it must be for Mrs Williams. And even though she felt more than a touch uncomfortable when she realised that Amber was the technician on duty, the patient wouldn't pick up on anything. By unspoken agreement they were polite and formal and, as always, Amber was kind to the patient, telling Mrs Williams in detail what to expect.

'Just stay as still as you can.' Amber explained. 'I'll talk to you through the microphone. We can see and hear you at all times, so just do your best to stay still and relax and we'll get this over with as soon as we can.'

The entire procedure took around twenty minutes, but for Bonita it was agony. She stood behind Amber's blonde head as Amber tapped away at the controls, images appearing on the screen. Neither woman attempted small talk.

'You're doing very well, Mrs Williams,' Amber said, leaning forward, pressing on a button and speaking into her microphone. 'I just need you to stay still for a few more moments, and then we'll be finished.'

'How is she?' Hugh asked, coming in as the investigation concluded. Guilt was a horrible thing to live with, Bonita thought as she looked at Hugh and Amber together. She knew that her discomfort today had nothing to do with Hugh and everything to do with herself. She had just assumed things had been over between the two of them, as they had been with herself and Bill—had been so wrapped up in her own grief, her own pain she hadn't factored the pain she might be causing another.

'How does it look to you?' Hugh frowned at the images. 'Doug, the medical registrar, is coming directly down to see her. I really thought she'd had a stroke.'

'Well, I'm not allowed to comment,' Amber said, 'but it all looks pretty good to me. There doesn't appear to be anything acute anyway.'

'Well, that's a relief. Right, let's get her back, then. Don't worry about calling for a porter,' he said as Amber went to pick up the phone. 'Bonita and I can get her back.'

Which sounded sensible, given he was going that way, but Hugh hung around, chatting to Amber and looking over the images, and Bonita's impatience grew.

'I need a hand to get her onto the trolley,' Bonita explained, giving him a very strained smile. Well, if Hugh wanted to play at porters he could damn well do their job.

But in the time they'd been away Mrs Williams had again improved. She managed to slide herself from the CT bed to the trolley, with only minimal assistance, even saying a clear 'Thank you' when Bonita covered her with a blanket.

'Probably a TIA,' Hugh said once they had settled her back into her cubicle. A TIA was a transient ischaemic attack. It looked at first like a stroke, but recovery was often near complete. Still it was considered a serious warning. Hopefully, with the right medical care Mrs Williams would be prevented from having a full stroke. 'Her neuro obs are good,' Hugh commented without looking at Bonita, 'though she's still hypertensive. Doug wants to arrange for a carotid Doppler.'

'Then he'll have to order that from the ward or Outpatients,' Bonita reminded him, 'as per procedure.'

'Is this how it's going to be, Bonita?' His words were as direct as his stare. 'I know I started this *procedure* nonsense, but I'm ending it right here. If we're going to work together as a team, then something has to give.'

'It already has.' Bonita flashed her eyes at him. 'I just handed in my notice.'

She didn't wait for his reaction—just got on with her work. And thankfully there was plenty. By the time lunch came around a much perkier Mrs Williams was sitting up on the trolley, surrounded by relatives and eating a sandwich, as Bonita, having caved in, tried to organise a carotid Doppler!

'Thanks for that,' Hugh said. 'She's being admitted to the medical ward. Nice old girl—I'm glad it wasn't a stroke.'

'Me, too.'

Cool but civil.

It was certainly an improvement on their last encounter.

She could surely live with that for a month. Though from here it seemed interminable.

The next patient was a sixty-year-old farmer with sudden onset of chest pain.

'Bruce Eames,' the paramedics introduced him cheerfully, their mood matching that of the patient. He was of solid, muscular build, a real salt-of-the-earth type. He managed a joke or two as they shifted him from the ambulance stretcher to the hard bed in the resuscitation area.

'Not exactly designed for sleeping!' Bruce grinned,

but Bonita could see the dart of fear in his eyes as he took in his surroundings. 'Do I really need this mask?'

'Just for now.' Bonita smiled, placing a probe on his finger to check his oxygen saturation. 'And don't worry about all these machines,' Bonita said. She taped over the IV the paramedics had inserted, just to ensure it didn't come out, then shaved a few areas on Bruce's chest before she attached the pads. 'They're so that we can keep a close eye on you. Here's the doctor to see you now.'

He'd come back too early from sick leave—Bonita could see that as he grabbed a drink from the water cooler before heading over to Bruce. Hugh's complexion had a sickly grey tinge, and though he chatted easily to his patient, from the beads of sweat on his forehead, Bonita knew he was struggling to see the day out.

'Have you had anything like this before?' Hugh asked as he took the history, but Bruce shook his head. 'Any heart problems?'

'Nothing.'

'You're not on any medication at all?'

'Nothing— Oh, the ambulance guys gave me some aspirin.'

'Who's your GP?'

'I haven't seen a doctor in twenty years—thank God. No offence.' Bruce grinned. 'You're just not my type!'

'None taken.' Hugh smiled back.

'He's as fit as a fiddle.' His wife joined them then. Bonita knew it was his wife without any introduction, just from the smile on her face, from the way she looked at her husband. It reminded Bonita of her mother all of a sudden. Normally she'd have asked Mrs Eames to take a seat outside for a moment or two while they ran some obs and did a quick ECG but instead she pulled over a chair and told her to have a seat. She was aware that her father's illness and death had changed the way that she nursed.

'OK, if you can just lean forward. Bonny,' Hugh said as he put on his stethoscope to listen to Bruce's chest, 'could you arrange an urgent portable chest X-ray and some morphine?'

'Sure.'

Quietly, she made the necessary calls, bagged the bloods that Hugh took and arranged a porter. She gritted her teeth then forced a smile as Amber came around in her lead coat to take the portable chest X-ray.

'Would you mind waiting outside for this; Mrs Eames?' Bonita asked, pulling a lead apron on herself. 'We'll only be a couple of moments.'

'Of course. I might ring Hannah,' she said to her husband, kissing him softly on the cheek, 'I'll be back in a moment, darling.'

And it was that quick! A row of ectopics flashed across the screen and Bonita frowned, but even before the machine raised the alarm Mrs Eames called her husband's name urgently.

'Bruce!' She said it once, then said it more loudly. 'Bruce!'

'Just wait outside,' Bonita said firmly. The wavy lines of ventricular fibrillation were on the screen now as the alarm kicked in. Bruce's eyes closed and his jaw suddenly went slack as Bonita called his name loudly.

She gave him a swift shake of the shoulders before lowering the bed flat and pulling out the pillows.

Mrs Eames's shout had everyone running before Bonita even had time to hit the emergency bell. Bonita flicked the machine to charge and commenced cardiac massage. Deb put out an emergency call and took over the airway as Hugh slapped pads on Bruce's chest and picked up the paddles of the defibrillator. Meanwhile, Bill, just coming back from lunch, guided Mrs Eames to the interview room.

Hugh told everyone to stand back, delivered the shock and ordered lignocaine as Bonita continued with the massage.

If there was a good cardiac arrest to have, VF was the best one, especially when the arrest was witnessed. The heart was still active, just fibrillating, and the drugs that were delivered combined with defibrillation. It meant that sometimes by the time the cardiac team and the anaesthetist had arrived, the heart was already beating effectively again—only not in Bruce's case.

On and on they worked. Amber had long since gone, Bonita was kneeling up on the bed now, her shoulder starting to hurt. She tried to comprehend how in just a few moments everything had changed.

'Let Deb do the massage,' Hugh ordered, and Bonita waited till Deb was beside her, their hand swiftly changing to allow for continuity. Now it was Bonita pulling up drugs, writing down the details, but with every minute that passed the outlook became more dire.

Bruce was in asystole now—without cardiac mas-

sage the line on the monitor was flat. Still they worked
on. The anaesthetist had intubated him, every drug had
been given, but his colour and oxygen levels were appalling. Bonita watched as Hugh looked at the cardiologist and he shook his head.

'I'm going to go and speak to his wife.' Hugh's voice
was measured and calm but there was this gruff edge to
it Bonita had never heard before at work. 'Keep going
till I come back.'

There was a side to nursing that Bonita hadn't really
considered till this point.

That, though death was almost a daily occurrence at
work, she might have to deal with it when dealing with
her own grief.

But other staff had been there before. Deb suggested
Bonita take over in the cubicles, which she did, but it
was like working on autopilot. She saw Mrs Eames supported by Hugh, walking, pale, scared yet somehow
dignified, and it reminded her so much of her mother it
was almost more than she could stand.

So, too, the closed curtains as they wheeled Bruce out
of Resus and into a side ward. So, too, passing Hugh the
pad so he could write the interim death certificate.

Just the horrible finality of it all.

'Why don't you go for coffee?' Bill suggested later,
when other relatives were arriving.

'I'll be OK.' Bonita shook her head.

'Come on.' Bill gave a sympathetic smile. 'I'll take
you up to the canteen.'

'She said she was OK!' Hugh snapped. 'Instead of
another extended break, Bill, could you please get the

blood results back from cubicle two, and I want to know why the paeds team *still* haven't been down to assess that child.'

'Mrs Eames wants to have another word, Hugh!' Deb popped her head into the nurses' area where Hugh was writing up Bruce's notes. 'She needs someone to go over again what happened.'

'Can't the cardiologist speak to her?' Hugh snapped uncharacteristically. The staff were used to his slight arrogance, but never where a patient or relative was concerned.

'He's back up on the ward.'

'Great.' Hugh whistled through gritted teeth. 'Deb, can you come with me?'

Whereas Luigi's death had been expected, Bruce's had been sudden. A lot of grieving had taken place before Luigi had died, but Bruce's family had just been plunged into it. And as much as her colleagues took the strain from Bonita, it still hurt.

His pregnant daughter arrived.

The son he had never got on with raced into Emergency, confrontational and upset, demanding from Bonita to know where his father was, what had happened, why he hadn't been called.

And it was too much.

Just too much, too close and too soon.

She didn't want Bill and the canteen.

Didn't want the staffroom and sympathy.

Or to try and cry quietly in the toilets.

So, taking herself off, Bonita made her way to the one place in Emergency that was quiet. She opened the door to the equipment cupboard, not even turning on the light, just heading for the vast chair that the night staff sometimes curled up in.

She jumped when she saw it was occupied.

She felt like an intruder who had crept in unnoticed. Worse than that, she felt like she'd crept in and an intruder had been. Everything she knew, everything safe was dishevelled and in disarray. She was appalled and stunned to see Hugh, her strong, dashing, confident Hugh, leaning forward, his head in his hands. And worst of all, he was crying.

'Sorry!' Coughing, sniffing, he wiped his face with the backs of his hands and stood up as if the chair itself had bitten him.

'What's wrong?'

'I'm fine!' Which was the most ridiculous thing he could have said. 'Just this bloody flu.'

'Hugh?' She caught his arm as he marched off. 'This isn't flu.' She'd never seen him cry, not once had he even seemed close. She wondered if he'd broken up with Amber, if her father's death, coupled with that of Bruce Eames, had made him suddenly think of his own father. Her mind whirred to find what could devastate him so. 'You haven't had flu, have you?'

'Leave it, Bonny.'

'Hugh tell me.' She was scared, scared to see him like this. Remembering all the times he'd comforted her, she wanted to do the same for him.

'I just miss him—OK?'

And he'd comforted her, comforted them all, been there and done the right thing on so many occasions.

And on one occasion he might have done the wrong thing—but at her bidding. Not once had it entered her head that he might need comfort, too. That Hugh had lost something just as precious.

'I miss your dad.'

'I know.'

'I just…' She'd never seen him flounder, this strong, eloquent man lost for words, and she held his hands as he went to walk out. 'I just needed some time to get my head around things.'

'You could have told someone.'

'I have…' He raked his hand through his unkempt hair. 'Amber's been great—she's tried to understand.'

'I meant at work,' Bonita croaked.

'What was I supposed to say? That I need compassionate leave because my friend's dad just died?'

'He's more than a friend's dad to you.' And she saw it then, the little flashes she'd glimpsed all coming together. She saw how he had been there, had helped, had been a doctor to her dad, had held it together, been the strong one—as if somehow it didn't hurt him as much as it hurt them. And in that second Bonita knew that it did.

Hurt even more perhaps because he was alone with his grief, because, as Hugh had pointed out, who could possibly understand that for him losing Luigi was harder than losing his own father?

'I'm trying to help Paul—he's taking it hard. I'm feeling bad about what went on with you…'

Yes, well!

Funny that half an hour ago she'd have probably

slapped him if he'd said that, but his grief was so palpable it made it hard to be angry. She realized the hell he'd been through these past weeks and months.

'It takes two!' Bonita pointed out, swallowing down a fizz of anger.

'I let him down.'

You let us all down, she nearly said, but she was making great leaps in self-control these days, so instead she tightened her grip on the hands she was holding and managed a very good impersonation of a gentle smile. 'Grief makes you do strange things. I remember on my midwifery rotation being told a lot of babies are born nine months after a good funeral.'

'You're not pregnant?' He asked in a 'that's all I need' tone.

'No, Hugh.' Bonita didn't even try to fake a smile, her hands dropping to her side. 'That's one thing you don't have to worry about.'

Yet still it was impossible to hate him—that would mean hating the man who had made her dad comfortable at the very end, hating the man who had supported her family, a man who was utterly bereft now and who, even if she regretted it, had brought her comfort in that long lonely time, too.

'You're leaving.'

'It's kind of hard to stay.'

'I've messed everything up.'

'It's not just you,' Bonita admitted. 'What with Bill and Emily. Then there's Amber throwing me daggers.'

On cue, Bill barged in.

'What the hell's going on? The place is steaming.'

'I was upset!' Bonita spoke in place of Hugh. 'With Mr Eames and everything...'

'Two minutes,' Bill warned, grabbing a few IV flasks. 'There's been a pile-up on the beach road—ETA 10 minutes.'

'Can we talk later?' Hugh's eyes were urgent as he spoke. 'About your dad, about things. Come to the apartment later.'

'No!' Instantly she shook her head. 'I don't want to see Amber.'

'Amber's not coming over. Please—I just need to talk.'

'She knows, doesn't she?' Her voice was shaking as she asked the terrifying question, shrivelling inside when he nodded.

'I had to tell her.'

'Did you?'

His pager was shrilling in his pocket.

'That new bar where I live...' He was heading out the door. 'Seven o'clock.'

'You shouldn't have told her!' Bonita grabbed his sleeve as he brushed past.

'I had to!' Hugh shouted at her for the first time. 'I had to tell someone!'

'And now she hates me,' Bonita sobbed as his pager screamed for his attention.

'Do you blame her?' His words were like a slap as he turned to leave, but they were nothing compared to what came next, nothing, because his next line had her recoiling, had her as dizzy and confused as if she'd been punched to the floor. 'With everything you've done!'

CHAPTER ELEVEN

'YOU look nice.' Carmel commented as, jangling with nerves and removing one of her silver bracelets so it didn't rattle quite so much, Bonita walked into the living room where her mother was lying on the couch, reading. 'Too thin, of course!'

'You're more Italian than the Italians!' Bonita smiled. 'How's the book?'

'Nice,' Carmel said. 'Thanks for getting this for me. It's nice just to curl up and...' She paused for a moment. 'Forget.' Then she grimaced. 'Not that I forget.'

'Escape?' Bonita offered, and her mum nodded.

'This is way better than those self-help books you bought me—according to them I'm insane.'

'You?' Bonita gawked. 'You're the most sensible, sane person I know.'

'Well, according to Einstein, insanity is doing the same thing over and over and expecting a different result.' She gave a tired smile. 'I thought if I cooked something he liked, if this meal was perfect he might get better. Mad cow, aren't I?'

'The nicest one I know,' Bonita said.

'I'll stick with romance.' Carmel winked. 'Are you coming back tonight?'

'Of course,' Bonita said, waiting for the inevitable, for the whos, wheres and whys, only they never came.

'It's good that you're going out.' Carmel's words merely added to Bonita's confusion.

'I won't be late,' Bonita said, because if she told her mother that then she couldn't be. She wished for the first time that Carmel would be just a little bit nosy, demand that she was home by ten, would *insist*, in fact.

'Well, if you can't get back for some reason, just fire me a text.'

'I told you, I won't be late.' Bonita insisted. 'Will you be OK?'

'And I've told you, I don't need a babysitter.'

'I know that. Still, it's your first night on your own….'

'And you need to get out,' Carmel said. 'Thank you, though…for being here.'

It felt entirely natural to cuddle her mother before she went out and just bliss when Carmel cuddled her back. Her heart was hammering in her chest, terrified, petrified at what lay ahead, wishing, wanting to stay here, to curl up in her mother's arms and not head out into the big scary world and put her heart on the line again.

'I'd rather stay in,' Bonita admitted, and even if Carmel had no idea why she was scared, she still held her.

'You know that you can't. We can't mope around here grieving for ever—there's a whole world out there waiting for you. Off you go.' She peeled her daughter off, gave her a lovely smile and a kiss on the cheek. 'I'll be sitting here when you get home, waiting to hear all about it. Though if you're late…'

'I won't be late!' Bonita said for the hundredth time. Because she wouldn't be.

If insanity meant doing the same thing over and over and expecting a different result, she was holding onto her mind. A drink, dinner, talk about her dad, talk about them a little bit—but there was nothing Hugh could say tonight that would have her toss her heart back into the ring.

Tonight was about moving on with their lives.

Tonight was goodbye.

So why, Bonita wondered as she teetered up the steps of the swanky new bar near Hugh's, was she wearing her best bra and knickers?

They'd never actually been out.

Oh, there had been barbeques and horse rides and a couple of work dos and more dinners than she could count, but they'd never actually been out, just them, before.

She'd never walked into a bar and ordered a drink and sat waiting for him.

They'd said seven, but she'd left at six-thirty, her nerves so shot that if she'd stayed home a minute longer, she'd have rung and cancelled.

So now, here she was, sitting at a table and staring out at Port Phillip Bay, catching her reflection in the window and wondering if she was wearing too much make-up, wondering just what it was she was doing there, wearing a skirt and waiting for Hugh.

It could hardly be called a date.

He needed to talk about her father and she needed to

find out why he'd told Amber, but there was something big that she needed to say.

Thank you.

For looking after her family and also for looking after her.

For making her say all the things she had needed to say to her dad so that she wasn't sitting filled with regret now.

And no matter how wrong, or how brief it had been, it had been more than a crush and more than sex, and it had been needed.

And maybe not just by her.

The grief that night had been shared by them both, Bonita could see that now.

And grief made you do strange things—like seek comfort from a source that was off limits, made forbidden arms a friendlier option than sleeping alone.

He was so good looking.

Bonita watched as he walked into the foyer, watched as heads turned as he came to the table, and the waitress, who had taken for ever to attend to Bonita, came straight over.

'A beer, thanks!' He smiled at Bonita's near empty glass. 'Do you want another?'

'Just water, please.' Bonita nodded to the waitress. One gin and tonic she hoped would be enough to give her courage—two and she might just start crying.

'How's your mum?'

'OK…' Bonita gave a smile so small it was barely there. 'I'm to send her a text if I decide to stay out!'

'Told you.'

Placing the menu on the table, finally he looked at her, and she could see the doubt in his eyes, knew he was wondering if it was his place to say that. She moved to put his mind at ease.

'I always thought he was the soft one and it was Mum giving me the hard time.'

'She knew what would upset him.' Hugh smiled. 'I remember when I first met you—you'd been out riding and were this grubby, muddy thing and I have to say I didn't really give you a glance. Then a couple of years on, one night you were going out to the movies with friends and your dad didn't want you to go. Your mum told him it was right that you did. Then you came down the stairs…' He laughed as he recalled what Bonita couldn't even remember. 'Your dad was down at the stables and you appeared with all this make-up and a top that was just a bit too tight and your mum was furious at you. She chased you up the stairs and told you to wash it off. If your dad had seen you, you wouldn't have been allowed to go out.'

'I gave her such a hard time.'

'She gave you a hard time, too…' Hugh smiled '…but she was actually making things easier for you.'

'I can see that now,' Bonita admitted, only she wasn't here about her mother. 'Thank you.' As naturally as breathing she took his hand. It was right that she should touch him, right he should feel the genuine gratitude her words conveyed. 'Thank you for making me see things clearly before it was too late.'

'He loved you so much,' Hugh said.

'He loved you, too,' she said, hating it that Hugh

closed his eyes, hating the regret that flitted across his face. The regret that was absent from her life, thanks to this man, because he had made her say the things she so nearly hadn't.

'Why do you think you let him down? Because you slept with me?'

Hugh nodded.

'You have no idea how much I loved your dad. Paul told me he was ill and then your mum rang me,' Hugh explained. 'Middle of last year she rang me and said she thought I'd want to know that things really didn't look good. At first I thought I'd come for a holiday…' The waitress was back, ready to take their orders, and they glanced at the menu, chose risotto because it was the first thing there, declined bread, and then Bonita agreed , even though she wasn't particularly keen, on a bottle of wine.

He'd just slotted in, Bonita realized. So many times Hugh had slotted in with their family, only she'd never actually stopped to wonder how they slotted in with him.

'You were going to come back for a holiday?' Bonita checked, when he'd tasted the wine and for now they were alone.

'I was always going to come back.' Hugh nodded. 'But hearing how ill your dad was, well, it kind of forced the issue.'

'Why did you leave?' For the first time she asked him.

'It seemed the right time to go.'

'Because you'd broken up with Amber?' she asked bravely, frowning when he shook his head. 'Because of your dad, then?' Bonita said, taking a sip of wine and then holding it in her mouth when he answered.

'Because of yours.'

She swallowed slowly as Hugh elaborated.

'You father and I had a row.'

'About?'

'His home, his family.' Hugh gave a tight smile. 'About how he'd welcomed me in with open arms, how he'd treated me like a son, and that he deserved respect.'

And she could almost hear her dad saying those words, knew Hugh was telling the truth.

'You're not a very good actress, Bonita! That morning, when your parents came home, you were supposed to be angry and upset, not blushing and awkward and smiling.'

'He knew we'd kissed?'

'No!' Hugh managed a laugh. 'Can you imagine what would have happened if he had? I'd be minus two kneecaps now!'

At seventeen she had imagined Hugh defiant and strong, and to hell with what her parents thought.

At twenty-four, somehow her parents' feelings mattered more.

'You had three months left of school, you didn't need to be messing up your head with silly crushes, your dad told me. He kept on that this was the most important time of your life. Can you imagine hearing that and knowing what had taken place, knowing that if they hadn't come home when they had…

'Bonny—as your dad told me—I was the last thing you needed.'

'You were everything I needed.' Bitter, bitter tears of regret stung her eyes. 'You humiliated me, Hugh, you told me I had a stupid crush.'

'You were seventeen!"

Two vast white plates were in front of them.

And they both declined cracked pepper and parmesan, even though, if she'd stopped to think about it, Bonita would have wanted it. Only she wasn't thinking about food, wasn't even thinking that she didn't like wine as she took a sip while Hugh spoke on. 'If I'd carried it on, stood up to your dad, what good could have come from it? You'd have left home, messed up your exams, your life.' He clamped his teeth together, his jaw tightening for a moment before he continued. 'Pretty much what's happened now. You don't have to leave because of me, Bonny. You don't have to leave your job and home. It's the last thing your dad would have wanted. I'll get another job, I'll move into the city, back to England...'

'It's not that straightforward!'

'It can be!' Hugh urged. 'I wanted to see your dad before he died, I wanted to have as much time with him as I could, I wanted to help your mum—to show them that they, to me, *are* my family.'

'What about Amber?'

'Amber?' Hugh gave her a bewildered shake of his head. 'Amber—we're friends—we went out years ago.'

'And now?'

'Friends.'

'Nothing else?' Bonita frowned when he nodded. 'Nothing at all?'

'OK, OK.' Hugh winced. 'One drunken night when I first got back, which we've both agreed to never discuss again...'

And it had to be true, Bonita realized, had to be true because she was grinning and he was cringing and no man, especially a man like Hugh, would admit to such a thing, unless they were being honest.

Really honest.

'So why does she hate me so much?'

'Because of the way you've treated me.'

'Me?'

'She warned me you were seeing someone before I came back. Then when you and Bill broke up I thought there was a chance, but you were so devastated about Bill, and so off with me…'

'You were going out with Amber…'

'Friends.'

'The wedding!'

'Friends.'

'I heard you're getting married.' Bonita refused to believe it, her mind screaming at her to remember the facts. 'You've got the ring…'

'Ah-h, that!'

'Yes, that!' Bonita spluttered. 'She told me if I came to your apartment again that she'd chuck a casserole…' She had to quash down her words as the waitress appeared.

'Is everything OK?'

'Everything's fine!' Hugh waited for her to disappear before confronting Bonita, speaking in harsh whispers, his fury matching hers. 'How do you expect her to be, Bonita? She's my friend. When I told her how you'd treated me after your dad's funeral…then rubbing my face in it later, holding Bill's hand in the canteen…'

'I was telling him about you.'

'Me?'

'He knows how I feel about you.'

Wine was quite nice really, Bonita decided, grabbing her glass as her words sank in. Wine was lovely with dinner because it gave you something to do with your hands, gave you a second to pause as you took a sip, as you decided whether or not to be brave, really brave.

Only the second she put down her glass the eager waitress was back, topping it up. Bonita just wanted her to go, wanted to be alone before she said it, before she took the biggest gamble of her life. She couldn't wait a second more…

'We broke up because he realised I liked you!'

She watched him process her statement. Like a sponge soaking up water, she could almost see him absorb each word, could see the adamant flicker of denial over his features, followed in an instant by realization of the possibilities. This thought process occurred for both of them and it was pointless to even pretend they could eat. Hugh called the waitress and asked for the bill, then changed his mind and thrust a pile of notes on the table. Then he took Bonita by the hand and they practically ran out of the restaurant.

'You broke up with Bill because of me.' They were in the street, he was pulling her hand, her heels clipping on the pavement.

'Bill knew I was still crazy about you.'

'Still?'

'Always.'

They were at his apartment now—well, they had to be, because he was taking out his keys, inviting her into the bit of his world she'd never been allowed to glimpse. And walking through the door she felt as if she was going home.

To the heady citrus scent that was him.

To his shoes in the hall.

To his books on the shelf and her family in a photo-frame.

Lots of her family…her father, her mother, her brothers—and in each picture was her.

'Six years ago I kissed a girl,' Hugh said. 'Supposedly just a kiss, but it was the most reckless, dangerous thing I'd done—not just to myself but to her. A girl who was forbidden because she was part of a family I adored, an angry, defiant teenager whose parents were running around trying to keep her from men. And the one guy they trusted was the one who wanted her most.'

And he kissed her then just to confirm it.

Not a stolen kiss, or a grief-laced kissed, just a kiss as if to prove that she was there.

And she kissed him back, not just because it made her feel nice but a big girl's kiss because she wanted to, because she could, and because there was absolutely nothing wrong in doing so.

They needed to talk, but they needed each other more.

And she knew when he led her to his bed that it was her bed now, too.

That wherever they slept they were home.

'You're wearing a skirt.'

'For you!' Bonita admitted as he took it off, crying at her own honesty. Crying at the passion that only he could evoke.

That the dream she'd been chasing was coming true.

No need to draw the curtains because all she wanted to do was see him. Peel off his shirt and run her fingers along those strong arms that had held her when she'd needed them. Finally understanding why there were times when Hugh had pushed her away.

The guilty secret that was the two of them was put to bed as he lay her down.

That he loved her family too, that he, even when he had been so cold, had been looking out for her made it so easy to hold him, to be bold, to look at the man who had lived in her dreams for a decade now and make those dreams a reality.

To make love to him.

Because Hugh needed her now.

It was so good to know when he held the peach of her buttocks and guided her down onto his erect length that she was giving back to him. There was no creaking bed, no chance of anyone knocking, just guilt-free exploration of him, feeling him. She smiled at the bliss of him inside her and felt utterly a woman as she moved her hips against his. There was no reason to hush each other as he rocked inside her. She was able to cry out when she came—and best of all to lie beside him on her side of the bed.

'That's my side,' Hugh whispered in her ear.

'Since when?' Bonita grinned as he dragged her across the bed and lazily climbed over her. She didn't really care where she slept, he could take whatever side he wanted so long as it was next to her.

'Poor guy…' She was in the crook of his arm, not

staring up at the ceiling but, as was infinitely preferable, the side of his chest. She ran her fingers along the flat stomach that had teased her, scarcely able to believe they were there.

'Who?'

'Bill.'

'I know—no one would listen when I said he was a good guy.'

'You've been crazy about me all that time?'

'No!' She thumped his chest. 'I pined for about six months when you went back to the UK, but after that I was doing fine without you, thank you very much! You just loused it all up by coming back!'

'Made you realise how much you wanted me!'

'Well, it didn't take long!' Bonita grinned. 'To get your arrogant, over-inflated ego back!

'What about you?'

'What about me?'

'Well, did you think of me?'

'Sometimes.' Hugh shrugged.

'How many times?' Bonita pushed.

'Oh, when I emailed Paul, or when I rang your parents…'

'And…'

'About three months into a relationship.' Hugh admitted, 'when she didn't make me laugh, or she didn't make me angry, or she didn't make me…' He smiled down at her. 'You run the gamut of emotions, Bonny.'

'Ouch!' Bonita winced, doing some frantic arithmetic. 'Six years, divided into three monthly slots, just how many women were there?'

'There were a couple that lasted longer.' Hugh grinned.

'How much longer?'

'Till I bought the ring and the wedding plans started, and no matter how right I told myself it was, I just couldn't convince myself…' He turned to face her. 'It wasn't you.'

'I wish he'd known…'

She could see the sun bobbing down over the bay behind Hugh's broad shoulders, lovely reds and oranges, and her father was missing it all.

Not just the weddings and the grandchildren, but knowing that the Hugh he'd loved, loved the daughter he'd loved.

'He did know.'

Hugh dragged her out of her pensive haze.

'How?'

'I told him.'

'You told Dad how you felt about me?'

'He said not to rush you. I was supposed to do it right…' Naked, gorgeous and utterly unabashed, he walked across the bedroom, opened a drawer and pulled out a black case. 'I was supposed to give you time to get over Bill, date you, and then one day…' He opened the box and watched her frown as she stared at what lay inside.

Massive, sparkly jewels, which were somehow familiar.

This distant hazy memory of a little girl being a girl and trying them on.

Dressing up prettily and being scolded by her mother for touching someone else's things.

'Zia Lucia…'

'Your dad gave them to me. He said that when the time was right…and if it wasn't, well, I was to give them back to your mum.'

'He trusted you with these…' She stopped then, looked up at the man she had always loved, who had, in his own way, always loved her, and realised what a stupid thing she'd just said. Her father had trusted Hugh with more than jewels—he'd trusted him with her.

'So the hospital grapevine did get it right.' Bonita smiled.

'Sort of…' He pushed the ring on her finger. 'Yes, I was crazy about a girl and, yes, I'd got the ring and was working my way up to telling her. Amber knew, and I guess she must have told someone.'

'Who told someone.' She kissed his lovely mouth.

'Who told someone,' Hugh said, kissing her back. 'Next time you hear a rumour, you come to the source!'

Oh, she could have kissed him for ever, would have kissed him for ever if Hugh hadn't pulled back.

'Come on, you—get dressed.'

She didn't want to get dressed, wanted to crawl back in bed beside him, wanted to make up for every minute that they'd ever been apart, but Hugh, as always it turned out, wanted to do the right thing.

Scrunching up the drive, stepping out of the car, seeing her mother come to the door, even though she wanted Hugh, she wanted her mother too, wanted to share with her this moment.

'I wasn't expecting you back.' Carmel smiled, hugging her daughter and then hugging Hugh, too. 'But I'm glad you came.'

EPILOGUE

STRANGE that out of all the Azetti siblings the one who liked the farm the least had turned out to love it the most.

Carmel had been advised by many not to make any major decisions for a year after Luigi's death—advice she had respected, almost to the very day.

But though she still wanted to oversee the business, the house, she felt it was just too big without Luigi. It was a house built for a family, only how could she sell the home and keep the business?

It had to be both.

Except one rapidly expanding family didn't mind living in the middle of a vinery and not having to worry about it.

Expecting twins, a sprawling farmhouse on the outskirts of town was just the thing for a busy consultant who liked, when he was away from work, to really feel as if he was away.

Carmel still owned the business, which meant she was a frequent guest at the kitchen table, and she never ceased to amaze her daughter.

This proud, independent woman more than coped. Always loving and respectful of her late husband, still she lived and loved her life. She moved to a gorgeous mews-type home in the centre of town, a ten-minute walk from the church with endless cafes and friends in-between. And she dropped in to see Hugh and Bonita, regularly at first, then extremely regularly, when her daughter needed her most.

Oh, and did Bonita need her now.

'She hasn't stopped crying!'

Hair piled on the top of her head, still in her pyjamas at six p.m., Bonita answered the door with a rather wild, slightly savage look in her eyes.

'She's cold!' Carmel said, picking up the devil child. Red in the face, tight black knots of curls on the top of her head, she snuffled into her grandmother as if she hadn't been fed in days!

'It's not cold, though!'

'Little girls feel the cold!' Carmel said, wrapping her in a bunny rug and cuddling her in as still she bellowed. 'You feed Alex!'

Alex—just pulling him from his crib had Bonita's breasts bursting with milk, this luscious baby, blond, content, happy to just twiddle Bonita's hair as he patiently fed. Bonita swore she saw him raise one eyebrow and smile a dribbly smile at his little sister's carry-on!

'Maybe we shouldn't go out.'

'It's your wedding anniversary,' Carmel pointed out above the screams.

'Hugh will understand—'

'Don't even go there!' Carmel interrupted. 'You get upstairs and get washed and dressed and put on some make-up! Alex and Lucia will be fine.'

Lucia.

Placing a sleepy Alex back in his crib, Bonita walked over to her daughter, stroked the crinkly, knotty curls, saw the little red spots on her cheeks from crying so hard. She felt the frantic *unease* that was ever-present in her daughter—and never could she love her more.

Her aunt, her grandmother, her mother all rolled into one—this tiny independent little lady who did things her way, much to everyone's delight and frustration.

'Go and get ready,' Carmel insisted.

So she did.

And it still felt awkward.

It still made her blush when she dressed for him.

Which was maybe how it should be.

Tired of him seeing her slobbing around in jeans and oversized tops, she'd splurged and bought a dress.

Black—which was the only safe option when you had a milk let-down reflex that could be triggered by a cat meowing.

Lightly spun wool, which was perfect for the cool evening wind that was blowing in.

And cut so low it was almost indecent—which would hopefully cheer up Hugh, who had left the house over twelve hours ago.

Oh, but she wished her father was here to see them.

To see that his wayward daughter actually hadn't strayed beyond the garden gate!

Shaking hands applied lipstick and perfume. She struggled with the earrings that nestled in their box, feeling the cool slip of stone from her aunt's necklace between her breasts as she put it on.

It was almost easier *not* to go out.

They were both so tired, it would have been far easier to scrap any idea of dinner out and just catch whatever sleep they could.

But not in the long run.

This love was worth dragging a weary body out for dinner with the most fabulous guy in the world.

And walking into the lounge, she saw him chatting with Carmel as she made him a quick cuppa, his tie somewhere over his left shoulder as he cuddled Madam and Alex. She saw the flash of *that* in his eyes as she teetered in on her new high heels, and she knew he felt the same way she did.

That Hugh Armstrong thought he was married to the most fabulous woman in the world!

The restaurant was superb—or it looked it from her view from the bar stool, as they waited for their table.

'Nice to get out?' Hugh checked.

'Yep!' Bonita smiled widely, then blew her hair skywards as she let out a breath.

She'd spent the whole day trying to shave legs, pluck eyebrows, paint toenails—things she'd normally have zipped through in half an hour but trying to express enough milk to leave for the twins…

'Hungry?' Hugh checked. 'The restaurant here is supposed to be superb!'

'Starving!' Bonita lied, because the toast she'd eaten just before her mother had arrived, so she wouldn't look like a pig at dinner, had actually filled her up. He'd brought her to the most fabulous five-star hotel in Melbourne, the restaurant was reportedly to die for and they needed this, Bonita told herself—dinner, just the two of them, *not* talking about the twins. This was how you kept the fizz in a relationship.

'Liar!' Hugh grinned, because he knew her too well.

'I'll start drooling when I see the menu!' Bonita promised.

'You look great.' Which was what a husband should say on one's first anniversary, but it was the way he said it that made the glass miss her mouth!

They didn't actually need any help keeping the fizz, Bonita thought, wiping her chin then sucking on her lemon and smiling over to him. There was a certain guilt that came with fancying your husband *so* much.

A feeling of unsolidarity as she sat at baby yoga and listened how her peers dodged their partners' advances, a flicker of shame as her OB told her they could gently resume sexual relations about two weeks after she already had! But they didn't have a guy who just adored you—wanted you—even when he'd seen you at your worst.

And they did have six years to make up for, Hugh had told her once.

'You look great, too.' Bonita smiled, staring down at his knee now, which was sort of between hers. 'What time did you book the table for?' she asked as she drained the ice in her empty gin and tonic.

'I didn't.'

'What?' Her eyes jerked to his.

'I was thinking about it,' Hugh said seriously, his knee pushing into the soft, squidgy inside of hers and making her tummy unfurl. 'I know we don't get out much, but when we do, we never seem to get to dessert.'

'Er, no...' Bonita agreed.

'We're always dashing home.' The pressure was firmer on her inner knee now. 'But we can't tonight because your mum's babysitting.'

'She is.' Bonita gulped.

'And I know how tired you are, and I know you'll have to feed the twins when we get in and because you're you you'll worry if we don't have sex on our first wedding anniversary.'

'That we'll be letting things slide!" Bonita said equally seriously, but her knee was pushing his back.

'So I made an executive decision.' He pulled a hotel card out of his top pocket. 'If you're starving, there's room service...'

'I'm not hungry.'

'And if your exhausted, there's a bed...'

'Come to think of it,' Bonita said, jumping off her stool. 'I'm actually not that tired!'

'I'm all yours till midnight!' Hugh said, dragging her to the lift. 'Actually, scrap that,' he said, as they landed on the fifth floor and frantically followed the arrows towards room 505.

'I'm all yours.'

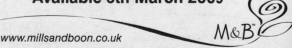

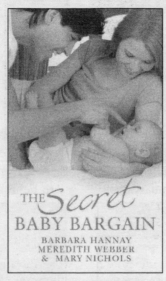

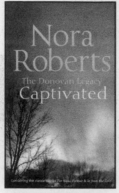
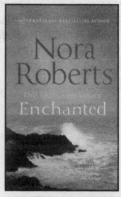
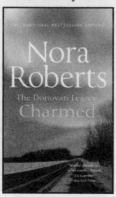
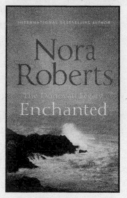

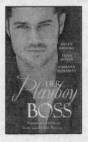

FREE!

4 Books
and a surprise gift!

We would like to take this opportunity to thank you for reading this Mills & Boon® book by offering you the chance to take FOUR more specially selected titles from the Medical™ series absolutely FREE! We're also making this offer to introduce you to the benefits of the Mills & Boon® Book Club™—

- ★ **FREE home delivery**
- ★ **FREE gifts and competitions**
- ★ **FREE monthly Newsletter**
- ★ **Exclusive Mills & Boon Book Club offers**
- ★ **Books available before they're in the shops**

Accepting these FREE books and gift places you under no obligation to buy, you may cancel at any time, even after receiving your free shipment. Simply complete your details below and return the entire page to the address below. You don't even need a stamp!

YES! Please send me 4 free Medical books and a surprise gift. I understand that unless you hear from me, I will receive 6 superb new titles every month for just £2.99 each, postage and packing free. I am under no obligation to purchase any books and may cancel my subscription at any time. The free books and gift will be mine to keep in any case.

M9ZEF

Ms/Mrs/Miss/Mr ....Initials..
BLOCK CAPITALS PLEASE
Surname...
Address..

....

....Postcode ....

Send this whole page to:
UK: FREEPOST CN81, Croydon, CR9 3WZ